Will Reason, Jonas Stadling

**In the Land of Tolstoi**

experiences of famine and misrule in Russia

Will Reason, Jonas Stadling

**In the Land of Tolstoi**
*experiences of famine and misrule in Russia*

ISBN/EAN: 9783337299644

Printed in Europe, USA, Canada, Australia, Japan

Cover: Foto ©Andreas Hilbeck / pixelio.de

More available books at **www.hansebooks.com**

IN

# THE LAND OF TOLSTOI

*EXPERIENCES OF FAMINE AND MISRULE*

*IN RUSSIA.*

BY

JONAS STADLING AND WILL REASON.

London:

JAMES CLARKE & CO., 13 & 14, FLEET STREET, E.C.

1897.

# PREFACE.

Amid the broken recollections of classic lore that begin to fade into the limbo of "the subliminal consciousness," as soon as we leave the discipline of our Alma Mater, is a Roman saying that it is better to do doughty deeds than to write about them.

The bearing of this observation lies in the fact that it is my friend, Herr Stadling, whose experiences and gleanings in the land of Tolstoi are here set forth. He has borne the fatigues of travel, gone in and out of plague and famine-stricken huts, and gathered from eyewitnesses and authorities the facts that did not come under his own observation. These he recorded in a Swedish work, "Från det Hungrande Ryssland." It has been my pleasant share, during a summer holiday on a pine-clad granite island between Stockholm and the Baltic, to co-operate with him in the rearrangement of the matter, to offer suggestions, and provide the whole with an English dress. While most of the matter is contained in the Swedish book just mentioned, it has been entirely rewritten, with complete change of form and many omissions and additions, for the English public. Some of the experiences in the relief work proper have been narrated in different language in *The Century Magazine* (June and August, 1894), and the story of Prince Khilkov has appeared, in other words and shorter form, in *The Sunday Magazine*.

The illustrations are reproduced from the originals used in the Swedish book. They are for the most part from photographs taken by Herr Stadling, and afterwards drawn by Herr J. Tiren, one of Sweden's foremost living artists.

WILL REASON.

Canning Town.

# CONTENTS.

# CHAPTER X.

## AMONG GERMAN COLONISTS.                    PAGE

# CHAPTER XI.

## IN THE CITY OF SARATOV.

# CHAPTER XII.

## PRINCE DMITRI KHILKOV.

# CHAPTER XIII.

## A RUINED FAMILY.

# CHAPTER XIV.

## OLDER RUSSIAN SECTS.

# LIST OF ILLUSTRATIONS.

TOLSTOI'S HEADQUARTERS AT RJASAN.

# CHAPTER I.

## FIRST ACQUAINTANCE WITH COUNT TOLSTOI.

Arrival at Rjasan—Tolstoi's Early Life—Education—His Opinion of the Universities—Unsuccessful Efforts to Help the Peasants in Years of Dissipation—Establishes Schools on his Estate—Tolstoi as "Peacemaker"—Educational Work and Opinions—Influence in Russia, &c.—Tolstoi and his Critics.

It was on a cold, stormy morning in March, 1892, the year of the great famine, that I arrived at the railway-station of Klekotki, in the province of Rjasan. In company with Madame B., who was also bound for the same place, I at once set out to drive to the headquarters of Count Tolstoi, distant some twenty-six miles across the plains, where he was hard at work relieving the needs of the starving peasants. The grey, woolly clouds were chasing each other at great speed; snow-wreaths whirled about us, and a heavy fall had hidden the road completely. At one or two points in the landscape we

1

could see a few trees that marked a landowner's dwelling, or a village with its church cupola and row of small, grey huts. At one part our journey took us for two miles along a road built by the Empress Catherine II., lined on either side with stately trees. It was heavy driving through the deep snow, so that we did not reach the River Don, on the further shore of which lay the village of Begichevka, our destination, until the afternoon.

The moment was now drawing near when I was, for the first time, to meet Count Tolstoi—a moment to which I had been looking forward throughout my long journey as to one of the most interesting occasions of my life. I was about to come into personal contact with a man whose greatness not even his bitterest enemies can dispute, in whom many an earnest seeker after truth discerns a seer and prophet, marking the dawn of a new era in the history of man.

Soon our driver drew up before a plain, one-storied wooden house, and called out, "*Vot dom Tolstova !*" ("This is Tolstoi's house.") About the premises were a number of peasants, carting loads of flour and grain. As we entered, we passed first through a kind of ante-chamber, densely crowded with *mushiks*, waiting to see the Count, then into a larger apartment that served as a dining-room. Tolstoi himself was not in, but I was shown into his private room behind the hall—a small apartment simply furnished with a sofa, a cot-bed, a few plain wooden chairs, and a large table covered with account books and papers. I found myself occupying the waiting time in speculations as to the impression Count Tolstoi would make on me. I could not succeed in divesting myself of the "great man" idea of the *Count*, the *aristocrat*, the *famous author*, the *great genius*. All these hid from me the image of him as a man, the brother of men.

After a few minutes, a young lady came in, and gave me a cordial greeting. I asked if she were the Count's daughter, but she replied, "No; I am his niece. My name is Kuzmin-sky." While I was speaking with her another young lady entered, with an energetic expression and lively eyes ; she, too, greeted me in good English.

"Countess Tolstoi?" I asked.

"They call me so," she said.

At the same moment a deep voice was heard in the hall, and the Count himself stood before me, dressed in a large sheep-skin coat of the kind worn by the *mushiks*. With a hearty grip of his strong hand he bade me welcome, asked about my journey, admired my Lapp dress, and showed me into a small room that I was to occupy. Then he told me to hold out my feet, and pulled off my Lapp boots. This was done so simply that they were off before I thought of protesting. Yet the spectacle of Count Tolstoi, whose greatness had been filling my mind a moment or two before, pulling off my boots like a common servant left me breathless with surprise. Then things took their proper perspective, and I saw the naturalness of it, and learnt more from this little unaffected deed of helpfulness than from all the learned lectures I had heard or all the volumes of theology I had read. I was in the presence of a man who had devoted a whole life to passionate search after truth and reality, and had found "the meaning of life" in following Him "who came not to be served, but to serve"; a man who not only talks about "*égalité et fraternité*," but whose life *is égalité et fraternité*."

I had come to do what I could to help in his work among the starving *mushiks*, but before giving an account of what I myself saw and heard while with this notable family in that sadly memorable famine year of 1892, it will be worth while to give a rapid sketch of the Count's life and character, as a man and the friend of men.

Count Tolstoi, the author, is well known, and has received his place among the foremost geniuses of the day. Leo Tolstoi, the philosopher and social reformer, has been amply discussed both by those who regard him as a new prophet, and those who look on him as a fanatic and a crank. The man Lyeff Nikolaievitch is comparatively little known. He has, it is true, told us somewhat of himself and his struggles after truth in his Confession, and throughout his other writings are scattered incidents taken from his own experiences. But he has said little or nothing of his work for his fellows, and what

he has told us has been liable to the failings of all auto-
biography. He has spoken of his life as it looks to himself.
But Oliver Wendell Holmes says somewhere that when we say
there are two people conversing there are really six. There is
A. as he appears to self, A. as he appears to B, A. as he
appears to God, and the same with B. Tolstoi has given the
first aspect; the second is the one we must take. With our
many burning social questions to-day, it is of more importance
to us to know what such a man as Tolstoi has done and is
doing to bring about their solution, than to be familiar with
the characters in "Anna Karenina," and others of his novels.
Moreover, I heard from some personal friends of the Count,
that his descriptions of his "wild oats" are very highly
coloured. To those who knew him, he belonged certainly to a
fast set, but on his personal character there was no stain. As
for the third aspect mentioned by Holmes, we must wait awhile
for that, if we are ever able to grasp it.

Tolstoi grew up without the knowledge of a mother's love;
she died when he was eighteen months old (he was born in
1828, August 28, old style); and his father left his family,
which was a large one, when the little Lyeff Nikolaievitch was
nine years old. So it happened that much of his early education was in the hands of relatives, of whom one, at least, is
described as hardly fitted to guide a youth's first steps in the
paths of manly virtue. In his home on his ancestral estate of
Jasnaja Poljana, in the province of Tula, he was under the
care of both a French and a German tutor, the former of
whom remained in the family until, at the age of fifteen, the
young Count entered the University of Kasan. For three years
he studied philology, history, and Russian literature. But he
soon lost faith in that "temple of wisdom," to which
Puschkin's words were thoroughly applicable: "As everything
in Russia is purchasable, so examinations and degrees of
learning also are a merchandise with the professors." Charac-
teristic both of the state of things at the university and the
views and tendencies of the young Count, is his description of
the teaching given there. "History," he said, "is nothing
but a collection of fables and details often meaningless or

absurd. The positive in it is a mass of dates and names of no value. The death of Prince Igor, the snakes that bit the hero Olef, &c.,—what are those things but nursery tales, and who needs to know if Ivan the Terrible married the daughter of Tomruck exactly on the 21st August, 1562, or if his fourth marriage, with Anna Alexijevna, took place in 1572? And yet they require of me that I shall know all this by heart; if not, I get a shameful "one" on my certificate. And how they write history! All is arranged after a given pattern. . . . Ivan the Terrible, *e.g.*, of whom Professor Ivan has had so much to tell us, was suddenly changed in 1560—something that has no interest whatever either for you or me—from a noble, virtuous, and wise ruler, into a mad, licentious, and terrible tyrant. Why? How? About this you may not even ask a question."

Small wonder that the young student, athirst for truth, sympathising warmly, though as yet half-consciously, with the downtrodden and oppressed, regarded this "temple of learning" as a useless institution. No doubt his lack of interest in many of the subjects had something to do with his being " plucked" at an examination, but it is also certain that this was largely brought about by one of those intrigues so common in a corrupt society. A hostile professor—hostile because of family reasons—refused to give him his due where he was incontestably efficient. This incident strengthened his determination to leave the university and give himself up to the work of elevating the peasants on his paternal estate, which had, by a combination of causes, not necessary to detail, passed into his hands.

He returned to Jasnaja Poljana in 1846, and flung all his energy into the task of raising both the economical and moral standard of peasant life. He failed, in spite of his ample means, warm heart, and indomitable pluck. The peasants would not let him pull down their rotten, old tumble-down huts, even to put up new and convenient ones at his own cost; they also refused to send their children to school. He found, as so many others have done, that good intentions alone are not sufficient to cope with ingrained evil, nor can the results of centuries of slavery be undone even in a lifetime.

The disappointed youth resolved to go to Petersburg in the autumn of 1847, to continue his studies, intending this time to take a degree in law. But the juridical hair-splitting of Petersburg satisfied him no more than the fables of Kasan. He returned to his estate in 1848.

It was at this period that the years of dissipation occurred that have been referred to above; then followed his experience as a soldier in Caucasia, and his successful career as a novelist. Still, through all these varied years he retained his love of the people unchanged; unlike some who have feebly tried to help the poor, and have drawn back into their selfish ease like a snail into its shell, at the first touch of what they loudly proclaim as "ingratitude." In Caucasia, as well as in European Russia, he was careful to keep himself in living touch with the people, not simply to study their life, but to give them real aid and sympathy. This love of men is reflected in his writings. He cared nothing for outward events nor outward greatness, but for everything that influences the moral development of the individual, though so slight as to escape superficial observation altogether. In a word, this young author cared for *man*, and made living men and women the object of his genius. His first book, "Utro Pomestchika" (The Landlord's Morning), and those that followed are full of that deep sympathy with the oppressed and the poor, that love of the people, that Tourgenieff sneeringly stigmatises as "hysterical."

Shortly after the Crimean War (Tolstoi bore his part in the siege of Sebastopol), he visited Western Europe, in order to study the school systems in use there, with a view to his work of raising the life of the Russian peasantry. On his return he began to establish schools on his own estate of Yasnaya Poljana.

The same year, 1861, saw the abolition of serfdom—in name, at least. Tolstoi probably saw more clearly than the rest of his countrymen the enormous difficulty of making this paper-emancipation an actual fact, and thus realising the ideal of the Reform Party. The first great difficulty was the settlement of the disputes that immediately arose between the landowners and the former serfs. The majority of the nobles were opposed to emancipation, and only a few had voluntarily liberated their bondsmen. To meet these difficulties the office of miravoj posrednik, or "peacemakers," was established, and the Count occupied this office in his own district, which he filled with untiring zeal. This was the only civil post ever held by him, so far as we know. His unswerving sense of justice often brought him into conflict with the landlords, but he cared about opinions as little then as now. On the other hand, he often had to refuse the demands of the peasants, but their faith in him had become so strong that they always acquiesced in his decision.

Besides this work, he threw himself heart and soul into his plans of education for the mushiks. As early as 1849 he had established a school for peasant children on his estate. Another succeeded in 1857, and the third in 1861. In this he himself conducted the instruction, with the help of four students from Moscow, and a German named Keller. From early morning till late at night he was engaged in active teaching, devising and trying new methods. The principal school was in his own house. All instruction was, of course, gratuitous, and the children were also frequently fed. In one form or another these schools have continued ever since. If closed as schools by the interference of police or priests, the children have been invited by the Tolstoi family "to tea," which feast included food for the mind also.

In connection with this work of teaching, Count Tolstoi edited for many years a monthly magazine called "The School," the contents of which were entirely devoted to education, and were of great interest. The fundamental idea of his "free schools" is the gradual realisation of the moral ideal, taken in its widest sense. Not so much development simply, as the *harmony of development*, should be the aim of all education. "*Therein lies the eternal error of all pedagogic theories*," says Tolstoi, "that they make development *per se*, the development of some special side of the child's being, their object and aim."

It is in the child itself, according to him, that the primary conditions for realising the ideal are to be found. "We must listen to the voice of the people," he says. The more he learned to know the young minds unfolding under his care, "listened" to their emotions, and watched the expression of them in their lives, the warmer grew his love for them, and his admiration for that simple poetry that surrounds childhood as an atmosphere. At the same time his faith in the so-called education of the upper classes, that carries them farther and farther from the true and natural, waxed weaker and weaker.

"Are the peasant children to learn from us how to write, or we from them?" he asks in his paper. He had set a number of boys of eleven or twelve to write down their thoughts and observations on different matters, or describe their experiences, and had made the astonishing discovery that they exhibited, as he expresses it, "an artistic power to which not even a Goethe could attain." This discovery made an overwhelming impression on Tolstoi. "I was frightened, and at the same time happy as a treasure-seeker, who on Midsummer Night has found the St. John's wort—happy, because I suddenly saw before me the philosopher's stone which I had been seeking for two toilsome years—the art of learning how to express one's thoughts; frightened, because this art evokes new wants, and a whole new world of wishes, which, as I saw at once, did not correspond to the surroundings in which these children live." It was not only a solution of the educational, but also of the religious question, that Tolstoi believed he had found in the life of these peasants, from whom in this also we have more to learn than they from us.

His paradoxes on the uselessness of what is commonly understood as education, art and science, are not to be taken as a condemnation of education, art and science in themselves. In one of his later works he says, "Art is not to disappear, but to become something else, better and higher." It is only in the service of selfishness that they are bad. The best proof of this is in his own untiring work in his schools, in his distribution of books and tracts among the peasants, and his gigantic scheme of a popular library, which is to contain a digest of the best that has been written by the best men in all ages, to be published in a popular form at one penny a volume.

After the radical change in his ideas and life, or rather the ripening of those ideas that had been germinating and growing within him all his lifetime, he devoted himself entirely to help and raise the downtrodden people by sharing their life. His attempt in Moscow, after his removal there in 1881, to aid the teeming masses of the miserably poor and degraded in that city have been most graphically described by himself in his book "What to do?" Here he says :—

"Through much painful struggle I came to see that I had a share in the cause of all this misery. I stood up to my ears in the mud, and wanted to pull others out of it! I, the parasite, I, the louse, which eats into the leaves of the tree, want to promote the health and growth of that tree! I now come to the following simple conclusion, that it is my duty to reap and use the fruits of the labours of others!

"By a long and roundabout way I reached the unavoidable result that was expressed a thousand years ago among the Chinese : 'If one man is idle, some one else dies of hunger.'"

Tolstoi despaired of being able to help the poverty and vice that prevailed in the city, and seemed inseparable from populous towns. He therefore left Moscow, to lead the life and share the toil of the peasants.

It is quite natural that such a man as this should have attracted many admirers and followers—many more of the former than the latter!—and that he should also have drawn upon himself many vehement criticisms and bitter calumnies. It is difficult to over-estimate his great influence both in his own and in foreign countries, although this has been greatly disparaged by some; over the youth of Russia it has been especially great. Banned by the censor, his later writings are being copied, distributed clandestinely, and read by millions. Hundreds, if not thousands, of young men have through his influence left the terroristic party and donned the armour of

Christ, by which to fight the powers of darkness and oppression. Several "Christian communities" have been established in different parts of Russia in order to put his principles into practice, and have thriven until they have been broken up by the police, or through the intrigues of enemies. A large number of his peaceful followers are now in exile either in Trans-Caucasia or Siberia, while others have "gone to the people," to share their life and toil in order to serve them and make their life richer and nobler.

In England itself there is a powerful testimony to his influ- ence in the large sale of his books, and the eagerness with which the articles from his pen that have recently appeared in the newspapers have been read; at the universities his books are well known, and thoughtful working men are familiar with his ideas. Much of his philosophy may be rejected, many of his results may be held to have come to him solely through the abnormal conditions of the Russian society in which he has had his origin and passed the greater part of his life. The present writers, in admiring the man, by no means accept all his ideas. But as a living force, as a man who thinks for himself and sets other people thinking too, it is difficult to compare him with any other figure of modern times.

Tolstoi's critics are many and of varied hue ; from the priests who frighten the peasants with stories of his branding all the *mushiks* who come to him for counsel and aid with the seal of the devil on their hands and foreheads, and the bishops who preach against him as Antichrist personified; to the officials and politicians who represent him as a dangerous revolutionary, seeking to rouse the people to armed revolt; and the gossips who circulate stories about his professing to be a vegetarian, while rising in the night to eat his beefsteak. A certain Russian professor, for example, has written a long series of articles in a Russian review, called the "Ruskaja Mysl," trying to explain Tolstoi's "peculiarities" from "his in- herited desire to live in the open air "; hence, all his work among the people, his relief work, *e.g.*, among the starving millions during the great famine, is only "a kind of sport."

We do not speak of thoughtful men who conscientiously

dissent from his opinions.  But when you have known this
greatest son of Russia personally, and seen this nobly-born
magnate and great genius daily devoting all the powers of his
mind, all the strength of his indomitable will, all the warmth
of his large and generous heart, to help and uplift the downtrodden, oppressed, and degraded peasants, and have seen, on
the other hand, the motley crowd of his critics and calum-
niators, fops, mammon-worshippers, courtiers, and priests, with
borrowed wisdom, drawing-room philosophy, fossil dogmas.
cut and polished, and a Pharisaism that will almost put to the
blush that of Judaic origin, it is as if a swarm of noxious
insects were buzzing round a giant ditcher, toiling in .the
sweat of his brow to drain a stinking and poisonous marsh,
and were raging over his attempt to destroy their para-
dise in which they have grown fat, attacking his perspiring
body, and seeking some open wound received during his noble
toil, in which to instil their corrosive poison, and fatten
themselves on his substance.

# CHAPTER II.

## CAUSES OF THE FAMINE.

Contrast of Famines in Russia and Western Europe—Condition at the Eman-cipation—Broken Promises—Insufficiency of Allotments—Action of Landlords—Prince Vasiltchikoff's Opinion—Proportion of Agricul-turists in Russia and other Countries—Nomadism—Capitalism and the Peasants—*Kulacks* and their Usury—*Kulacks* and Officials—Oppressive Taxation.

THIRTY-FIVE millions of people *starving*, at the close of the nine-teenth century, with its marvellous network of railroads and other means of communication, its wonderful development in all the means of production, and its loudly boasted organisation of labour, in times of peace, and in a country endowed with unlimited natural resources! This is so remarkable a phenomenon, that it can only be explained by a concurrence of abnormal causes.

It is well known that years of dearth and famine decrease both in intensity and frequency as civilisation and means of communication develop. In England, for example, during the fifteenth century, when in normal years food was cheap, labour well paid, and wealth, as it was known at that time, more generally diffused than in any century since, there were times when the crops failed through bad seasons, and the population, limited by its crude husbandry and without foreign or colonial cornfields to draw upon, suffered severely by disease and death. Under the cruel Corn Laws of later times, which shut out the people's bread to fill the pockets of one class, the same phenomenon was seen. In Western Europe, generally during the middle ages, famines occurred on the average every eighth or tenth year, and were accompanied by great mortality among the poor. But in the present day, by the remarkable develop-ment of international trade and the opening up of gigantic corn areas in different parts of the world, these years of dearth have become a thing of the past, in such countries as have adopted the enlightened policy of interdependence, with some measure of domestic freedom.

Russia, however, is a remarkable exception to this rule. Of course, famines occurred in the olden time. In the Nikonian Chronicle, which covers the period between 1127—1303, there are eleven years of famine recorded. In 1128 the population of Novgorod lived on the bark and birch of lime trees, and in 1229-30 a large part of Middle and Northern Russia was devastated by famine. But during the last two and a-half decades the years of dearth have *increased* to such an extent that in many parts the peasants may be said to be in a chronic state of famine. The semi-official journal, *Novoje Vremja*, for October 7, 1891, says that scarcely a year passes without a visitation of some part of the Empire. This is borne out by the terribly increasing mortality among the peasants. The average rate of mortality in the whole of Russia is about 34 per 1,000, and, contrary to the experience of Western Europe, where the death-rate is higher in the towns, in Russia it is the rural population that yields the higher figures. Among the peasants of Central Russia, for example, the frightful rate of 64 per 1,000 has been reached. In 1885 a Medical Congress was convened at Moscow for the purpose, among others, of investigating the causes of the growing mortality among the peasants. The Congress decided that it was due to the insufficent quantity and bad quality of the food, *i.e.*, to chronic famine.

The explanation of this extraordinary state of things can only be made by reference to the course of events since the emancipation of the serfs. During the period of serfdom, which is usually understood to date from the decrees of Boris Godunoff, tying the serfs to the soil on which they worked, to the abolition under Alexander II. in 1861, the peasants were certainly often subjected to great cruelty, but their masters had a direct pecuniary interest in keeping them from starvation.

In the introduction to the Act of Emancipation, the Govern-

ment made the following well-sounding promise :—" To provide
the peasants with the means of satisfying their wants and
enable them to fulfil their duties toward the State " (*i.e.*, to
pay taxes) ; " for this purpose they shall receive in inalienable
possession allotments of cultivable land and other belongings,
which in this Act are to be specified."

How has this promise been kept?

The so-called "*dvorovije*," or serfs attached personally to
their lords, and not occupying any land, became proletarians
in the cities. The serfs proper did receive allotments, which
were handed over to the "mir," or village community, which
was to be responsible for the payment of the "redemption
money" for the land as well as the taxes. The Government
paid out the landlords in a lump sum, so that the peasants
were henceforth responsible directly to the Government for
everything. The price paid to the landlords was supposed to
represent the capitalised "*obrok*" or rent (about 9-12 roubles
per allotment). But the valuation was actually made, not on
the market value of the land, *but on the supposed loss to the
landlord caused by the emancipation*, which in most cases
reached a much higher figure. To illustrate by a parallel,
it would have been the same in the United States if, on the
emancipation of the slaves, the liberated negroes had received
allotments and been made to pay the cotton planters the
purchase-money for their freedom, instead of simply a fair
rent for their land.

This was the first hardship imposed on the unfortunate
*mushiks*. In the second place, the allotments were ridiculously
insufficient to supply even their limited needs. To maintain a
peasant family at least ten to fourteen hectares are required.
(A hectare is about two and a-half acres.) To understand
this apparently high estimate, as it would be considered in
England, it must be remembered that out of the produce the
peasant had to pay the extraordinary high rent referred to
above, and the Government taxes, which in Russia are, of
course, far heavier than in England, and also that the survival
of the "three field" system and other drawbacks of Russian
agriculture made the produce of far less value per acre

than with us. But, as a matter of fact, one-fourth of the peasants received only 0·8 hectares to "each male soul" (*i.e.*, adult able-bodied man), and about one-half received from two to three hectares. Even if free from debt and taxation, the peasants could not live on these plots more than 150-180 days in the year. Either then they must rent land, which is only accessible to them at unreasonably high prices, or leave their homes and become proletarians or slaves. But, of course, they were started with a heavy debt, and the taxes are ruinously oppressive. The annual "redemption money" has amounted to 185-275 per cent. of the real rentable value, and the taxation for the Army, the Church, and other Imperial purposes increases yearly. Moreover, the increase of population has led to a still further decrease in the size of the allotments, making the position of the unhappy *mushiks* still worse. For it must be noticed, *pace* Malthus, that miserable conditions of life, so far from being a " check " to population, are direct stimuli, except in the case of sudden and over-whelming disaster. According to official statistics, collected by the Government in 1878, the allotments in fifteen govern-ments averaged only 1-2 hectares per "male soul"; in some parts it did not even reach one hectare.

In the third place, the landlords have taken advantage of the ignorance and misery of the peasantry and their own authoritative positions to cosen, cajole, or terrify them out of their most valuable pasture and forest land, and have after-wards rented it out to them again at prices they could fix at will.

Prince Vasiltchikoff, Chairman of the Agricultural Congress at Petersburg in 1886, speaking of the position of the peasants, said: " Since that time (1871) the agricultural proletariat has increased with alarming rapidity. Through statistical researches, made by the State authorities in Moscow, it has been proved that the agricultural proletariat has increased by 25 per cent. This shows that one-fifth of the entire population of the Empire, and one-third of the rural population in Russia proper, or about *twenty millions of souls are agricultural proletarians, i.e.*, as many as the

entire number of serfs at the emancipation.* And I do not
dare to affirm that the life of our agricultural proletarians is
more tolerable than that of the former serfs."

It must be remembered that in Russia the agriculturists
form the great bulk of the industrial population. In France
the non-agricultural labourers form 23 per cent., in Italy 25
per cent., in Austria 27 per cent., in Germany 32 per cent.,
and in England 53 per cent. of the whole population; in
Russia they only form 1½ per cent. These figures, moreover,
show no signs of increase, but rather of diminution. From 1866
to 1885 the non-agricultural industrial classes have decreased
by 0·08 per cent. Of the 110,000,000 of inhabitants only 1½
millions are non-agricultural labourers. In fact, the agricultural labourers of Russia are almost equal in number to the
entire (non-agricultural) industrial population of the rest of
Europe.

Owing to the impossibility of earning a living at home,
explained above, the Russian peasantry is increasingly " on the
move." In some governments, e.g., Nishni Novgorod, entire
villages thus migrate with the women and children. Cattle
hey usually have none. A few years before the late famine
of 1891-2, more than 60 per cent. of the Russian peasants
did not possess either horse or cow. No wonder that in many
places the women drag the plough !

The peasants are, as a rule, clever at handicrafts, which
they practise on the large estates as they wander through
the country, but the blessings of increasing "free" competition cut down their pay to a minimum, so that they often
have to beg their way. Meantime their home goes to ruin,
family ties are loosened, their plots of land are left untilled,
their houses and implements are either seized for taxes or fall
into the hands of the *kulacks* (usurers). Numbers emigrate
to Siberia, but this is hampered by unreasonable regulations,
and many are sent back. Meanwhile the mortality continues
increasing, being now generally 40-60 per 1,000.

To describe in detail the whole system which has reduced

---

* In 1858 the serfs of the landlords numbered 10,447,149 "male souls ";
the " serfs of the State," 9,149,891 ; and the " serfs of the domains," 842,740

the Russian *mushiks* to hopeless misery would be to write the internal history of Russia for the last half-century, but some of the principal points may be mentioned. Since the emancipation a new element has entered the life of the peasants—capitalism, with its invariable result of proletarianism. Before this the *mushik* was a chattel, a part of his master's capital, to be maintained in as an efficient condition as the rest of his goods. Afterwards he was forced

A MUSHIK FAMILY.

into the arena as a nominally "free" *competitor* with his former masters in the struggle for existence. It did not need the inspired insight of a prophet to foresee on which side victory would lie—on that of the capitalists on the one hand, armed with all the formidable weapons of modern finance, with absolute autocracy for their ally, or of the *mushiks* on the other, with their ignorance, servility, and fatalism bred of centuries of serfdom, in which they were

2

treated and driven as cattle. We have mentioned that the lands allotted to them were insufficient for the maintenance of life; they lacked also the means and knowledge of the best modes of cultivating what they had.

More must also be said of the systematic exploitation and oppression on the part of the estate owners and the authorities. The landlords, who had in former years been accustomed to live upon the industry of their slaves, had neither energy nor skill to cultivate their lands in a proper manner. Many of them rapidly ran through the " emancipation money " without applying it to the improvement of their estates. Swiftly on the abolition of serfdom followed the development of the railroad and steamboat traffic, which raised the value of the forests and the produce of the land enormously. Immediately a devastation of forest land and impoverishment of the soil began. Immense tracts of timber were ruthlessly felled, to the great injury of the climate and soil, and crop after crop of wheat was raised on the same fields without replacing by manure what was taken away, until the land was completely exhausted. At the same time that the conditions of the peasantry made them unable to participate in the increased value of agricultural produce, seeing that they were unable on their small plots to produce for the open market, rents were raised against them to a terrible extent.

In fact, the entire system of finance and steam communication was used as a gigantic apparatus for sucking the life-blood of the people. In the first place, the cost of construction was enormous. The difficulties presented by the physical features of the country were much more favourable in Russia than in Finland, for example. Yet the cost in Russia was three times as much as in Finland (sixty to one hundred thousand roubles per kilom. as against twenty thousand roubles per kilom). *This difference went in no measure to the working man,* for labour was cheaper in Russia than in Finland. Again, though private railways have paid very well in Russia, the companies have succeeded through bribery in obtaining State subsidies, which in 1883 amounted to 781,888,800 roubles (a rouble is about 2s. 3d.). The smallest amount of common-sense is sufficient

to see that all this is in the last result squeezed out of the
workers. Besides this, railroad statistics show that the chief
travellers are the peasants, who are forced to use the cars, not
in profitable enterprise, but in their wanderings in search of
the means of subsistence, out of which a heavy payment has
to be made for railway tickets. About three-fourths of the
peasants lead this nomadic kind of life.

In the most intimate connection with the railroads are the
banks, as is natural in a pre-eminently agricultural country.
The money market and the railway traffic correspond in their
rise and fall. It is from the great banking institutions that
have risen in the last few decades that the money flood is
periodically sent out to all the villages in the country, and
returns thither, after having finished its work of nominally
providing capital for agricultural operations, but really of
fleecing the peasants. This is partly through a shameless
system of usury by which the *mushiks* have to pay 200-300 per
cent. interest, and partly by custom, somewhat akin to what
used to be forbidden in England as " forestalling " and
"regrating." Immediately after harvest agents appear on the
scene, and take advantage of the peasant's need of ready cash
wherewith to pay their taxes to buy up their produce at a
shamefully low rate ; they must have money to pay their taxes
or they will be flogged nearly to death by the police. Before
the new year provisions run out, and the *mushiks* are face to
face with the alternatives of buying back their produce at
exorbitant prices, leaving their homes to look for work elsewhere, or begging.

The moneylenders who thrive so well by draining the life-
blood of the peasants are usually known as *kulacks*, literally
*fists*. Some interesting figures have been collected by several
Russian authorities as to the extent of these gentlemen's
operations. It seems that the peasant, in his distress, applies
to anyone who has money to help him, and among his creditors
are found merchants, priests, deacons, nuns, village scribes,
surgeons, noblemen, military men, teachers, and such peasants
as have managed to get a footing above their fellows. But the
professional money-lenders, or *kulacks*, are his great resource.

We will give some examples of the methods by which the peasants are fleeced. It is very usual when, *e.g.*, a loan of twenty-five roubles is made, for one month, to require a repayment of fifty roubles; should these not be paid on the exact day, a fine of five roubles a week is exacted. Among the cases investigated by our author, the annual rate of interest ran up to 120-140 per cent. in eighteen instances; 88-90 per cent. in four others; and to 60 per cent. in twenty-eight more.

Frequently the lending is done on a kind of pawnbroking system; clothes, household goods, agricultural implements, stock, and land being pledged as securities. In other cases, the borrowers pledge their labour, which is exacted at the busiest season of the year and valued often at half the market rate of wages. If, for example, a borrower has engaged to be responsible for the complete working of a piece of his creditor's land—that is, to plough, sow, and reap it, he gets no more than two or three roubles per hectare, while the customary price is seven or eight roubles.

In the village of Tcherdakli, government Stavropol, the peasants borrowed 100 roubles from the *diatchok* or sacristan, for six months. As a "mark of gratitude," *i.e.*, interest, he got from them the use of one and a-half hectares of good land for sixteen years.

In the village district of Starososnimskaja, in the spring of 1886, ninety peasants borrowed from a *kulack* the sum of 1832·70 roubles, and pledged themselves to repay it on August 1 following, in 6,109 puds of rye, which the *kulack* valued at 28-30 copecks a pud. In addition to this, they had also to pay 2,125 puds of hay, of which 1,000 puds were estimated at four copecks each, and the rest at five copecks. At the same time that these peasants were compelled to sell their grain at thirty copecks per pud, their creditors were selling to other hard-pressed peasants at seventy-five copecks to one rouble per pud.

In 1885, the peasants in Malouza, district Novo Usensk, borrowed 300 roubles from a merchant for half a-year, and gave him in payment seven yoke of the best draught oxen, two large ploughs, two waggons, and two water casks; these last are especially well made, and of considerable cost.

A *MUSHIK* ON THE TRAMP.

In ten villages of the district Nikolajevsk, the annual rate of interest was found to be 250 per cent.; in fifty-three others it was 90·8 per cent.

During the bad seasons of 1888-9, most of the peasants in

the two districts just mentioned were compelled to sell all their cattle and sheep. There was nothing left to pawn, so the *community* began to borrow, on security of the communal land; according to figures given in that year, 56 communer had already so pledged their land, and 107 were in debt to *kulacks* and merchants.

In the district of Bugulminsk, the population is largely composed of Tatars, Mordvins, and other non-Russian peoples. The *kulacks* have taken advantage of the greater ignorance of business matters to exact many times the amount really due. For example, a man borrowed 155 roubles for a year. He could not pay up promptly, so his creditor seized his barn, all his straw-thatched outhouses, one hectare of his crops, his gate, and a quantity of his fencing.

Another, a Tatar, had borrowed 291·50 roubles, and when he could not pay, lost his dwelling-house, all his outhouses, his horse, his cupboard, his samovar, and his clock.

Two peasants borrowed twenty-eight roubles, and had in return to reap rye for two days with two men, to plough the land with their own horses for fifteen days in the spring-sowing, and to plough the fallow land also for fifteen days.

In another case three peasants borrowed twenty-seven roubles from a nun, from March 2 to October 11, on condition that failure to pay, should forfeit all their property, beasts, implements, bees, and all their clothes, and that no question was to be raised before the authorities about it.

These are simply a few instances taken here and there as examples of a general practice. I. M. Krasnopjorov gives the following figures as the result of his investigations. These are the latest we have been able to get, but by no means represent the state of things in quite recent years, when matters have become, necessarily, much worse. It is understood that these figures are in connection with this forced borrowing.

| | | | | |
|---|---|---|---|---|
| The peasants lose by forced sale of grain | ... | ... | 21 | per cent. |
| ,, | ,, | ,, purchase ,, ... | ... 97 | ,, |
| ,, | ,, | piecework on the land | 60 | ,, |
| ,, | ,, | harvest work ... | 50 | ,, |
| ,, | ,, | daily labour ... | 39 | ,, |

The economic position in the government of Samara in 1889 was as follows :

| | |
|---|---|
| Peasant holdings under cultivation ... | 48,468 |
| Communal land in pledge or leased out | 453,917 hectares |
| Arrears of taxes to Government | 5,808,459 roubles |
| Debts to usurers ...  ...  ... | 1,170,932 „ |

These facts and figures relate to times *before* the famine. During my visit I made the acquaintance of a liberal man of great practical knowledge and high position, who described the condition of things as follows :

"At present the peasants are slaves in the power of the *kulacks*, who have a kind of agreement or monopoly with the authorities for stripping the people to the bones. No one can have any transactions whatever with the peasants without the permission of the officials, and these take care that those so privileged shall be men of their own kidney. It is only in name that the peasants are free; virtually they are in worse slavery than before the abolition, for it was to the interest of their owners to see that they did not starve to death. If the *kulacks* do "good business," the officials get their share. If the peasants should steal a bundle of hay from the rich *kulacks*, they get three years' imprisonment, with flogging besides. If these gentlemen or any of the officials rob a peasant of all he has no notice is taken of it."

"But do not the *kulacks* and other capitalists show some sympathy with the people in such fearful distress as the present ? "

"You can see yourself what kind of sympathy it is," he said ; "that meal that you bought in Zemljanki, consisting of chaff, sawdust, and dirt, is a very good example of it; this is what they sell or lend to the *mushiks*. I do not know of one solitary instance where a *kulack* has opened a soup-kitchen, let us say, for the starving. I know of many where they have lent one rouble for the purchase of a coffin for a peasant's near relative, and demanded three in return ; or where they have provided the starving with a little food, on condition that they pledge themselves to give their work in the busiest times for several years!

" It is very common for a *kulack* to lend five roubles, and receive back fifteen, and if it is not punctually repaid, to take all the debtor's property. If at any time a peasant should dare to bring him to account, the *kulack*, who is hand and glove with the magistrate, is acquitted, and the peasant in his turn is hauled before the *natchelnik*, who is a little Csar in his *volost*, and convicted of some offence or other. And it is forbidden to say a word about the doings of these gentlemen in the papers.

"Both *kulacks* and officials are using the opportunity presented by the famine to complete the slavery of the *mushiks*. When the peasant cannot pay the Government taxes, which is an utter impossibility just now, they are sold up entirely, to their last cow, their sheep, their household stuff, and clothes. When there is nothing more to take, they are flogged and driven to borrow money from the *kulacks* to pay the taxes, pledging their labour for longer advance. The taxes frequently amount to more than 260 per cent. of the entire produce of their holdings, and form a powerful link in the chain that binds them to the triumphant car of capitalism and tyranny."

I expressed my astonishment that the Government should attempt to collect the taxes when they must know that the people were dying of starvation.

" It is not only so," he said, " but six per cent. is added to arrears, which are often, by the way, the invention of the collectors. If threats are of no avail, birch rods are used to squeeze the last copeck out of them, though their wives and children are dying of hunger. In a village in Vistka, where people were famishing, the ' fatherly Government' seized the last provisions of the destitute peasants, in the shape of 300 hens, and sold them to a rich *kulack* at about a penny apiece to pay off arrears of taxes.

"In another district, which had suffered not only from famine but also from one of the fires that are so frequent in Russia, the inhabitants turned in their distress to their ' little father ' in St. Petersburg, praying, not for assistance, but simply that the taxes might not be exacted. In reply there came a collector, who used the direst threats to them that he would exact

THE WIDOW'S LAST COW.

the taxes and the last copeck. The poor men sold all they had, in their fright, till everything was paid, except two villages, where there was nothing left to sell. But it was of no avail. More than fifty peasants were first flogged and then thrown into prison. This happened on June 1, 1891, and is reported in the Petersburg paper *Nedjela* for June 21. In the same number you will find that the district officials, when they heard of the deficit, imprisoned the village *starosta* also, because, in official language, 'he had been guilty of negligence.'"

"How can the peasants put up with all this?" I asked.

"They are far from satisfied with it," he said. "They make war in their fashion against the landowners and capitalists, steal from them all they can, and take every opportunity of defrauding them. They are in a great majority, but have no combination. On the other hand, the landlords and capitalists are allied with the soldiery, police, and authorities in general. It is already a war between two hostile forces, whose interests are opposed to each other, and it is only a question of time for this conflict to assume a fierce aspect. Tolstoi and his friends, and the different sections of the Liberals throughout the country, are working for peaceful reform; the revolutionary party, on the contrary, desire an upheaval by any means whatsoever."

I myself saw something of this pitiless exaction of taxes during my stay among the famine-stricken districts, notably in the case of a poor widow. One of my *mushik* acquaintances informed me that the *ispravnik* (chief of police) was coming to the village to collect arrears of taxes, and would seize the last cow of this poor woman. I put my Kodak under my cloak, and hurried to the place. The *ispravnik* had not yet come, but was expected every moment. The poor woman was standing with her arm thrown over the neck of the cow, which she had managed by great struggles to keep through the famine, and now it was to be taken from her " to support the State." I took a Kodak picture of her as she stood, but when the *ispravnik* approached I judged it prudent to take myself and photographic apparatus off, much as I should have liked a portrait of the official himself. Afterwards I saw his man leading the cow away, and had at least the satisfaction of assisting to console the widow for her loss.

It must be clear to all, from these facts, that the bad crops were not the real cause of the great famine, but simply the incident that made the chronic need apparent; the destitution itself is due to the causes indicated.

" Unless we are willing to let dust be thrown in our eyes," says the prominent Russian Professor Issajev, " we must admit that under other conditions of civilisation and development, with a wiser use of our natural resources, we should not have left so wide a breach for the devastating forces of nature, such as the direction of the winds, the scanty rainfall, and the consequent drought."

# CHAPTER III.

## TOLSTOI ON THE FAMINE.

COUNT TOLSTOI had for some time foreseen that such a famine must inevitably come, and had warned the authorities of it. He had also, long before they had any correct ideas of the extent and nature of the distress, or had taken any measures to obviate it, laid before them such proposals as would, if adopted, have lessened its terrible ravages to a considerable extent at least. Such were the establishment of public works on a large scale to give remunerative employment to the people; the regulation of the prices of provisions by a fixed standard, and forbidding the hoarding of flour, &c., while the people were starving; the opening of free eating-houses in adequate numbers and capacity in the famine-stricken villages; the organisation of all available voluntary forces in rational relief work, &c. But the "powers that be" in St. Petersburg not only refused to listen to his warnings or to take his advice, but devised a fiendish policy of persecution against the noblest man their land contained. His warnings were treated as revolutionary threats, and made the basis of a report of a "widespread Nihilistic conspiracy." He had offered the Russian papers an article suggesting the best modes of meeting the distress; they refused it. According to his usual custom, he allowed it to be published by the press of other countries. In England *The Daily Chronicle* gave an English translation, in which the meaning of one sentence was not made clear. Tolstoi had said that the peasants must not only be fed, but roused from their hopeless apathy and lifted up from their deep debasement. On this sentence *The Moscow Gazette*, the principal organ of fanatical and autocratic "obscuration," fastened, making the meaning to appear as "the peasants must be roused *against the authorities.*" Prince Stcherbatoff, father-in-law of a former editor of *The Moscow Gazette*, wrote a bitter article, which that paper published, the purport of which was that "this evil" (*i.e.*, Tolstoi and his work) "must be exterminated." This led to other attacks in the press, and if Countess Tolstoi had not journeyed to St. Petersburg and obtained a private audience with the Tsar, matters would probably have been pushed to extremities. To one holding Tolstoi's faith, and it is *faith*, not mere opinion or sentiment, there could hardly be a more cruel mode of attack. Many letters came to him from all quarters after the article appeared in *The Moscow Gazette*, from university men down to simple peasants who could scarcely frame a legible letter, asking "Is it possible that our dear Count, who has taught us by word and deed to follow the teaching and example of Christ in not resisting evil, but blessing those that curse us, and doing good unto those that hate us, has fallen so far, as *The Moscow Gazette* says, as to proclaim the doctrines of hate and bloody revolt, instead of the Gospel of love, self-sacrifice, and patient endurance?" But the Count paid no attention to these attacks, and during my stay with the family I never heard from him or any of its members a word about the matter, or even the names of his persecutors.

For some time the local authorities and the Government disputed as to the very existence of the famine, the former asserting and the latter denying it, until the matter was placed beyond denial by authentic accounts of numerous deaths from starvation in different provinces. In England, however, we can hardly throw stones at the Russian Government, since we have had our own authorities gravely asking whether there were actually men who had real difficulty in finding work, and regarding the negative "information" of their own red-tape bound bureaus as more reliable than the statements of those who passed their lives among the workers and knew their circumstances intimately.

When the terrible character of the evil could no longer be disputed, the Government began to take steps for its relief. They issued circulars to all the village authorities, who were to fill in the required details and return them to headquarters. From this information they expected to know who needed help, and to distribute the relief accordingly.

Count Tolstoi, in criticism of these measures, pointed out that the failure on the part of the Government to understand the true causes of the distress made them unable to devise effective means of relieving it. Bad crops were not the cause, which lay deeper than the palliatives proposed by the Government could reach.

"The activity of the Government, having for its outward object the feeding and preservation of the well-being of forty millions of men, is met (as we have seen) by insurmountable obstacles.

"First. It is impossible to determine the *degree* of the people's need, since they may, in order to support themselves, show either a maximum of energy or complete apathy.

"Second. Even were this determination possible, the amount of bread and money required for this purpose (at least one thousand millions of roubles) is so great that there is no hope of acquiring it.

"Third. Granting the possession of this money, the gratuitous distribution of bread and money among the people would only weaken its energy and activity, which, more than anything else, is at this difficult time necessary, to maintain its well-being.

"Fourth. Allowing the distribution to be so made as not to weaken the activity of the people, there is no possibility of distributing the relief justly, and in consequence those who are not needy will get the share of the really poor, the majority of whom will remain all the while without help, and perish."

In another of his articles on the famine, which were not allowed to be published in Russia, he says : " It is in this vicious circle that the Government is moving, and there is no getting out of this *circulus vitiosus*. For the task that the Administration and the municipalities have set themselves is nothing less than to feed the people. To feed the people! Who is it, then, that has undertaken to feed the people? It is we, the officials, who have taken upon ourselves to feed those who are always feeding and always have fed us. A suckling babe wants to feed its nurse, a parasite proposes to feed the plant that nourishes it! We, the governing classes, who do not work and live upon what other people produce; we, who cannot take one step without them, *we* are now going to feed them! The very idea has something grotesque in it. Not to speak of all other wealth, we may say that the bread is directly produced by the people themselves. All the bread existing is sown, raised, havested, threshed, and distributed by the people. How is it, then, that this bread is not now in the hands of the people, but in ours, and that we are obliged, by a peculiar and artificial process, to return it to them, calculating so and so much for each individual? It is evident that we have taken it without paying for it, and have taken too much, so that we must now return it; but this restitution presents many difficulties. What then must we do? I believe we must begin by not taking what does not belong to us.

" Some children had a horse given them, a real live horse, and they went out for a drive. They went on driving, driving, always driving, up hill and down dale. The horse was all in a perspiration; it lost its breath, but always went on obediently. All the while the children shouted and cheered, boasted to each other as to who best knew how to drive, and always urged the horse to gallop. It seemed to them, as it always does, that when the horse galloped, they galloped, and they were proud of this gallop. So they amused themselves without thinking of the horse, forgetting that it lived and suffered. When they saw that it slackened its speed, they raised the whip, struck it, and shouted still more. But all things have an end, and the good horse's strength was exhausted. In spite of the whip, it slackened its speed. Only then did the children recollect that the horse was a living creature; that it is usual to give horses food and drink. But they would not stop, and tried to find a way of feeding the horse while running. One of

them took a handful of hay from under the seat of the
carriage, jumped down, and ran alongside of the horse, holding
out the hay to it.  But this was uncomfortable.  He jumped
back into the carriage, and the children devised other means.
They took a long stick, fastened the hay to one end, and,
sitting in the carriage, offered the hay to the horse.  They
thought of numberless ways, except what ought, above all, to
have entered their minds : step out of the carriage, wait, and,
if they really pitied the horse, unharness it.

"Do not the well-to-do classes, in their relation to the
labourers, in all times and in all countries, act just as those
children in urging on the horse which carried them ?  Are not
the governing classes doing the very thing that these children
did, in trying to feed the horse without stepping out of the
carriage, when they are trying, now that it has spent its
strength and must refuse to carry them further, to find means
of saving the people, of feeding it without changing their
relation to the people ?   They devise all kinds of means
except the one that appeals to the mind and heart : cease to
gallop, and step down from the horse, which they pity.

"The people are suffering from hunger, and we, the governing
classes, are very anxious, and desire to help them.  For this
purpose we form committees, hold meetings, collect money,
buy flour and bread, and distribute it among the people.  But
why do the people hunger ?  Is it possible that this should
be so hard to understand ?  Is it absolutely necessary to
calumniate them, as some arrogantly do, saying that the
people are poor because they are lazy and drunk ?  Or must
we deceive ourselves by saying that the people are poor only
because they have not assimilated our civilisation, but that
from to-morrow we will set ourselves to the task of initiating
them into all our science, hiding nothing from them, so that
then they will doubtless cease to be poor ?  Therefore we do
not need to be ashamed of living at their expense, because it
is simply for their own good !

"Must we hunt for the sun by candle-light, when everything
is so clear and simple, especially clear and simple to the people
at whose expense we live and eat ?  It may be allowable for

3

children to imagine that it is not the horse that carries them, but that it is they themselves who are going along; but we grown-up folk can very well understand how the famine has come upon the people. The people hunger because we consume too much. To us Russians this fact ought to be all the clearer. Industrial and commercial nations, like the English, who live upon their Colonies, may yet be unable to see this clearly. . . . But as regards ourselves, our connection with the people is so immediate, so evident, it is so clear that our wealth is produced by their misery, or their misery by our wealth, that it is impossible for us not to see why the people are suffering from hunger. Is it possible that the people, in such circumstances, in which they are born, *i.e.*, with these taxes, this insufficiency of land, this neglected condition and this savagery, having to perform this immense amount of labour, the fruits of which we enjoy in the shape of comforts and amusements—is it possible, I say, that these people can escape hunger?

" All these palaces, these theatres, these museums in the capitals, the cities, and small centres of population are produced by the people, who suffer and continue to produce all these things that are useless to themselves simply because they get their food thereby. That is, through this forced labour, they save themselves from the famine that is always hanging over their heads. Such is their constant position. We continually keep the people in a situation in which they never can keep themselves from hunger. This is our method of forcing them to work for us. This year the strain has been too great; the bad harvest has shown us that the string has been pulled too tightly. But what has happened is nothing extraordinary or unexpected, and we ought to understand why the people are starving. Knowing the cause, it is very easy to find the cure. The principal means of cure is not eating up their portion.

" This concern of society for the relief of the distressed people is like that of the founders of the Red Cross during war. Then the energy of some is devoted to massacre; this massacre is considered as the normal condition. On the other hand, a new activity is brought into being, of a contrary tendency, having for its aim the healing of those who suffer from the massacre. All this is excellent, so long as the war, the exhaustion and oppression of the people are considered as normal; but when we pretend to pity the men killed in the war and the sufferers from the famine, would it not be simpler not to kill, and, consequently, not to invent the means of healing? not to rob the people of their substance, and all the time we are so doing pretend to be concerned about their welfare? For the last thirty years it has become almost fashionable to profess a love for the people—for 'our younger brother,' as they say. Our society persuades itself and others that they are greatly concerned about the people's condition, and express their concern in mutual reproaches for the lack of sympathy with 'the younger brother.' 'For thirteen years I have reproached others for their lack of love for the people; what further proof is needed of my own love for them?' All this is a lie. Love of the people does not and cannot exist in our society.

"Between a member of our leisured classes—a gentleman dressed in a starched shirt, an official, a landlord, a merchant, an officer, a scientist, an artist, on the one hand, and a peasant on the other, there is only one link; the one that makes all peasants —working-men in general, 'hands,' as the English call them— necessary to work for us. We cannot hide what we all know.

"All the interests of each one of us—of science, of our occupation, of our artistic interests, of our family life—are such that we have nothing in common with the life of the people. The people do not understand the 'gentlemen,' and the latter, in spite of their belief to the contrary, neither know nor understand the life of the people.

"Voltaire said that if people in Paris could kill a mandarin in China by simply pressing a button, very few Parisians would deprive themselves of this amusement.

"Not to speak of the generations of workers who perish in the idiotic, painful, and demoralising work of the factories for the pleasure of the rich, the entire agricultural population, or at least an enormous proportion of it, is forced through insufficiency of land for their maintenance to such a fearfully intense work that it destroys their physical and moral powers, simply for the purpose of giving to their masters the possibility of increas-

ing their luxury. It is with the same object that merchants
compel the whole population to drink, and thus exploit it.
The people degenerate, the children die prematurely, and all
in order that the rich, the "gentlemen," the merchants, may
be able to live to themselves with their palaces, their dinners,
their concerts, their horses, their carriages, their flirtations, &c.

"Why deceive ourselves? We have no need of the people
except as an instrument, and our interests (by whatever argument to the contrary we comfort ourselves) are always
diametrically opposed to the interests of the people. 'The
more they give me as salary or as pension, *i.e.*, the more they
take from the people, the better for me,' says the official.
'The more the people have to pay for bread and other
necessary products, *i.e.*, the worse off the people are, the better
for me,' says the landlord. 'The longer the war lasts the
more I shall make,' says the manufacturer. 'The less paid
for wages, *i.e.*, the poorer the people are, the better it will be
for us,' say all the upper classes. What sympathy can we
have, then, for the people? Between us and them there is no
link but animosity—the link between the master and the slave.
The better off I am, the worse for the people, and *vice versâ*.

"All life in Russia, all that is past, and is passing at present,
confirms what I say. At this moment, when, as they say,
people are dying of hunger, have the landlords, have the
merchants, or the rich folk in general, modified their lives?
Have they ceased to exact from the people, to satisfy their own
caprices, a work that is frequently false? Have the rich given
up ornamenting their palaces, eating luxurious dinners, riding
their thoroughbreds, following the hounds, dressing themselves
in the height of fashion? Do not the rich at this very time
hold stores of seed and flour, expecting a still greater rise in
the price? Are not manufacturers depressing the wages of
their workers? Are not officials receiving higher salaries? Do
not all the educated classes continue to live in the cities—for
some purpose they consider very elevated—and to eat in them
the means of living which are imported there, for lack of which
people are dying?

"It is under these circumstances that we all at once begin to assure ourselves and others that we pity the people very greatly, and that we want to help them out of their misery, which we ourselves have brought upon them, a misery which is necessary to us.

"This is why those people's efforts are in vain, who with unchanged lives desire to come to the people's aid by distributing the wealth they have first taken from them.

＊          ＊          ＊

"If a man of the leisured classes really wants, not to help, but to serve his people, the first thing he ought to do is to understand clearly his relations to them. When nothing is undertaken the lies, though they remain lies, are not very hurtful. But when, as now, one wants to serve the people, the first thing to be done is to reject the lies and get to understand our relations to them. And when these are clearly seen, i.e., the fact that the people give us the means of life, that their poverty is caused by our riches, that their hunger comes from the satisfaction of our appetites, we can begin to serve in no other way than by ceasing to do what ruins them.

"My thought is this : it is love only that can save men from all miseries and calamities, including famine. But this love must not be limited to words, it must be expressed in actions. And these deeds of love consist in giving one's morsel to those that hunger, as not only Christ but also John the Baptist has said, i.e., to make a sacrifice. Therefore, I think that the very best thing to be done by those who understand the need of changing their mode of life, is to go this very year and live among the starving peasants and spend a certain time with them.

"I do not say that all who wish to help the *mushiks* ought absolutely to take up their abode in a cold hut, dwell among vermin, live on ' lebeda ' (a kind of weed), and die in two months or a fortnight; I do not say that whoever does not do this, does nothing useful. But I say that to act exactly thus, to live among them and die in two months or two weeks, would be very good, very beautiful, just as beautiful as to carry pardon and die among the lepers, as Father Damien did. But I do not say that every one can or ought to do this, and that all else is nothing. I say that the more a man's actions approach this, the more profitable will they be to himself and others, and that whoever approaches the ideal, however little, will do good. There are two extremes; on the one hand to give one's life for our fellows; on the other, to live an entirely unchanged life. Between these two extremes all men are to be found; some who act as Christ's disciples have left all to follow Him; others are like the rich young ruler, who turned and went away when he heard the Master speak of a changed life. Between this we find the different Zaccheuses, who change, but only partially. But to become like these last we must always aim at approaching the first.

"All who understand that the way to aid the starving peasants is by breaking down the barriers that separate us from them, and on this account change their mode of life, necessarily rank themselves somewhere between these limits according to their physical and moral powers. Some, as soon as they come into the country, will eat and sleep with the sufferers; others will live apart, but establish eating rooms and work there; a third set will help distribute the provisions and flour; a fourth will give money; a fifth—I can imagine such persons—will live in a famine-stricken village and do nothing but spend their income and help the casual starvelings that come in their way.

" I do not know, and I do not wish to say, if the people, the entire people, shall have enough to feed upon. I cannot know this, for independently of the famine, an epidemic may break out to-morrow, or an invasion cause the death of the people; or to-morrow a nutritious substance may be invented capable of feeding the whole world; or, simplest of all, I may die myself to-morrow, without having found out if the people have had enough food or not. The important thing is that I have not been charged with the task of feeding forty millions of people in a certain territory, and that I cannot attain this outward object, viz., to feed and save from calamity a fixed number of men, but that I ought to think of saving my soul, and bring my life as near my conscience as possible. I cannot do more than one thing : to use my powers as long as I live for the service of my brothers, regarding all without exception as my brothers.

" Strange to say, as soon as we turn from the task of solving questions of the outward life, as soon as we forget the forty millions, the price of bread in America, &c., in order to consider the problem that is true and proper to man, the question of the inner life, all the preceding matters are solved in the best manner. All the starving millions would thus be fed in a satisfactory way. On the other hand, the activity of the Government, having only an external object, the feeding of forty millions, is met, as we have seen, by insurmountable obstacles.

" No other activity can avoid these impediments in the way of Government action . . . and attain to great results that are inaccessible to Government action, than that which has an inward object—the salvation of the soul—and which always consists of sacrifice. It is this that, in the face of starvation, impels a peasant woman in a famine-stricken village, when she hears beneath her window the words " For Christ's sake " (commonly used by beggars), to hesitate before causing discontent, to take her single loaf of bread, as I have seen more than once, put it on the board, cut off a piece as large as the palm of her hand, and give it, making the sign of the cross at the time.

" For this inward activity, the first obstacle—the impossibility of determining the degree of the need—does not exist. The orphans of heaven ask for alms; the woman knows they have no resources and gives. What is impossible to an official, who is concerned with lists and documents, is easy to those who live among the needy and have in view only a small number whom they can help.

" The second obstacle—the enormous number of the poor— exists as little as the first. There are always poor people, and the whole question is, what portion of my powers can I devote to them? The woman who gives alms does not need to calculate how many millions of poor there are in Russia, what is the price of American flour, &c. There is a single question for her: how to use her knife on the loaf so as to cut off a smaller or larger slice. Small or big, she gives it, knowing that if all helped according to their ability every one would have a piece of bread, no matter how great the number of the poor.

"The third obstacle exists still less for the peasant woman. She does not fear that the slice of bread given to the orphans of heaven may weaken their energy and make them used to begging, for she knows that these children understand very well what that slice of bread that she cuts for them costs her—they see that she gives her last, or almost her last bread.

"Neither does the fourth obstacle exist. The peasant woman is not concerned as to whether she really must give to those that now stand at her window, or if there are others in still greater need, to whom she should give this slice. She pities the children of heaven, and gives to them, knowing that if all did the same there would be none dying of hunger, either now in Russia, or anywhere at any time.

"It is this kind of activity, having a moral object, that has always saved, and always will save, men. And it is this that ought to be adopted by those who want at this painful time to serve others.

"It saves people, because it is that smallest of seeds that produces the largest tree. One, two, or a dozen men living in the country, and helping according to their power, can do very little. But this activity is contagious; it is because of this power of communicating itself to others that an activity inspired by love is so important. An outward activity, expressing itself in gratuitous distribution of bread and money, according to official lists, only engenders bad feeling, greed, jealousy, hypocrisy, untruthfulness; whereas a personal activity of love evokes, on the contrary, the noblest sentiments—love and willingness to make sacrifices. . . . Herein lies the force of the activity inspired by love, that it is contagious, and therefore its influence is limitless. As one candle lights another and thousands of candles are thus set burning, so one heart kindles another, and a thousand hearts are set burning. Millions of roubles of the wealthy will achieve less than will a small abatement of greed and a little increase of love in the great mass of men. Love has only to increase, and the same miracle will take place that was accomplished in the distribution of the five loaves; all will be able to satisfy their hunger, and there will still be food to spare."

TOLSTOI TAKING NOTES.

# CHAPTER IV.

## RELIEF WORK IN RJASAN.

Countess Tolstoi's Letter—General Organisation—An Illustration of the
Position—Defects of Government Relief—Tolstoi's Methods—Visit to a
Famine-Stricken Village—Countess Maria Tolstoi and Her Father's
Work—"Traits of Civilisation"—Destitution, Disease, and Death—Miss
Kuzminsky and the *mir*—More Starving Villages—Tolstoi's Difficulties—
Some of His Helpers.

" DEAR SIR,—It is so difficult to give advice in such a matter as
beneficence.  Any help in such a distress is welcome, and an
organisation of relief for the famine-stricken in Russia could

do very much good. But organisations (private) are not permitted in Russia; every one does for the help of the people what he can.

"If any one would like to send considerable sums of money, it could be sent either to the committee of the Grand Duke Tsarevitch in St. Petersburg, or to the committee of the Grand Duchess Elizabeth in Moscow; or if you prefer to direct money in private disposition, my husband and all my family would do our best to spend it as usefully to the profit of the national distress as possible.

"I think that if you would come to Russia yourself, you could help very much, as personal help is wanted nearly as much as money help. But the life in those famine-stricken villages is very hard; one must bear very much inconvenience; and if you have never been in Russia and have no idea what a Russian village is, you will not endure life in it.

"The famine is dreadful! Though the Government is trying to do as much as possible, private help is very important. The horses are dying for want of food, the cows and all the cattle are either killed by the peasants, or are falling dead from starvation. A very small part of them will be left.

"We were thinking, if we were to receive considerable sums of money, of buying horses when spring comes in the South of Russia, so as to give our peasants the possibility of working. Our peasants can do nothing without cattle. But those are only plans. At present we have so much to do to keep the people alive. How dreadfully sad it is to see our poor suffering peasants so helpless and looking for help, so full of hope when they meet any one who shows them pity and interest! If you try, Sir, to do anything God will bless you.—Yours very truly,

"COUNTESS S. TOLSTOI.

"January 20th (Old Style), 1892."


It was this letter, in answer to one of mine, that had brought me over to Russia, with contributions from English and American friends, to help in what small way was possible the Tolstoi family in their energetic and self-denying efforts among the starving *mushiks*. In the following pages I give some account of what I saw, from notes jotted down at the time in my diary. But a few words of introduction are needful to explain something of the system on which the Count and his helpers proceeded.

I met the Countess Tolstoi at their house in Moscow on my journey through. Here she carried on the correspondence concerning the relief work, while her husband held his head-quarters at Rjasan, and the young Count Lyeff Lvovitch made Samara his centre of active operations. Countess Sophia Andreevna Tolstoi is tall and stately-looking, and retains the freshness and elasticity of her youth to a remarkable degree. Her power of work is simply wonderful. I saw a great pile of letters and telegrams she had received that day from all parts of the world. Some related to the department of relief work under her own care, which may be called the wholesale department; she was responsible for buying the immense quantities of different food-stuffs required, and despatching them to Rjasan and Samara. Others consisted of appeals for help from starving districts, but most were concerned with the financial part of the work, contributions from friends in different countries, inquiries, &c. In all this she was without the help of any secretary. "It has grown to be a habit with me," she said, "to answer all letters myself. Otherwise I cannot feel perfectly satisfied."

As regards the relief work proper, carried on by the Count and his son, it must not be imagined from what has previously been quoted from his criticisms of official methods, that Tolstoi himself neglected organisation or method, depending entirely on individual impulse. He recognised the futility of it all as a *cure*, but for the present purpose of helping the starving peasants in their terrible emergency he was quite alive to the importance of so ordering the work as to be most efficient. His view of the case was well put in the conversation I had with him on the matter. He said : "I will use an illustration to give you an idea of the state of things. Suppose this little round table placed in a distillery and covered with bottles of different sizes, all of which are filled with spirits. Beneath the table is a fierce heat that causes the contents of the bottles to evaporate, after which, in the cold air above, it is condensed and discharged in two streams, one going into the great reservoir of the capitalists, the other into that of the Government. Now, since all these bottles have been emptied, and are, therefore, unable to produce any more, they must, of course, be filled again to some extent in one way or another. A large pail is therefore taken, dipped into the great reservoir, and its contents poured over the bottles on the table, but the greater part falls outside the bottles. We are now trying to put funnels into the bottles to avoid this running outside."

A more intimate acquaintance with Government methods helped me to understand the significance of this figure. Flour was distributed monthly, according to prescribed rules. In many cases the drinking habits of the miserable *mushiks* led them to sell it at once for *vodka,* and in some it was at once seized by pitiless creditors. Supposing that neither of these calamities occurred, it lasted only for fifteen or twenty days, leaving the poor family to starve until the next distribution. Hence the sickness and death-rate went up with a bound in the latter part of each month. Much sickness was also caused by the lack of fuel among the *mushiks,* who were thus forced to eat the food raw, having no means of cooking it. There is no wood in this part, and straw is the fuel used, which of course had suffered the fate of the crops generally.

Still worse was the system of selection employed by the Government. No help was given to "labourers"; *i.e.,* those able to work, or to those possessing horses and cattle. It was entirely left out of consideration that there was no work for these unfortunate people to do, and no food for their cattle. Again, there was little hope for the "black sheep," that is, the sectarians, the Stundists, persons of non-Russian extraction, and all who were not *personæ gratæ* to the "powers that be" or their representatives. Further, expenses were shamefully heavy, and large quantities of flour were stolen, adulterated with sand, chaff, &c., or allowed to spoil. I noted more than one case of this kind that came under my own observation.

Tolstoi's "putting in funnels" meant, then, the relief of those overlooked by the officials, and whatever might be done to remedy these defects. It was not easy. Even the discovery of the most needy was far from being as simple as it looked. To our notions, all the *mushiks* would have qualified *en masse* under that heading, but to the Russian workers there were grades, "and in the lowest depths a lower deep"! Another obvious idea was to apply to the *starosta* (head man of the

STAROSTA.    MARIA TOLSTOI.    MISS KUZMINSKY.

CONSULTING THE STAROSTA.

village), or to the pope, but alas! the *starosta* is not always one in whom there is no guile, nor is the pope always a saint. The only reliable method was for the Count and his assistants to go into the villages themselves, and compile from individual inquiries the lists of names and details needed for wise and efficient aid. Then these were verified by the calling together of the entire village community, or *mir*, when the lists were gone through and discussion held as to the best means of relieving the most distressed. It is probable that these tables were the most exact statistics in Russia.

The principal means of relief was by eating-rooms, where two meals a-day were served free to the most needy. Where the villagers had a supply of flour, warm food only was served; in other places warm food and bread. Special rooms were opened later for the children.

Another branch was the supply of fuel; about four hundred cords of wood were distributed during the winter, either free or in return for work done. Then the horses were cared for as much as possible; large numbers were sent to other parts where fodder could be got, and three hundred were placed in a large stable built for the purpose.

Work materials in the shape of flax and bast were supplied to the *mushiks*, that they might both work at their own clothing and make shoes, which the Count bought at full price, for distribution among the poorest.

Then there was the provision of seed and replacement of stock, with a view to prevent, as far as possible, a repetition of the famine. This was usually done on condition of a moderate return being made after the following harvest, and the income from this source was destined towards establishing homes for destitute children.

The work in Samara was on the same model. I can now proceed to give incidents taken from the notes in my diary.

Before 6 a.m. the starving *mushiks* began to gather at the headquarters. Half-an-hour later they filled both the yard and the ante-room, where they stood with heads uncovered, silently waiting their turn to see the Count. Tolstoi himself, his daughter Maria, her cousin Miss Kuzminsky, and two others were busy writing down the names of the applicants or distributing relief. The ravages of the famine among the members of the evil-smelling, motley crowd were evident in the haggard looks of some and the swollen faces of others.

The young Countess had been up very early in the morning to attend to household matters before joining in the relief work, which lasted until the time came for breakfast, and after that for visiting the villages. Breakfast (at 9 o'clock) consisted of *kasha* (a kind of porridge), bread-and-butter, potatoes and other vegetables, tea and coffee, the young Countess Maria acting as hostess. Her elder sister, Tatiana, had also been at headquarters, but had had to return home on account of failing health. Maria Lvovna or "Masha," as the Count calls her, is a devoted follower of her father.

It had been arranged that I should accompany the Countess Maria on her round through the villages. Dressed in a polashubok (see illustration), felt boots, and a cap of Siberian lambskin, she opened the door of my room and called out " Ready." In my Lapponian dress I came out and took my place at her side in a *sani*, a primitive and unpainted sleigh, drawn by a well-fed, little black horse. Just as we were starting, I found that I had forgotten my gloves. "Here, take mine," said the Count, who stood by the side of the sleigh. Off we went at whirling speed, the Countess holding the reins herself. I believe that Russian ladies beat those of all other countries, even in America, in horsemanship. I have often seen them driving a *troika*, or sleigh, with three horses abreast. Certainly the Countess knew how to drive. In a few minutes we had passed the Don and were out on the desolate plains. The air was keen and biting, and a blinding snowstorm swept over the steppes ; the road was destitute of the customary marks, and we soon lost our way. After driving for some time with the snow whirling about us so that we could not see the length of the horse, she drew rein and said, " I think we must turn back home. Soon we shall see nothing." " Do you know the direction of the village to which we are going? " I asked. " Yes." "Then let us try to get there." "All right. Get up, Malchik!" (Little Boy). Off we sped westward along an ice-covered ridge, and after a time found the road again.

The Countess told me that she had worked for a number of years among the peasants trying to help them. She had had a school for peasant children on their estate, but as she did not teach them to cross themselves nor to worship the pictures of the saints, the priests had her school closed. Then she invited the children to her house to tea, and continued to teach them over the tea-table.

Talking about their home and the large number of strangers
coming to see her celebrated father—often, no doubt, out of
mere curiosity — I remarked that he was said to deny the
immortality of man. "This," I said, "I have never been able
to understand, as being incompatible with his view of life and
way of living."

WAITING FOR HELP.

"My father deny the immortality of man!" she exclaimed.
"You should have heard him recently in a circle of friends.
As our shadowy dreams, he said, are to our present life, so
this shadowy life is to our future existence." Speaking of
God she said, "They try to define what God is and what He
is not, but whatever beautiful and grand words they use, I say

that He is infinitely more than that. I like best of all to call Him Father. Is it not beautiful to think that the highest good is our Father ? "

Our conversation turned to the literary works of the Count,

COUNTESS MARIA TOLSTOI.

and she told me how he came to write his satirical play, "The Fruits of Civilisation."

"It was one winter night, and we had just finished our work for the day. 'Let us have some fun,' said my sister Tanja. 'Yes, let us improvise a spiritualistic *séance*.' Father joined in, and wrote down a sketch of the play to be improvised;

4

this he afterwards finished, and it was published under the title of ' The Fruits of Civilisation.' "

The play was performed three times ; once was in Yasnaja Poljana, and a second time in the town of Tula, the Count's eldest daughter, Tatiana, playing the part of Tanja (the heroine being named after her). The third time it was played by a company of aristocratic amateurs at Tarskoje Selo, the summer residence of the Tsar, in the presence of sixteen grand dukes and duchesses, and other high dignitaries, numbering about 250 persons—of course, " for a benevolent purpose." It was a great success. The high-born audience laughed, and applauded the biting satire, the point of which was directed against their own society ! What a grotesque scene ! On the Emperor's private stage, the victory of the people is represented by members of the highest aristocracy ! But who in these circles thinks of this bitter self-mockery ? Pungent means are required to amuse persons enervated by idleness, epicurism, and licentiousness—so they laugh at the amusing surface, without being touched by the author's deep pain and sympathy with the oppressed, that throbs through the whole piece.

By this time we saw through the storm a long row of what looked like snow-covered mounds. It was the village of Pinki. Approaching nearer, we found that the mounds were peasants' huts, half buried in the deep snow-drifts. The village looked poor and desolate in the extreme. No smoke was rising from any of the huts, every other one of which was roofless. No living body was seen about ; all appeared to be ruin and death.

We stopped at one of the *izbas*, in which the Count had opened a school and eating-room. For some time after our entrance we could see nothing distinctly, but our feet told us that the naked soil served as floor. When our eyes grew accustomed to the gloom we saw a number of benches, and standing between them about thirty children, silently looking at us. The teacher, an intelligent young man, approached and saluted us. In one corner were a couple of elderly people. From the neighbourhood of the oven came heavy breathing and coughing, and, lying on top of it, we saw three children,

covered with black small-pox. I suggested that these ought to
be removed at once, and the Countess replied that it would be
done as soon as possible, but as there were no hospitals, and
almost every house was infected, it was not easy to isolate the
sick. These poor children had been brought to the school,
"because it was warm there."

Leaving the Countess to attend to the school and eating-
room, I went through part of the village from house to house.

In *izba* No. 1 I found one cow, three elderly people, one of
whom was lying on top of the oven, sick with typhus, by the
side of two children in the last stages of black small-pox.

In No. 2 was a child with black small-pox, an old man with
typhus, and two women whose bodies were all swollen. No
cattle—all starved : no fuel, no food.

In No. 3 a curious sight met my eyes. When I entered
the small hut, the earthen floor of which was frozen hard, I
saluted, but got no reply, nor could I see anyone. I was about
to go, but heard heavy breathing, and a sound like sweeping
proceeding out of the oven. All at once a pair of feet
wrapped with rags protruded, and in a moment a big *mushik*
crept out of the opening, followed by a sickly-looking woman,
shivering and pressing her right hand on her brow. I asked
what was the matter. "*Golova bolit*" (my head aches), she
answered. "Have you no children?" "Yes : look here!" she
said, bursting into tears and pointing to what looked like a
bundle of rags on top of the oven. It proved to be two
children, one on the point of death from hunger or consumption, and the other in the extremes of black small-pox. The man,
tall and strongly built, stood with drawn stony face and hollow
eyes, his tangled hair sticking out in all directions, motionless
on the frozen floor, a picture of hopeless apathy. No cattle,
no food, but what was given from outside.

No. 4. Two grown people and two children, both ill. As
she moved the rags that covered one of the children the
mother burst into tears, and I saw great drops rolling down the
cheeks of the poor disfigured girl herself. Something stuck
in my own throat as, unable to utter a word, I gave the poor
woman a silver coin and passed out.

No. 5 contained a woman, disfigured by a disease shockingly common among the peasants, and two sickly and forlorn-looking children.

No. 6 sheltered three families, one cow, one horse, and two sheep, all huddled together to protect themselves from the intense cold. It was a strange sight to see the fine-looking *dyadushka*, or grandfather, with snow-white hair and beard, climb out of the crib to which the horse was tied, come tottering up to me on his aged limbs, and salute with a deep bow. I told him that friends of the *mushiks*, in foreign lands, had sent me with help to their suffering brothers in Russia. In a feeble and trembling voice he said, "What good people! May God bless you!"

On my return to the school I found it changed into an eating-room, filled with about forty persons, young and old, who sat down to eat, after crossing themselves and saying their prayers. The dinner, consisting of black rye bread and pea soup, tasted very good. When the Countess had arranged for the opening of an eating-room for little children we started to return home.

"What is your impression from your first village visit?" asked the Countess.

"Terrible," was all I could say. "Are you not afraid of catching small-pox and typhus?"

"Afraid! It is immoral to be afraid. Are you afraid?" she replied.

"No, I have never been afraid of infection while visiting the poor," I said. "It is terrible to see such hopeless misery. It makes me sick only to think of it."

"And is it not shameful for us to allow ourselves so much luxury while our brothers and sisters are perishing from want and nameless misery?" she added.

"But you have sacrificed all the comforts and luxuries of your rank and position, and stepped down to the poor to help them," I rejoined.

"Yes," she said, "but look at our warm clothes and all other comforts, which are unknown to our suffering brothers and sisters."

AN EATING ROOM.

" But what good would it do to them if we should dress in rags and live on the edge of starvation ? "

" What right have we," she retorted, " to live better than they ? "

I made no reply, but glanced wonderingly into the eyes of this remarkable girl, and saw there a large tear trembling; something seemed to press on my heart and threaten to choke me. " But how is it possible that the authorities permit such a terrible state of things ? "

"I don't know," was the short and significant answer.

In the evening the Count seemed quite downcast. " I feel really ashamed of this work," he said. " We don't know what real help there is in it. We are prolonging the existence of a number of the starving peasants for some time, but their misery will go on all the same ! "

" You also help them spiritually," I said. " You are doing a good work."

" I don't preach," he said. " I am so bad myself that I cannot preach to others. And we do not know what is good and what is not; when we think we do something very good, it may be quite the reverse. The real good is in the will and the motives of our deeds."

Next morning I started out with Miss Kuzminsky on a visit to two villages to arrange for the distribution of wood. The plan adopted was as follows : It was left free at the homes of the most destitute. Those not so badly off had to fetch it from the railway station, and from the least needy some return in work was expected.

We reached the first village after a rapid drive of two hours over the snow-covered plain in a bitter cold, and stopped at the house of the *starosta*. Inside we found him, his wife, four children, the grandfather, one cow, one foal, and three sheep, gathered in one room, lighted dimly by an opening of about eighteen inches in diameter. A large table stood on the soft earthen floor, and a bench ran along one side of the room; there were no chairs. We paid some visits at individual *izbas*, and then the *mir* was summoned to the *starosta's* house. This was a work of no great difficulty, as almost the entire population of the village was following us as we went. Soon the *izba* was crammed with *mushiks*. Miss Kuzminsky took her place behind the table, and by request I sat beside her. Then the proceedings began. Miss Kuzminsky had a list of the most needy. To the first, a poor widow with four children, all nodded assent, crossing themselves. Then came Alexis B——. There was a low murmur through the room, and a *mushik* said, "Certainly

FROST AND FAMINE.

he has no fuel, but neither have any of us, and he has a horse." Ivan K—— was mentioned. "*Otchen bedni!*" (Very poor). So the entire list was run through, opinions being freely given on each case, while the sheep and the cow every now and then expressed their opinion in their own language. Miss Kuzminsky made an excellent president, calling the speakers to order when they spoke too many at a time, or wandered from the subject. The *mushiks* themselves behaved in a gentlemanly

manner, and when they grew a little warm, there was nothing
of the disorder that would ensue in European gatherings, if
each one's character was canvassed as openly as at these
meetings of the *mir*.

The atmosphere was simply stifling, partly owing to the
vermin and the cattle, and I was astonished that Miss
Kuzminsky could stand it for over an hour without the least

MISS KUZMINSKY AND THE PEASANTS.

complaint. In this village also we found many sick folk,
mostly suffering from black small-pox or typhus.

On another occasion I went out with another guide, a young
nobleman who had joined Tolstoi's band of workers. It was
an intensely cold Saturday morning, and a greenish-yellow
band along the eastern horizon threw a dim light over the
snow-covered plain. We were bound for a distant village that
had appealed for help. Soon our shaggy little horse was white
with frost. The sun rose and gilded everything with his

light, but a sense of desolation oppressed us as we drew near the village. No smoke was rising anywhere. Most of the *izbas*-were roofless, having been stripped for fuel. No living creature was to be seen, except two or three skin-covered skeletons of horses, picking a blade or two of old and rotten grass in front of a recently-dismantled *izba*, and a few forlorn-looking dogs, almost too starved to move from their places on the dirt-heaps in front of the huts. Death or desertion had emptied many of these, and in almost every house we entered there were persons sick of typhus, small-pox, &c. All the help received from the authorities was consumed, most of the cattle had died, and for food they used a kind of bread made of dried and powdered grass, chaff, straw, and leaves from trees. Those who were not ill with fever, &c., were almost too weak to move or speak.

We reached home just before Count Tolstoi, whose good spirits were in great contrast to our weariness. He talked and laughed merrily, and his eyes fairly beamed with joy. The cause of his delight was soon told. He had finally overcome all obstacles and established his children's eating-room. A simple matter this, to our ideas, but it had cost him many a weary day of struggle against difficulties. The mere procuring of suitable food was hard enough, but there was also the ignorance, superstition, and folly of the *mushiks*, and the bitter opposition of the clergy to overcome. The *mushiks* wanted the children's food brought to their homes, but Tolstoi knew well that in that case the children would get but little of it. Then the priests frightened them with tales of learned theologians having conclusively proved out of the Book of Revelation that Tolstoi was veritably Antichrist. The story of his branding the *mushiks* on the forehead to seal them to the power of the devil has already been alluded to ; in this foolish and wicked story which was preached from the pulpit, it was said that the Count paid the peasants eight roubles apiece as purchase-money. Only the Sunday before a Bishop had delivered a special sermon in the second-class waiting-room at the railway station at Klekotki, before a crowded audience, dishing up all these fables and denouncing the Count in the strongest terms as Antichrist, who was seducing them with food, fuel, and other worldly goods. The Orthodox Church, he said, was strong enough to "exterminate Antichrist and his work."

No wonder that many were frightened. But one of the *mushiks* in my hearing, settled the matter to his own satisfaction in a very logical way. "If the Lord," he said, "is like his servants, the popes and officials who oppress and rack us, and Antichrist is such a person as Tolstoi, who freely feeds us and our children, I had rather belong to Anti-Christ, and I shall send my starving children to his eating-room." Later on, the peasants sent their children by thousands.

After our late dinner, while the Count was busy and the *mushiks*, crowding as usual to his headquarters, I took a walk, and noticed a *gendarme*, probably stationed there to keep a watch on what was going on. Besides this open representative of the Government of Petersburg, there was a crowd of detectives, swarming in or about Byegitchevka. Sometimes they would come disguised as applicants, asking for help and denouncing the authorities; sometimes as friends, volunteering their services. The Count's experienced eye, however, soon detected these, and he politely told them that they were not wanted.

The evening of the same memorable Saturday saw a gathering of helpers and friends from different quarters, who had come to spend that night and part of the following Sunday in consultation and friendly intercourse with their master. Of this highly interesting group, of whom two were women, none were above middle age, and all were educated, some possessing a high degree of learning, and all from prominent families. One had been a Fellow of Moscow University and was about to be nominated to a professorship, when he suddenly quitted the University and "went to the people." In *mushik* dress he shares the peasant's life and toil, helping them in every possible way, believing this to be a better object of life than the attempt to beat Greek and Latin into the heads of the Russian upper class youth. Yet he was no dreamer, but a man of imperturbable calmness of mind, acute understanding, and deep knowledge of human nature. Two years ago, he

travelled, mostly on foot, through all the provinces of this vast
empire, visiting and studying all kinds of sectarians, working
his way as a day-labourer, and securing in return only food and
lodging.

BEFORE A DISMANTLED *IZBA.*

# CHAPTER V.

## TOLSTOI'S TABLE TALK.

War—An Expensive Conscience—Modern Religious Sects—Religion and Invention—The Russian Sectarians—" The Café of Surat "—Attitude to Political Governments—Western Literature and Mammon—Forthcoming Books—Is Tolstoi a Christian ?—The Nature of His Christianity.

AT evening, sitting round the boiling samovar or the tea-table, Count Tolstoi would converse with his friends on different subjects. Out of kindness to me, the conversation was often carried on in any of the Western languages, but when it grew animated it insensibly glided into Russian, which I but imperfectly understood. What I did not understand, however, was for the most part kindly translated by one of the company.

Naturally, the terrible distress and the incidents of relief work formed the staple matter of conversation, but at times other topics were introduced. Here I give a merely fragmentary account of some talks on more important subjects. Speaking of modern militarism, Count Tolstoi asked me once about the feeling of the people in my country towards the Russians. I told him that the pagan idea that certain nations were our natural enemies, and the abominable system of educating children in that unchristian belief, was gradually giving way to sounder and more Christian views, and added that our *people* certainly had no enmity towards the Russian people, and that many of our most thoughtful men were looking to Russia when in these days they wanted to find those who could afford to keep a conscience and follow its behests.

After a moment's silence, the Count said, " I like that expression—to afford to keep a conscience. But I tell you, *it is very expensive !* " Then he spoke of his great hopes for the future, from the gradual change in popular opinion in favour of Christian relations between the nations, *i.e.*, that they are awakening to the fact that we are all brothers, and cutting themselves loose from the pagan official tradition, inculcated and supported by the established churches, that we are enemies.

Speaking of the religious question, he referred to the fact that Protestant churches have been and often are quite as intolerant as the Roman and Greek churches, and that Nonconformist denominations have the same tendency. He showed thorough acquaintance with the Nonconformist and Pietistic movement in Western countries. In his view, this movement in its first beginnings fulfilled an important mission in rousing the people from their spiritual stupor, and breaking the fetters of ecclesiastical tyranny and formalism. But already it has largely lost its power for good by failing to follow the teaching and example of Christ; it has followed the example of the State churches in allowing organisation and money to play a more prominent part than practical Christianity.

It is this stepping aside from Christ's Christianity which has at all times led to the decline of religious denominations. Modern ecclesiastical and denominational Christianity, with its politics, its religious business-system, its dogmas, its formalism, its intolerance, is altogether artificial and opposed to the true interests of man. Christ's Christianity, on the other hand, satisfies his deepest needs, both in his private and social relations.

Tolstoi had received books and papers descriptive of themselves, both from the Salvation Army and the Mormons. Of the latter he said: "I have read their books with much interest. It is remarkable what a prominent part invention plays in the different religious systems. It differs largely, however, in degree. With Joseph Smith we might say that it constitutes 90 per cent., whereas with Moses it amounts to 10 per cent."

Concerning the modern Christian sects in general, he said: "Above all things Christians ought to put themselves into a natural relation to one another and the world at large, *i.e.*, to follow Christ and realise His teaching in daily life, instead of wasting their time and energy in organising sects, building churches, supporting clergy, and fighting each other's dogmas."

Of the present religious movement in Russia, which has certainly raised the Sectarians to a much higher level than the Orthodox peasantry, Tolstoi has a high opinion. He gave interesting accounts of peasants who have both grasped and retained a firmer hold upon practical and central Christian ideas than many learned theologians. One night he read a deeply interesting letter from an old Stundist peasant, who had taught himself to read and write at the advanced age of sixty, in order to be able to read the Bible for himself. This letter is translated and given in the account of the Stundist movement later on in this book. When he had finished reading it, he said, "I tell you, these men are real heroes!"

Russian peasants very frequently consult the Count, either personally or in writing, about their perplexities on religious or moral questions, or come to him as a friend to confide their opinions to him, and discuss the matters in point.

His sympathies, like his views, are broad enough to comprehend what is good and true in all men and creeds. This is shown both in his writings and his conversation. True, he criticises narrowness and combats error, and that not infrequently in vigorous terms, but this is not for the mere pleasure of opposing others. His desire is to prepare the way for truth and make openings for the light. To come into personal contact with this man, and listen to his words, is to feel at once that you are under the spell of a passionate lover of truth and righteousness.

There is a fable written by the Count, and published in the *Vestnik Europi*, called "The Café of Surat," which will be of interest, as it contains the ideas he frequently expresses in different forms in his conversation, and may fitly find a place in his "table talk."

### THE CAFÉ OF SURAT.

In the Indian town of Surat was a café, where travellers and strangers from all parts used to resort, and many folk were gathered together.

One day there entered a learned Persian theologian. He had spent his whole life in studying the being of God, and had both read and written many books on the subject. He had thought, read and written so much about God that he had lost all power of right thinking, and became muddled in his head to such a degree that he had lost faith in God altogether. When the Persian King heard of this he banished him from his kingdom.

After having belaboured his brains all his life concerning the First Cause, this unhappy theologian had become so confused that instead of perceiving that he had himself lost his mind, he began to think that no greater mind ruled the world than his own.

This theologian had a slave, an African, who accompanied him everywhere. When the theologian went into a café, the African remained outside in the court, and sat on a stone in the sun; so he sat at this time driving away the flies. The theologian threw himself on a divan, and ordered a small cup of opium, which was brought to him. When he had finished the whole cup, and the poison began to work in his brain, he turned to his slave and said,

"Now, wretched slave, tell me, is there a God or not?"

"Of course there is," said the slave, and pulled out a little wooden idol from his girdle. "Here is the God that has protected me all my life in this world. It is made of a bough of that holy tree that is worshipped everywhere in our land."

The other customers in the café heard the conversation between the theologian and his slave, and were astonished. The question seemed to them odd enough, but the slave's answer more so.

A Brahmin, who heard what the slave said, turned to him, and exclaimed, "Miserable fool! how is it possible to believe that God can be hidden in a man's girdle? There is only one God—Brahma. That God is greater than the whole world, for he created the whole world. Brahma is the one great God, the God to whom temples have been raised on Ganges' shores; the God who is served only by his priests, the Brahmins. These priests alone have knowledge of the true God. Twenty thousand years have already passed, and how many revolutions have taken place in the world, yet these priests have remained what they always were, because God, the one true God, protects them."

So spoke the Brahmin, believing that he had convinced them all. But a Jewish money-lender, who was present, answered him.

"Nay," said he, "the temple of the true God is not in India. And God does not protect the Brahmin caste. The true God is not the God of the Brahmins, but of Abraham, Isaac, and Jacob; and the true God only protects His own people, Israel. From the beginning of the world God has continually loved and does love our people only. And though our people are now scattered throughout the whole world, that is merely to try them, and God will, because He loves us, gather His people again in Jerusalem, and once more rebuild that wonder of the ancient world, the temple at Jerusalem, and raise Israel to the lordship over all other nations."

Thus said the Jew, and burst into tears. He would have gone on with his speech, but an Italian who was there broke in on him.

" You do not speak the truth," he said to the Jew, "you do not describe God rightly. God cannot love one nation more than another; on the contrary, if He did in former years protect Israel, eighteen hundred years have now passed by since God's wrath was kindled against His people, and as proof of this wrath of His, He cut off their existence and scattered them over the whole world, so that their faith is not only no longer spreading, but only exists in a few places. God shows favour to no nation, but He calls all who wish to be saved into the bosom of the Roman Catholic Church, outside which there is no salvation."

So spoke the Italian; but a Protestant clergyman, who was among the company, changed colour and answered the Catholic missionary.

" How can you say that salvation is only to be found in your religion ? Learn to know that they only can be saved who

5

serve God in spirit and in truth after the law of Jesus, according to the Gospel."

A Turk, a customs officer in Surat, who was sitting smoking his pipe, turned at this to the two Christians with an earnest look.

" It is useless for you to be so certain of the truth of your Romish religion," said he.  " Your faith has already been superseded by Mohammed's teaching for six hundred years past.  Moreover, as you can see yourself, Mohammed's correct doctrine is spreading more and more both in Europe and Asia, even in enlightened China.  You yourself recognise that the Jews are rejected of God, and that the proof of it is that they are abased, and their faith is no more on the increase.  Only those who believe on God's last prophet shall be saved—and of these Omar's followers alone, and not those of Ali, for these are unbelievers."

At this remark the Persian theologian, who belonged to Ali's sect, wished to reply.  But at that moment a general dispute arose between all the strangers of different religions and creeds.  There were Abyssinian Christians, Indian Lamas, Ishmaelites, and fire-worshippers.  They all disputed about the essence of God, and how He ought to be worshipped.  Everyone maintained that only in his land was the true God known and worshipped as He should be.  All quarrelled and shouted at one another.  A certain Chinese alone, who was there, a disciple of Confucius, sat quietly in a corner and took no part in the hubbub.  He drank his tea, and listened to what the others were saying, but himself kept silence.  The Turk, who caught sight of him during the dispute, turned to him and said: " Help me, dear Chinese.  You are silent, but you can very well say something to support my contention. I know that just now different religions are being introduced into China.  Your merchants have more than once told me that you Chinese look upon the Mohammedan religion as the best of all, and willingly embrace it.  Come to my assistance, and say what you think of the true God and His prophet."

" Yes, yes ! " chimed in the others, as they turned to him.

The Chinese Confucian shut his eyes, thought awhile, and

then opened them, while he drew out his hands from the wide sleeves of his dress, folded them on his breast, and began to speak in a quiet, mild voice.

"Gentlemen," he said, "it seems to me that it is just their own pride that more than anything else prevents men from agreeing in religious matters. If it will not weary you, I will make this clear by a parable. I journeyed from China to Surat by an English steamer, which was on a voyage round the world. On the way we stopped at the east coast of Sumatra to take in water. At noon we went ashore and sat by the seaside under the shade of some cocoa palms, not far from some native villages. There were representatives of several different nationalities in the company. While we were sitting there a blind man came to us. He had become blind, as we learnt later, from looking too long and keenly at the sun. In consequence of his continual gazing at and thinking about the sun he had at the same time lost both his sight and his reason. Since he was perfectly blind he had become fully convinced that there was no sun at all. He was accompanied by his slave, who settled his master in the shade of a cocoa palm, picked up a cocoanut, and began to make a night-light from it. He made a wick out of the fibre, pressed oil from the nut, and dipped the wick in it. While he was occupied with this the blind man sighed and said, ' Well, slave, what do you think now? Did I not tell you that there is truly no sun at all? See how dark it is, yet men say that there is a sun. But if so, what is the sun?'"

"' I don't know what the sun is,' said the slave; ' it doesn't matter to me; but there is a light, I know that. Here is a night-light that I have made, that gives light enough for me to serve you with, and get things ready about the cottage,' and he held up his cocoanut shell, ' Here,' he said, ' is my sun.'

"A lame man was sitting there with his crutches. He listened, and began to laugh. ' You have surely been born blind,' said he to the sightless man, ' if you don't know what the sun is. I will tell you what it is. The sun is a fireball, and this fireball rises every day out of the sea, and goes down every evening among the mountains of our island. We all see it, and you would too, if you had your sight.'

" A fisherman, who also sat there, said to the lame man, ' It is very evident that you have never been outside your island. If you weren't a cripple, you would have been to sea, and known that the sun does not go down among the mountains on our island, but just as it rises out of the sea in the morning, so it goes down into the sea every night. I am telling the truth, for I see it with my own eyes every day.'

" An Indian heard him. 'It amazes me,' he said, ' how a sensible man can talk such rubbish. How can a fireball possibly sink into the sea and not be quenched? The sun is truly no fireball—the sun is a god, and that god is called Diva. The god drives in a chariot round the golden mountain Speruvia. Sometimes it happens that the fierce serpents Ragn and Keta attack Diva and swallow him, and then it gets dark. But our priests pray that the god may be delivered, and then he is set free. Only ignorant men like you, who have never been out of it, could imagine that the sun shines only on your island.'

" A captain of an Egyptian vessel, who chanced to be there, struck in. ' Nay,' he said, ' that, too, is folly. The sun is no god, and he does not only go round India and that golden mountain of yours. I have sailed far and wide, both in the Red Sea and the Arabian Gulf; I have also been to Madagascar and the Phillipine Islands, and the sun shines on all lands, and not India only. He does not go round any particular mountain, but rises by the Japan Isles—that is just the reason they are called Japan, because in their language it means "The Sun's Birth"—and sets far away in the West, beyond the British Isles. I know this, because I have seen it myself, and have heard a great deal about it from my grandfather, and my grandfather sailed to the world's end.'

" He would have gone on talking, but an English sailor from our ship interrupted him.

" 'There is no country where they know so much about the sun's course as in England. The sun, as we all know quite well in England, doesn't stop anywhere, but keeps on going round the world.' But not knowing how to explain it quite clearly, he pointed to the pilot, and said, 'He's a much cleverer chap than I, and can explain the way of it more clearly.'

" The pilot was an intelligent man, and had listened in silence to the conversation till he was appealed to. But now, as they all turned to him, he began to speak, and said : ' You are all mistaken, both you and the rest. The sun does not go round the earth, but the earth round the sun ; besides this, the earth turns round its own axis, so that in the course of twenty-four hours Japan, the Phillipine Islands, and Sumatra, where we now are, also Africa, Europe, Asia, and many other countries beside, turn towards the sun. The sun shines not only on the earth, but on many other planets which are like the earth. Those of you who are willing to be convinced of this have only to look up into the sky and then on yourselves here ; you will no longer believe that the sun shines only for you or your own land.' So spoke the wise pilot, who had travelled widely round the world, and gazed much into the heavens.

" Yes, the mistakes, divisions, and strife of men concerning religious questions come from pride," went on the Confucian. " As it is with the sun, so also about God. Every man will have his special god, or, at least, one for his native land. Every nation desires to shut up in its own temple what the whole world cannot contain. And can any temple compare with that which God Himself has built to unite in it all people in one religion and one faith ? All human temples are built after the pattern of that temple—God's world. In all temples there are founts, arched vaults, lamps, pictures, inscriptions, law-books, offerings, altars, and priests. In what temple is there such a baptistery as the ocean, such a vault as the sky, such lamps or candles as the sun, moon, and stars, such pictures as living men who love and help each other ? What inscriptions concerning God's goodness are so easy to understand as the blessings that God has everywhere lavished on us for our happiness ? What law-book is so plain and clear as that written in man's own heart ? Where are offerings of such worth as those offerings of self-sacrifice, that loving human beings make for their neighbour's sake ? And where is the altar that can compare with a good man's heart, on which God Himself receives the offering? The loftier man's thought of God, the better his knowledge of Him. And the better he knows God, the more nearly will he approach Him, and resemble Him in His goodness, mercy, and love to the human race. But let not him who sees God's full light, that fills the whole world, condemn or despise the superstitious man, who in his little idol sees only a ray of the same light; neither let him despise the unbeliever who is blind and sees no light at all."

So spake the Chinese, the disciple of Confucius, and all in the café were silent, and no longer disputed as to which religion was best. So ends the parable.

The position of Tolstoi and those who think with him with regard to the political government of the world has been greatly misrepresented in many quarters. It is true that they repudiate all worldly authority in general, because they are convinced of the equality of all men, and regard the unnatural relations that now prevail between the masters and the bemastered as a consequence of evolution on wrong lines. But a violent revolution against the present powers would be equally contrary to their principles, because they believe the command " Resist not evil " to be fundamental in morals. On these grounds they disapprove utterly of the " physical force " policy of the terrorist party.

Tolstoi and his friends do not think much of Western literature. They say that like everything else in the present system of society it is dominated by money-power, and consequently betrays great laxity of morals. According to them, money plays the most powerful part in the production of books. The object of their making is money, and because they are made to sell, their contents are such as to be pleasing instead of true. The judgment of the critics is biassed, and these influence the choice and sale of books. Moreover, the publishers, who are powerful and wealthy themselves, exercise great pressure on the press and critics generally; and the retail booksellers are also under the same pressure of pecuniary motives. Hence it follows that the vast flood of Western literature that issues from the press is tainted in its source, and poisoned throughout by the deadly influence of Mammon. The most revolting example of this they consider to be the composition and sale of hymns to the love of God and books concerning Jesus, all with a view to amassing money ; a proceeding that is in most violent contrast to the whole life and teaching of the Master. Everyone knows that Tolstoi himself is consistent in this ; that he retains no copyright in his works. It may not be so generally known that in Russia his books, forbidden by the censor to be printed, are written out by hand at immense cost, and distributed at a price much below the value of the labour of copying them. It seems scarcely credible that this laborious process should be necessary in these days of automatic compositors and rapid presses, yet who knows whether the influence of the works so copied and circulated in manuscript is really less than that of the enormous mass of printed literature that issues from the press of Western Europe ?

Tolstoi told me once that he desired to write two books before his death. One was to be a kind of counterblast to the increasingly martial spirit of the time, that seemed almost personified in the young German Emperor. This has since been published under the title of " The Kingdom of Heaven is Within You." It is, as the Count meant it to be, a kind of summing up of the case against all use of physical force.

The other, that has not yet appeared, was to be the history of some Russian colonists, who had unknowingly settled outside the frontier of Eastern Siberia. There, away from all interference from Government officials, they had built up a little commonwealth of their own by the simple development that sprang from the natural satisfaction of their common needs, and passed several years in peace and quiet happiness. But one fine day the authorities discovered them. It was true they were beyond the frontier and outside the Russian jurisdiction, but that was a small difficulty in the eyes of the paternally benevolent Government. They simply shifted the frontier so as to include the colony, and thus conferred on the unwilling people the inestimable blessings of life under an autocratic despotism, with its accompanying delights of excessive taxation, police supervision, forced military service, landlordism, established ecclesiasticism, &c. Yet some people do not know when they are well off. From that day the happiness and prosperity of the colonists has become a thing of the past. The question has often been put by prominent religious people in England, "But is Tolstoi a Christian?" Well, that depends entirely on your conception of what a Christian is. If it is a matter of creed or ritual, no doubt Tolstoi would have to be rejected by most of the divisions into which nominal Christians have fallen. Tested by the standard of the Greek Church, he is not, for he has no belief in the validity of their ecclesiastical traditions, the powers of the priests, the efficacy of their pardons, the utility of saint worship, &c. Or by the Romish test, he thinks nothing of the infallibility of the Pope, the Immaculate Conception, the power of priestly absolution, of ecclesiastical bannings or blessings. He is outside the Anglican fold, for he has no faith in "orders," or in the apostolical succession. "Evangelicals," so called, cannot claim him as one of them, for he does not accept their theories about the inspiration of the Bible or the exact relations of the Persons of the Trinity, or their favourite explanation of Christ's work of salvation. What is left of the Christian faith, you ask?

Tolstoi is not so much concerned with beliefs about, as faith in, God and Jesus Christ. He believes in God as a child believes in his father. That is, he trusts His wisdom and His love, although he feels unable to give metaphysical definitions of these attributes, and precise explanations of the manner in which they work. To him God expresses all that is good, noble, true, pure, and beautiful. He believes in Jesus Christ as the Leader of men through the difficulties and perplexities of this world, as the Deliverer from what is really evil, as the Way of Life. He tries to follow Him, to obey His commands, that his own life may grow, and his faculties be developed to a fuller understanding of the truth.

This may be wofully insufficient, according to the views of those who themselves think they possess clear and true doctrines, and that "except a man so believe he cannot be saved," but it is remarkably like what Christ required of men Himself. And of the two, this simple faith, this earnest endeavour to *be* and to *do* right, costs a man far more than the effort merely to *think* right.

Moreover, judged by the standard of dogma, Tolstoi could not be a Christian, according to one division of Christians, without being a heretic according to the others, but in sight of this attempt to live his life in harmony with the teaching of Christ, he is at one with all earnest and sincere men of every denomination whatever.

It is true that Tolstoi can no more avoid dipping into doctrine occasionally than the rest of us, and his recently published book on "The Four Gospels" shows that he, too, can be led by the use of subjective methods to critical results that can hardly stand the test of objective facts. It is true that in his " Kingdom of Heaven is Within You " he uses arguments that seem to many of us to be invalid, and draws inferences from Christ's words that strike us as unwarranted, and that in his books generally he expresses opinions that are no more certainly true than other men's opinions; and, of course, he believes in them, as we all believe in our own, and very rightly, so long as we really think them, and do not merely reflect the opinions of those about us.

This is no more than to say that Tolstoi is human ; that he is not himself the Truth, but only a disciple seeking to find and obey the Truth ; that he is not the Light himself, but one who is earnestly trying to open out his whole life to the Light, that under its vivifying rays he may grow as God meant him to grow, that the dark places of wrong within him may be purified by the Light, and all that is good bear much fruit. Only a disciple, yet, with all his faults and errors, of which probably no one is more conscious than himself, nearer the Master by far than many of us who wisely sit in judgment on them ; a disciple who, by his renunciation of the riches, power, and dominion of the world that came to him by birth, by his sturdy and uncompromising struggle against what he honestly believes to be evil, by his self-sacrificing deeds

of mercy and love among "these least," has honourably
earned the right to the name of " Christian," which, with
multitudes of " professors " more orthodox than he, is
merely a conventional label of respectability, a badge
assumed light-heartedly, a wearing of the Master's colours
that is belied by a carelessness about the faithful execution
of His orders.

# CHAPTER VI.

## SPRING SCENES IN SAMARA.

EARLY in March, 1892, on a bitterly cold morning, I left Count Tolstoi's headquarters in the Government of Rjasan, to accompany his son Lyeff Lvovitch and another young nobleman, Paul von Birukoff, to the young Count's centre of operations in the government of Samara. "Where shall we meet next?" said Tolstoi to me as we parted; "perhaps in Sweden, or beyond the Mississippi!"

As we went towards the railway station of Klekotki in our sleighs, we met a long *oboz*, or baggage-train, of more than a hundred horses, bringing fuel and food for the relief work. Our own train, according to the habit of Russian railways, was several hours late. We travelled third-class, following the Tolstois' usual custom, taking our baggage into the car with us. Long distances prevail in this country, so a traveller's equipment usually consists of portable bedding, food, and a tea-set: you can get hot water on the cars. Every nook and corner of the train was crowded with luggage and packages of different kinds. The passengers, also, were of assorted varieties—Russians proper, Mordvinians, Tcheremiss, Tatars, and Bashkirs. Of these, the Tatars held a dis-

tinguished pre-eminence in my eyes, by reason of their
cleanliness and politeness. The young Count called them
"real gentlemen," and told me that they were the most
honest and sober people in all Russia, and consequently filled
positions of trust as a rule. He gave a good character also to
the Bashkirs, but in my own experience I found them of a
slyer and more cunning disposition than the Tatars. The

A GROUP OF TATARS.

Mordvinians and Tcheremiss are of Finnish race, inhabiting
the forest regions of Kasan and its neighbouring districts,
which have been their home as far back as history reaches.
Nominally orthodox, they are at heart pagan, and in secret still
offer sacrifices to the spirits of the forest. They were very
picturesque in appearance, with their olive faces, black
moustaches, dark Mongolian eyes, and white caftans of coarse
woollen homespun. The Tatars and Bashkirs are Moham-

medans ; they and these semi-pagan tribes, including also the
Votyaks and Tchuvashi, their neighbours, are on a very high
moral level, being industrious, sober, and honest.

I could not sleep at all the first night. The smell, the
vermin, and the presence of diseased *mushiks* were too much
for me ; I had frequently to go out on to the platform—the
cars are of the American pattern—on account of nausea.
But the famine had one incidentally good result : there was

THE YOUNGER TOLSTOI'S HEADQUARTERS AT PATROVKA.

a general absence of drunken people ; the first I noticed was a
priest.

During the night a prison car, whose small windows were
protected by iron bars, and on each of whose platforms stood
two *gendarmes* in grey, armed with rifle, revolver, and sword,
was attached to our train. It was filled with convicts bound
for Siberia, including both genuine criminals and those whose
political or religious opinions made them obnoxious in the eyes
of a suspicious Government. I noticed, when I got a glimpse
through the double doors, some comely girl faces among the
crowd of rough and shaggy *mushik* heads. Even children are

not infrequently sent to Siberia for political or ecclesiastical reasons.

Birukoff had brought bandages and antiseptics, and occupied himself each day with washing and dressing the sores of the *mushiks*, and speaking words of cheer to them.

The second night, also, I could not sleep a wink; it was not merely the heat and the stifling, poisonous air, but there were a number of suspicious individuals about, and thieving is of very common occurrence on the cars. The third night tired nature would be denied no longer, and I slept soundly. At five a.m. the Count woke me to see the Volga bridge, and an hour later we were in the city of Samara, whose elevated position on the east bank of the Volga, and public buildings and churches, give it a striking appearance.

We stopped here a day to transact some business. The place was crowded with starving *mushiks*, suffering from spotted typhus, black small-pox, and scurvy, begging for bread by day and sleeping in hovels and cellars at night. Very many of the rich had fled to Paris or Nice. Private relief-work was chiefly carried on by foreigners. Two Germans, Herr Koenitser and Herr Wakano, fed respectively fifty and a hundred people daily. An Englishman, Mr. Besant, with means brought from Great Britain, gave each day two meals to four hundred of the sufferers. The Russian helpers were mainly sectarians; a Molokhan lady, a widow, worked assiduously and quietly, according to her means, among the poor. It was the same in the province. The English Friends, supported Prince Dolgorukoff's medical expedition to Eastern Samara, and dispensed much help through their agents. The young Count Tolstoi's funds, by which he carried on his extensive work, came mostly from foreign countries, chiefly England and America.

At one a.m. we were at the railway station, but the train was not. All was quiet as death. In the second-class waiting-room we found a number of men, women, and children, covering about a quarter of an acre of flooring, making night musical by snores in various keys, surrounded by immense piles of luggage. Lyeff Tolstoi came in with the tickets, after sending an express telegram to the place to order horses, and told us the train was belated seven hours! In stoic calm he spread his cloak on the floor and joined the company of sleepers, and after a cup of tea we did the same. At nine the coming of the train was announced for mid-day; it proved to be two p.m. The cold was 30° Réaumur (about 35·36° Fahr.). On the way a priest told us that in his village, which contained 1,600 people, there was only one horse left; all the rest were starved or killed.

At Bagatoye we left the train, it being then dusk. We found that one of our cases of canned goods had been stolen, and that the *express* telegram, despatched from Samara twenty hours before, had not yet been forwarded. We had, in consequence, to send for conveyances to the nearest village, *Sani*, each drawn by two small shaggy horses, tandem fashion. On the way the Count beguiled the time by telling me stories of the nomadic races who had lived on these steppes, and fought heroically for their freedom.

We lodged that night with a *mushik* acquaintance of the Count's, who seemed to be considerably above the usual run. Not only was his place much cleaner than was common, but it had a plank flooring. We slept on the floor in thick blankets, the lamp overhead burning all night. In the morning our hostess poured water over our hands as we washed, a Russian custom of hospitality. After a breakfast of tea and bread we pushed on, and soon arrived at Pakovka, the village which Count Lyeff used as his centre. His headquarters consisted of a one-storied *izba*, divided by partitions into three small rooms; one for sleeping, one for entry, reception-room, and kitchen, and one for dining-room, parlour, and office. The second was constantly crowded with *mushiks*. No sooner had we arrived than we were besieged. The Count went to work at once, and all the time I was with him he took but few hours of rest by night or day.

That was Saturday. One of our drivers had been a fine, neatly-dressed youth, who had told me of his connection with the Molokhan sect, and on my expressing a wish to be present at one of their meetings had offered me a hearty welcome. Birukoff and I went next day, at 9 a.m., and found in a large *izba* about two hundred people collected; the women and children were toge-

ther nearest the doors, and the men inside. They had been
told of our coming, and on our entrance rose together in greeting ; our coats were taken, and we ourselves led right through
and given seats at the table.   Like most of the sectaries, the appearance and demeanour of these powerfully-built, though now
emaciated folk, indicated a higher degree of intelligence and
culture than that of the Orthodox peasants generally.

As soon as we were settled, the congregation rose again, and
struck up a very strange kind of chant.  The words were from
a chapter of the New Testament, read out verse by verse by one
of the leaders.  The music was a kind of canon or round, of
which the motive remained the same, but which was subject to
variations to suit the different words of the text.  Like all
Russian songs, it was in a minor strain, and made a deep impression on me, despite its primitive, almost wild character.
These simple, wailing tunes have been shaped during centuries
of remorseless persecution, and express the striving after light
and freedom of many thousands of souls.  They were now sung
with great feeling and life by the whole assembly.   I give an
attempt at reproduction of the motive of the chant:—

After the singing, one of the leaders read Matt. xxv., containing the parables of Jesus concerning the Virgins and the
Talents, making short and practical comments as he read.  Then
the meeting was open to all, and several of the older members expressed their views tersely and to the point.   I must say I found
this mode of proceeding more instructive and helpful than many
of the set theological sermons I have listened to, although these
*mushiks*, who had frequently *taught themselves* to read in
advanced years and under extreme difficulties, had no other
source of instruction than the Bible and their observation of

life. I translate some of my notes, in which I jotted down a few of their comments :—

"The fire in the virgins' lamps is insight into truth. But it is not enough to have *fire;* one must use, and, above all things, have *oil.* What is this oil? It is the *will* to do good expressing itself in action, *i.e.,* good deeds. We can have light and great insight, and not live up to it, like those spoken of in

STAROST.       P. VON BIRUKOFF.      COUNT L. TOLSTOI.
TOLSTOI'S CHIEF HELPER.

another parable, who build their house on sand, that is, hear the word without doing it afterwards. This is the most important matter in the whole of Christianity, yet is most often neglected by those who profess to be Christians, who occupy themselves with a lot of doctrines and ceremonies rather than doing the will of God. The kernel and centre of good works is love to God and man, love showing itself in self-sacrifice for the suffering brother, as is proved by Christ's words concerning the last judgment—only those who have fed the hungry, clothed the naked, visited the sick, &c., will enter into His glory."

· Birukoff also, at request, not only commented on the passage, but gave an address on the words, "The Law and the Prophets were until John; from that time the Gospel of the Kingdom of God is preached, and every man entereth violently into it."

There was not room in Tolstoi's *izba* for more than himself and chief helper, Ivan Alexandrovitch Berger, so I had to get quarters elsewhere. I found these in the afternoon, in the *izba* of the village "*Pisar*," or scribe, a young unmarried man and his widowed mother. I had breakfast with these good people, but dinner and supper with the Count. Another member of this household I shall always remember with affection. He was from our first acquaintance one of my most intimate friends, shared my bed frequently, took tea and milk out of my saucer, and was always brisk and cheerful, however gloomy our surroundings. True, Vaska was "only a cat," but he has many a time brought me no little comfort when returning from scenes of hunger, disease, and death.

The free kitchens in Samara district were on the same plan as those of Rjasan, except in minor points where local circumstances led to alteration. Here, too, deputations from distant villages came with appeals for help, and when the workers returned from their rounds they brought the same tales of typhus, scurvy, black small-pox, &c., caused by the famine. Here is a sample of a day's work, extracted from my diary, Wednesday, March 24.

6 a.m. The bells call the Orthodox to early mass. It is Lent, and this early Mass is celebrated every day. The head-quarters are already besieged by a crowd of applicants. Not professional beggars, with well-worn, stereotyped petitions and blessings, but a timid manner of making their wants known. "Our food is all gone long ago; we are starving. Help us." "My wife and children are sick, and I have nothing for them; help us with a little tea and sugar, and something for *kasha* and soup!" "We have a horse and cow, which are starving.

SPRING SCENES IN SAMARA.

We are so grieved to lose them now that spring is so near. Help us with a little fodder."

A little girl is led up to the Count, and in a voice hardly audible for suppressed tears, whispers "My mother died last night, and I have nothing for my little brothers and sisters."

While at breakfast fresh batches of petitioners arrive, among them some Bashkirs and Tatars from great distances, with terrible tales of misery and pestilence. "Our own provisions gave out long ago. The Government help is not enough to keep us alive. Nearly all our cattle have perished. Our sick ones and our children are slowly dying of starvation."

One of the helpers and myself drove to a neighbouring village to look into the sanitary conditions. First we came to a row of clay huts, something like the adobe huts in New Mexico, but much poorer. The snow had drifted above many of their flat roofs, the location of which could be found by the smoke from *kisjak* (fuel of dried manure and straw) that rose here and there. An opening in the drift let us inside, and we found that a small window had also been kept clear. Before our eyes were of use, our ears caught the sound of heavy breathing and moaning. Then we saw on the oven a woman of middle age suffering from spotted typhus. To our questions she gave only incoherent replies. A man of about the same age, dressed in a shirt of dirty sackcloth, girt round the waist with a rope, his uncombed hair on his forehead, and his glassy, sunken eyes fixed in an expression of despair, sat by the side of the oven, and on a bench lay a little five-year-old boy in rags, and suffering from hunger and scurvy. Two wooden benches and a small rough table on the earth floor were all the furniture they had.

"Have you any cattle?" "No, we had two cows, but had to kill them." "Any fuel?" "Only what our neighbours give us." "Any food?" The man produced a hard piece of black rye bread, all that was left of the Government supply.

A second hut contained an old man of seventy, a woman of forty, dreadfully scored about the face with disease, and two emaciated children, sick, on top of the oven, slowly perishing of starvation. The father had been carried off by spotted typhus, and the grandfather had come to look after the family. The same story—no cattle, no fuel, two loaves of bread, a few peas.

In a third hut, larger than the foregoing, we found five persons, a calf, and two sheep. Two of the five persons were down with typhus, the rest were suffering from scurvy. The other huts we visited simply repeated the story with variations.

I visited one of the free kitchens the Count had opened.

APPLICANTS FOR AID.

About fifty guests came, each with his wooden bowl and spoon. Most of them crossed themselves as they entered—there were not so many of the "unorthodox" here—and when all were assembled they sang the "table prayer" in chorus. The first part is to *Bogo matjer*, God's mother, the second consists of extracts from the Lord's Prayer, the third is a prayer for the Tsar. The food consisted of bread, pea soup, and *kasha*.

In addition to the clay huts of the village, there were sheds that had been thatched with straw. But they had been dismantled for fuel, and now presented a *bizarre* appearance, as the bare wooden framework, with branches of willow wattled in, gave something of the appearance of a deserted rookery. Miserable skeletons of horses were here and there plucking the remains of some of the thatch that had been pulled off.

While we were away Prince Dolgorukoff had arrived, and I was introduced to him on our return. This Prince, as was said above, was conducting a medical expedition in Eastern Samara, the expenses of which were partly borne by Friends in England. This was a very timely aid, as there were no hospitals, and, in fact, no sanitary arrangements whatever. *On paper*, there was to be a store of medicine for every *volost*, or

VILLAGE STREET IN PATROVKA.

district of villages, but when we made inquiries the whole "store" consisted of "only three bottles containing some unknown liquid"! Two physicians, two surgeons, and six volunteer nurses constituted this expedition. They took dinner and supper with the Count, and though the accommodation was cramped the company was good, and all went well.

It was late that night when I reached my "room." This was a small corner behind the oven, on the top of which my host and hostess slept. But I found sleep hopeless. The pictures of the saints I had seen in the daytime seemed to move about in lifelike fashion. I shut my eyes many times in hopes of dropping off, but they opened of their own accord just as often. The church bell tolled "One." The *lampadka*, burning before the saint in "the holy corner" of the outer room, spread a dim light, and through a crack in the wooden partition I could see an ugly old saint staring at me, while on the oven's top my hosts snored lustily. I tried to sleep again, but it was no use. I lit my lamp, looked at my watch—it was 2 a.m.—and tried to read, but my thoughts wandered. I glanced at the wall, and there was life and motion! I had already tired myself out in warring with the vermin, which taught me to suffer in silence. Therefore, I left these travellers in peace. I thought of the morning, when at last I could get out of this dark and stifling prison into the fresh air and light of the sun. I peeped into the other room, and was surprised to see that the *lampadka* of the holy Nicholas was going out, so I decided to let my little lamp, which illumined no saint with shining halo, but a swarming multitude of ——, burn on till the sun should supersede both lamp and *lampadka*. With longing after the sun and the fresh air I at last fell asleep.

After spending the night once in another peasant's house, my good host asked me in the morning if I had slept well. When I said "No," he inquired if I had been visited by "*klop*." Not having heard the word before, I asked what it was. Rising quickly and running to the wall, he picked off a bug and brought it to me in his hand. "*Vol klop*" (this is *klop*), he said. He looked astonished when I expressed my strong aversion to "B flats," declaring "they are good for cleansing the blood."

*Saturday, March* 27.—As I sat at breakfast, the door opened, and a small, piping voice was heard on the other side of the partition: "*Barin gatav?*" (Is the gentleman ready?) "*Sei tschess*" (Immediately). The voice belonged to a little, lively and agreeable little *mushik*, who was to drive us over to Birukoff's headquarters at Petrovka, some twenty miles away over the steppes. We found a strong headwind blowing, and out on the steppes the storm was very bad, so that it was with the utmost difficulty that I could see the horse in front of us. It was a wonder to me how Vasutka, my driver, who looked like a little snow goblin on the sledge, could find the way. In one valley we did lose it, and the poor horse struggled helplessly in the soft snow. Vasutka began to beat the poor animal, who struggled hard, shivered, and looked piteously round at us. " Stop that," I cried to him, and jumped out to unharness the horse. The cold seemed to me much harder to bear out on these steppes than the same degree of frost on our own northern fells ; my hands began to freeze as I outspanned the horse, and it was with the greatest difficulty that I kept my face from becoming frost-bitten.

We managed with ropes to haul the horse out of the drift on to some harder tracks, but had to repeat the process several times. The horse was getting exhausted, and it seemed probable that we should have to spend a day and night in a snowstorm out on the steppes. "Vasutka, do you think we shall get out of this ? " " *Gospod znajer* " (God knows). " Are you afraid ? " " *Nitchevo !* " This last word is hardly trans-latable ; it is a kind of vocal shrugging of the shoulders.

However, at last we hit the road again, and by good hap kept it until we reached our journey's end.

Birukoff was out, but the peasants, after gaping and whis-pering about my outlandish dress and broken Russian, showed me to his room. It was about 10ft. by 6ft. His box-bedstead was made of roughly-nailed boards ; there were two wooden stools and a table, on which lay a Russian New Testament, a French philosophical treatise on Pythagoras, and some lists and account books belonging to the relief work. In about half-an-hour he came home, tired and hungry, but cheerful as usual, and we had a late dinner. Like his master Tolstoi, Birukoff is a vegetarian, and lived on the same food that he served to the peasants.

The usual crowding in of applicants took place during the meal, and after attending to them we went off to a committee meeting concerning some new eating-rooms. The members of this committee impressed me very favourably by their bearing and speech. They clearly felt that they were not in the pres-ence of officials, whom they hated and feared, but turned to Birukoff as a friend ; he, on his part, met them with unfeigned cordiality and respect. I was introduced, and the object of my journey explained, after the business was finished. One and all rose up, and in chorus thanked me, and asked me to convey their thanks to all the friends abroad who had contributed through me.

It was evident from what was brought forward at this meeting, that in spite of all denials from certain quarters, numbers were dying directly of starvation, and not simply from diseases occasioned by the famine. It also appeared that many families had mixed clay with the bread. I keep a sample of this as a grim memorial.

When we came out there was a considerable crowd assembled to see " the first foreigners who had visited their village." I was by this time so used to the curiosity of the peasants that it roused my wonder when I was *not* followed by a crowd. This happened to me once, where I saw women and children peeping round corners or out of windows, and then hastily drawing back. The riddle was solved when I reached my lodging. My companion, with whom I had been speaking in German, told me that the women in the village had said, " He doesn't use Christian speech, and he is not dressed like a Christian. He must be the *tjort* (devil) himself."

Von Birukoff had had to overcome endless opposition from the different authorities before he could succeed in his work ; yet he had triumphed to an extraordinary degree, and astonished me with his indomitable doggedness and pluck. He had charge of the north-eastern wing of the Count's army of warriors against pestilence and famine. Already he had established forty eating-rooms, and hoped to double that number.

One of the most heartrending features of the famine was the multitude of orphaned children, whose parents had fallen victims to starvation or typhus. In Samara alone they numbered many thousands, and, without friends or relatives, wandered from village to village seeking help for themselves and little brothers or sisters. Many were fed in the Count's eating-rooms, but it was impossible to help more than a small number of the great multitude.

Here is an entry from my diary: April 14th. Got no rest during the night. About midnight a number of starving people.

STARVING ORPHANS.

wandering from village to village in search of bread, came and asked for food. The pitiable folk seemed in hopeless despair. In the outer room they kept talking and whispering, now and again breaking out into sobs and crying. The number of starving beggars roving about is increasing alarmingly. One crowd after another has passed through the village during the day, very many of whom have been children. As I was eating my breakfast this morning I saw a large number of child-beggars approaching my lodging-place across the plain. It was no new sight, but very painful on that sunny April morning to see these pinched and starving little ones. One girl of about nine, carrying a little child, looked as if she might have been thirty or more. A little way off stood a boy, looking on the ground with a sorrowful expression.

" Where do you come from, little children ? " I asked.

" From the village of G—— " (in the neighbourhood).

" Who is the little one in your arms ? " I asked the girl.

" My little brother."

" Where are your parents ? "

" They have died in the ' disease ' " (spotted typhus).

" Have you no relatives ? "

" Many have died in the disease, and others have gone away."

" What is your name ? " I asked the boy just mentioned.

" Ivan Petrovitch A."

" Where are your parents ? "

" I have no parents ! " And the poor little fellow burst into tears. The other children told me that his father died a month ago, and that his mother was buried yesterday. All of them, I discovered, were orphans.

Yet it was one of the things that astonished me most in Russia, to find that so many of the upper-class people in the cities tried to deny the existence of any extraordinary famine, and that while the cities themselves were swarming with the starving peasants. Once a well-fed and warmly-clad " gentleman " on the cars said to me, in an authoritative tone, " The distress of the *mushiks* is not so great as people make out. They are accustomed to no other condition, and are contented and happy. The *mushiks* are *cattle*."

Not only so, but at first the authorities prohibited the giving of relief by private persons, and when that was no longer possible invariably gave them the cold shoulder, and even set detectives in large numbers to spy on their proceedings.

In Moscow, for example, a certain Madame Marosova, who offered to support 10,000 famine-stricken people at her own cost, *was forbidden to do it,* and one of Colonel Paschkoff's large establishments, in which 500 people were fed daily, was closed by the police in the famine year 1892, in Petersburg, under the eyes of the Procureur of the Most Holy

GOVERNMENT LUILDINGS IN PATROVKA.

Synod and of the "Little Father" of the Russian people. Even in the destitute villages out on the steppes of Samara detectives were watching those who were devoting all their powers to feeding the hungry, while official representatives of these "powers (of darkness?) that be," who were doling out a horrible mixture of chaff, sand, and dirt, instead of the flour provided by Government, were left unmolested. Of course, I do not know what these "ministering spirits" reported about our work, but I am sure that if they told the truth they could in no way describe the methods of relief as "dangerous." The loyalty of the addresses of thanks from the peasants ought to have satisfied the very Pobiedanostseff himself. Here is a specimen.

## ADDRESS OF THANKS.

On behalf of the meeting in the village of Samovolovka in the district of Patrovka, and in the name of persons belonging to the eating-room, who number forty, no more and no less,

CHURCH IN PATROVKA.

and who, from their whole sincere heart, and with the unanimous consent of the entire meeting, have the honour of thanking

First, and above all, the Heavenly Tsar, and

Next to Him the Earthly Tsar, Alexander Alexandrovitch, with his whole family, and the Most Holy Synod, with all its nearest councillors, and finally

We have the honour of thanking Your Highness Count

Tolstoi, and you, Mr. Merchant, Paul Ivanovitch, for all your benefactions to us, for your food; and if we had not received alms from both quarters, from His Imperial Majesty the Emperor, and from Your Highness Count Tolstoi, we would have been in a terrible state, we would hardly have been alive. From our whole, sincere, and grateful heart we again thank you, and we remain very satisfied with your arrangements, and we will thank you many times for many years. We shall be very, very content.

Some weeks after my visit to Petrovka, the following incident happened there. I had it, not from Birukoff himself, who, like Tolstoi and his helpers generally, makes it a rule never to tell about how they are treated by priests and officials, but from another, a thoroughly reliable person.

Herr von Birukoff went one day on certain business to the house of a *Kulack* in the village, where he met the priest of the place. The host set tea, and wine and *vodka* before them. The priest took both tea and *vodka*, but Birukoff, being an abstainer, took tea only. The former soon got "a little fresh," and began throwing out innuendoes against Birukoff and his helpers. "People come now from all parts," he said, "and give so much food to the *mushiks* that they completely spoil them, but they never go to church, but set the peasants a bad example, and do not live according to the Bible." "What do you mean?" said Birukoff; "speak plainly, and don't insinuate."

"Well, I mean that you care nothing for church or Bible, and live like heathens."

"I love and revere the New Testament," said Birukoff, "and earnestly try to carry out its contents in my life. I always carry a New Testament with me and read it every day. Have you a Bible?" And he took out his Testament and put it on the table before the priest.

"I have my Bible on the desk in church."

"Yes, and there it may lie. You don't read it yourself, nor teach the people from it, nor try to fulfil its contents in your life. What fruit does your Bible bear if it lies in the church? Neither your own nor your people's life shows any fruit of the Gospel." Then Birukoff read some portions of the Sermon on

the Mount and other parts of the New Testament which teach
how a Christian should live.

Then the priest got into a rage, snatched the Testament and
flung it out of doors, exclaiming "Does the Gospel bear such
fruit then?" and flung himself out by the same way.

*     *     *     *     *

It is "the great Lent," with its multitude of services. Early
and late the Pope, dressed in his "rjassa," a long gown with
wide arms, a long staff in his hand, and accompanied at a
distance by the "psalm-singer," walks slowly and majestically
to the church, where the bells are rung in rapid time. Behind the
priest and his pomoststchik come troops of people of all ages
in single file, bowing and crossing themselves as they enter the
church. It is "*Blagovestshjenije*," Annunciation Day. An icy
cold wind drives the newly-fallen snow over the plains as I go
with the crowd to church, which is filled to its utmost capacity.
The barbaric Eastern splendour of the interior, the number of
saints in their silver frames, the gaudy decorations, the costly
robes of the priest, and the elaborate ritual contrast painfully
with the malodorous motley crowd of ragged, emaciated, and
dirty men, women, and children. These incessantly bow and
cross themselves, and kneel before the pictures, while the priest
walks round those of the Virgin and the Christ, swinging "the
holy Kadjilnitza" or censer, and the "psalm-singer" sings
the Mass with a strong "gin-bass" (produced through drinking
much gin). Powerful as his voice is, it is drowned by the
coughing and the screams of the babies.

On either side of the "*ikonastasis*," a large screen before the
altar, stands a small desk within a rough wooden enclosure,
where a man is busy all the time selling "holy" wax candles.
The poor usually buy the cheapest kind, at about five copecks,
and light them before their favourite saints. A brisk business
is carried on in this kind of merchandise, the value of which is
greatly enhanced by the priest's "consecration." The net
proceeds are divided betwen the clergy and the church.

There is a strong draught through the church, yet the air
is unspeakably foul. The whole service, with its mechanical
ceremonies, its prayers, and chanting in a language unintelligible

to the people, the emaciated and haggard appearance of the
congregation, many of whom were disfigured by syphilis and
small-pox, and all of whom bore the unmistakable impress of
degradation and slavery, make the most painful impression
on me.

During the famine the people attend church more assiduously
than usual, hoping by this to conciliate the Deity. For the priests
they have neither love nor respect; it is merely ignorance and

A MUSHIK'S FUNERAL.

superstition that hold them under their sway. The popes, as the
village priests are called, belong to the " white priesthood," and
are compelled to marry; the members of the "black priesthood"
live in enforced celibacy.   The popes have no salary, but have
ample power of deriving a good income from the compulsory
fees for the numerous religious ceremonies. The nice parsonage
in our village testified to better times in the past, and the well-
fed appearance of the priest showed that, although his income
had been badly reduced, he had not been inconvenienced by
starvation.   Ceremonial fees vary according to circumstances;

baptism of an infant costs from fifty copecks to several roubles ; a wedding five to twenty roubles, a funeral one to ten roubles. The rich pay much larger sums. Then the priests receive a great deal in kind. Ten times a year they make their rounds through the villages, when each family must contribute something. At the great festivals he comes to hold "moleben" or

DELIVERED BY DEATH.

prayers in their homes, when they must give him at least twenty-five copecks, some pastry, ten eggs, &c. In this village there are four hundred homes, so he does not do so badly.

It must not be supposed that these offerings are all given willingly ; on the contrary, the priest has often to threaten and quarrel with the peasants before he can collect them. Sometimes the dead lie unburied for days, because their friends cannot pay what he asks. A baptism or wedding may be more easily postponed, but in the end the peasants have to give in. Where sectarians are numerous it is most difficult for the priest to get so much, but the police are on his side, and he can get them harassed, imprisoned, or even banished.

Take as an illustration the following conversation between peasants, telling of their different priests. One narrates how, in the village of F——, a peasant went to the priest to arrange for his wedding. "Ten roubles," demands the priest. The peasant haggles about it. "Well, you shall have it for five then, not a copeck less." Three roubles are offered, on the plea of poverty, but the pope will not give way for a long time ; at last, however, he agrees, and on the appointed day they meet for the ceremony.

The priest begins. According to Russian custom the couple should be conducted round the *analoj* or reading-desk three times, but the priest stops after the first round. "Little father," says the bridegroom, "according to law thou shouldst take us three times round the desk." "Three times for three roubles ! " exclaims the priest. "One is enough for thee."

Then the bridegroom notices that the priest does not hold the crown over their heads, according to custom, and says, "Little Father, why dost thou marry us without a crown ? " "Wilt thou, then, have a crown also for three roubles ? Thou are jesting, little brother. This will do." At the end the priest should give the couple a little wine, but none is forth-coming. The peasant stretches out his hand for some, saying, "A little wine, little father ! " "So," shrieks the priest "thou wouldst have wine, too, for three roubles, thou little rascal ! " Nor is any given. So the edifying ceremony ends.

The other peasants shook their heads, saying, " *Voj, voj,*" such a " *batuschka* " (little father).

"With us," begins another, "the priest is better in that respect ; he does not gnaw the flesh from our bones, but——"

"What then ? "

The peasant shuts his eyes and shakes his head.

"Does he drink ? "

" Drink!   Drink!   And when he gets his spells, oh !   And he is fearful when  he gets drunk.   Then he fights and carries on like a mad dog.   One night, not long ago, when the village had barely gone to rest, the large church bell began to ring.   The whole village ' rolled out ' to see where the fire had broken out.   We all looked round, and could see nothing. We ran to the church steeple, and there we saw the *batuschka* standing, with only his shirt on, banging away with the clapper of the large bell.   ' Little father, what is the matter ? '   we cried.   ' I—hic—have—hic—been fighting—hic—with the old woman—hic—and—hic—I want you—hic—to help me lick her.' "

General laughter among the peasants.

Sometimes the priests take revenge on peasants for low pay-ment or any other cause, by refusing to give children the names selected, and substituting others frequently of an insulting kind.

*          *          *

Coming out of the church I wander off to the steppe to get a little fresh air.   On my return I see at a distance a group of people slowly coming up the village street, and recognise a scene enacted every day.   It is a funeral procession—not of Dives, with silver-covered coffin, heaped with flowers and carried on a catafalque by eight or ten bearers, preceded by priests in flowing, ornate vestments, singers and picture-bearers ; no, it consists only of four men bearing on their shoulders a coffin of rough, unpainted boards.   As it approaches I recognise in one of the bearers a strongly-built *mushik* with regular and beautiful though now emaciated features, who called on the Count last night and got two roubles to buy a coffin.   Often these poor people had no means even to procure a coffin for a dead relative.

It is not merely the custom of the country that makes me uncover my head as these men, bowed by want and sorrow, slowly pass on their way to the dismal cemetery on the steppe outside the village with the remains of their brother whom death has delivered from nameless misery.

Even in the midst of starvation and disease there occur

scenes that move to laughter. One day I came to Count
Tolstoi's dwelling, and found one of the young *mushik* women
employed about the place almost crazy with despair; loudly she
wailed and bemoaned her evil lot. I thought that surely her
husband or some one dear to her had died, but when I asked
what was the matter, the young Count replied :

" Her husband got horribly lousy. She wanted to clean him
up a little, so put his sheepskin in the oven, but the heat was
too fierce, and the coat and all its population was burnt up!
When her husband discovered it he stormed, scolded, and beat
her, so that now she is afraid to go home."

*Hinc illae lacrymae!* I had the satisfaction later of presenting
them with a new sheepskin, on condition that he should not
beat his wife, and she should try to keep it free from vermin.

Another curious scene was witnessed when some good-souled
ladies of Warsaw sent two large bales of clothes to be distributed among the needy. There were all kinds of fine raiment
—mantles, vests, stockings, and costumes of various descriptions.
I waited to see if there were any *corsets* in the lot, but evidently
the Polish ladies thought their far-away sisters in Samara were
not sufficiently cultured for this article of dress! It was great
fun to see how eagerly the peasant women and girls came
running up with hands outstretched to get some of the finery,
threw the silken wraps over their old sheepskins with delight,
and in high glee bore off their treasures to their home.

On another day there came a poor old woman in sad trouble
to the Count. With tears running down her wrinkled cheeks
she threw herself on her knees before him. When he had got
her up again and encouraged her a bit, she drew out of her
sheepskin cloak a ragged bundle, which she undid and took out
another rag tied up in a knot; this also she untied, and produced a something tattered and torn almost beyond recognition,
but which turned out to be a rouble-note. Then she told her
story.

" 1 am a widow from the village of X." (here she produced a
document from the village scribe attesting the truth of her
story), " and have a small plot of land. After my cow died of
starvation, and we ourselves were threatened with the same

SNOWDRIFT AT THE END OF APRIL.

PEASANTS CUTTING THROUGH THE SNOW.

fate, my son went to Uralsk to look for work. After some weeks he sent me a rouble to buy some seed. With the note tied up in a bit of rag I set out, but lost it on the way, and only found it again after a lot of trouble and searching. A calf had got hold of the rag and chewed it, so that my rouble was all bitten to pieces. Then I went to the village authorities, and they told me to come to your worship, Lord Count." Tolstoi changed her damaged note for one for five roubles, and gave her besides help in other ways.

The week before Easter we received an invitation from a gentleman to spend the holidays at his residence. The snow was still lying deep on the ground when the young Count, one of his helpers, and myself set out. Here and there on the hill-tops or on the sunny slopes it had melted in spots, and on these some miserable-looking cattle, amid the carcases of others of their kind that had succumbed, were feeding on the sparse, old grass. The eye rested with pleasure on these bare patches, looking like islands dotted in a sea of ice, formed by the endless stretches of white snow, that reflected with almost unbearable brilliancy the intense sunlight. Overhead the lark was singing his beautiful song, while beneath the snow is heard the purling of many streams as the water rejoices in its first freedom from the fetters of winter. Looking westward from an elevation on which we stopped to enjoy the scenery, we saw the golden cupola of the church with the village clustering round—the scene of our toils during the last month. The thought of the contrast between this bright and lovely spring morning and the unspeakable human misery that has engulfed us all this time, made the former seem one of Nature's most bitter ironies.

Our host gave us a cordial welcome, and did all in his power to make our stay pleasant, giving us with open-hearted hospitality the best the house afforded. On the farm was a large number of horses, kept for the celebrated "kumiss treatment." Kumiss is a special preparation of mare's milk, considered good for certain classes of invalids; often in summer-time there would be fifty patients under treatment at the farm. Only Bashkirs and some other Asiatic herdsmen

THE KUMISS FARM.

HERR FÄLTVÄBEL.

have the skill required to prepare this drink properly; the Bashkirs and Tatar element was considerable in the neighbourhood. Besides these there were two other Asiatics who

JASHKA.

*MUSHIKS* WAITING FOR THE DISTRIBUTION OF SEED-CORN.

contributed very largely to our pleasure. One was called "Herr Fältväbel, a camel of considerable intelligence, who became a universal favourite. On his broad back we enjoyed short trips in the neighbourhood of the farm. He arranged a special entertainment for us on his own account, when, with

Dr. B. on his back, he lay down on a clear space out on the steppe, to which he had waded through deep snow, and absolutely refused to stir. At last a Tatar floundered with much difficulty through the drifts to the spot, and persuaded him to get up and return home. "Jashka," the other Asian, was a little white ass, who speedily rivalled " Herr Fältvübel " in the popular esteem. I give portraits of both, taken with my Kodak.

The evening of our arrival black clouds began to gather, and when we retired about midnight a heavy storm was raging; fierce gusts of wind threatened to tear the roof off the house, while the hail beat furiously against the windows. Not only was the storm without, but, in my case at least, within also. I had received that day a letter from Southern Russia, and now opened it and read, among other things, "The father of the family is banished" for being a sectarian. "His wife, who has been forbidden to accompany him, is hopelessly ill from sorrow and suffering, and her six children, who surround her, are starving. . . . She receives no relief from the Government, because she is— a sectarian. . . . Several families are in the same predicament."

All sleep is banished. My thoughts roam everywhere. Back to the childhood when all was bright and joyous; in the heart love, hope, and faith; in the world order, justice, and truth. Forward to the rude awakening, to the grim realities of life, especially the horrors I had witnessed of late, in the midst of which I now was; to the holocausts of human lives, the rivers of blood and tears, shed to gratify the lust and caprice of tyrants; rivers that have not watered and fertilised the lands, but in their fierce torrent have washed away the fruitful soil, leaving whole regions desolate and bare, both in the past and to-day. Where is that law of progress of which we boast? Civilisation after civilisation in the past, rotten with its own corruption, has been swept away by barbaric hordes, in their turn to rear anew the fabric of fresh civilisation, and in their turn also to fall before the avenger. Here, to-day in Russia, are thirty-five millions of hard-working peasantry struggling against starvation and pestilence; the rich continue in luxury and idleness, the Government is exacting the last mite from the oppressed people for the instruments of international murder; the preachers of religion proclaim submission and self-denial, with reward in the next world, while they themselves live in affluence and grab all of this world's wealth they can, and while preaching the Gospel of the Cross hunt down the "heretics" as wild beasts. The miserable peasants have cried to heaven that their children may be delivered from starvation, but the brazen gates have remained closed. They write letters, piteous in their very illegibility, to authorities asking for justice, and receive no reply, or are punished for their audacity in complaining; they knock at doors that will not open to them, they speak to persons who will not listen. They understand nothing of the system of official society, with its forms, its laws, its etiquette.

On my table is a pamphlet containing two sermons by a German pastor on "The Famine and Our Sins." Whose sins? Why does the punishment fall on the innocent? Are these peasants' sinners above all others that they should suffer and the oppressors go free? What have those poor orphan children done that they should wander by thousands over the steppes, starving and freezing to death, or surviving only to lead a life of misery and degradation? What is their *sin* to merit so great a "*punishment*"?

"Faithless pessimism," you exclaim, in your comfortable homes. Maybe so, but these *were* my thoughts at the time, however I may look at things when the deep stirrings of emotion have passed by. But would it not be well to consider, not so much the frame of mind into which these sufferings and cruelties threw me, but the *facts* themselves? Optimism is a grand thing, if you have first faced the terrible suffering and evil in the world; faith is magnificent if, while comprehending the depths of woe and sin, you yet can put unwavering trust in God. But the optimism that is based on wilful ignoring of ugly facts is either callousness or cowardice, and the "faith" that is exerted for other people

in their distress without doing all in our power to help is a
ghastly impertinence.

At Easter time the orthodox go to church on the evening
before "Long Friday," and the service continues until
after midnight on Easter Eve. That night the *mushiks*
believe that the dead stir, that they can even hear them
moving about and talking in their graves, if they lie with
ears pressed to the ground. So they take food and *vodka*
into the graveyards for the use of their buried relatives, and
even in the terrible need of the famine this rite was not
altogether neglected.

Easter morn rose fine and clear; all about us was heard the
customary greeting, " *Christos voskresje*," with its reply and a
kiss. For forty days this formula is used, not only when
friends meet, but at the head of letters of all kinds, in business
and on all occasions of importance, even in the collection of
debts! Among the educated, this and other church ceremonies
are so neglected that the *mushiks* regard them as having a
peculiar religion of their own.

At evening the company separated; some returned to their
posts, others remained a few days longer at the farm.

With the break-up of the winter, all communication on the
steppes is interrupted, because of the swollen streams, fed by
the melting snow. We had, in consequence, to wait a fortnight
for our letters.

It was time to begin the year's agriculture, but no *mushiks*
were seen in the fields, except one or two who were working for
a *kulack*. The others had neither seed for sowing nor horses
for ploughing. There was seed in the public storehouses of
the Government, about one-third of what was needed, but when
the peasants sent to inquire of the authorities, they received no
reply. Despairing, they appealed to the Count for aid. But
he could at first do nothing, having no means; fortunately,
however, he received considerable remittances from Countess
Tolstoi in Moscow, who sent on money collected in America
and other places. At once he got horses and seed, and by
working night and day, two hundred of the most needy were
helped to sow their holdings. Large numbers left their homes

"THE GRAVES OF MY FRIENDS."

to look for work, but there were not many who could afford to hire labour.

My stay with Count Lyeff drew to a close. It had been decided that when the Volga traffic was open, I should go to Southern Samara and Saratoff to arrange for the opening of free eating-rooms for the sick and convalescent.

The evening before my departure I paid a number of farewell visits to friends in Patrovka. As I returned, I saw a curious piece of evidence of the straits to which the peasants were reduced. A poor *mushik*, with a shaggy little horse, was driving a plough over the land *made altogether of wood*. I found that many peasants had pawned all their implements to get money to pay their taxes, or to buy food.

There was still one visit to pay. I was up at sunrise next morning, and went to the cemetery to have a last look at the graves of those who had died in the famine. All was quiet in the village, except for several cocks that were scratching on a dunghill before an *izba*, and crowing their welcome to the day. It seemed as if I should be able to make my little pilgrimage to the graves of my friends unobserved, but on reaching the burial-ground I saw a number of peasants digging graves for their dead at that early hour. I took a photograph of them, and of the fresh graves that told of Death's winter-harvest in the famine-stricken village.

It was May when I left, yet the young Count was still feeding twenty thousand people a day, and helping the needy in countless other ways beside. Almost all that summer he worked on, distributing the food that came through friends outside. Later on, twelve additional car-loads of American flour were sent him by the Anglo-American Committee in St. Petersburg. The terrible strain of the hard work and the care involved in directing this vast and difficult relief in Samara entirely broke down his health, which, I am sorry to have to state, has not as yet been restored in this summer of 1895. Truly he is one of those who have been willing, like their Master, to lay down his life in self-denying toil and sacrifice for the sake of others who can never repay him.

I got permission to accompany a physician, sent out by the

Governor of Samara to inquire into the sanitary condition of
the district, on his return journey.  We met at a village seven
miles off, where I found him engaged in a four hours' dinner
with a Government official.  In high spirits they drove off in
the latter's carriage, I following in our *tarantan*.  Eight miles
of fast driving brought us to a priest's house, where we were
invited to tea and wine.  The doctor and the official took leave
in Russian fashion, kissing each other three times, and we set
out on our thirty miles to the railway station, the doctor
ensuring our punctual arrival by plying the driver with *vodka*.
I was tired, and asked the doctor to get my ticket, giving him
a ten-rouble note—the fare was six or seven roubles.  As we
got into the train he said my ticket was all right, but in one of
the intervals of my dozing on the train, I overheard him say to
the conductor, " This gentleman is sent from America with
bread for the starving; he ought to have a free passage."
The conductor agreed, but at Samara the doctor returned me
—not the ten-rouble note, but *my change*.  I had been inclined
to agree to his request that I should get some of the American
gifts sent to him for his relief work, but this little incident
changed my mind.

COUNT LYEFF TOLSTOI, JUNIOR.

8

# CHAPTER VII.

## A POLICY OF DEATH.

THE ignorance and superstition of the Russian peasants,
which strikes a visitor so forcibly, may be unhesitatingly
attributed to the deliberate policy of the Government, and not,
to the character of the peasants themselves. It is true that
during the short reform period under Alexander II., in the
early sixties, a considerable number of well-equipped schools
were established in connection with the *zemstvos*, or district
governments. When, however, the wave of Liberal policy was
followed by the backwash of reaction, these schools were
gradually crippled, and under Alexander III. the nadir of
education was reached. His attitude may be accurately
gauged from his speech to the people on the occasion of his
coronation—"Peasants you have been, and peasants you will
remain!" This sentiment was embodied soon after in a
*ukase*, according to which only a small section of the people
were to share in educational advantages, and even for these
favoured few "the measure of instruction shall be in
proportion to the status of the person having children to be
educated." In pursuit of this policy the boards of education
in Saratov and other places have resolved that " the instruction
in schools shall be so limited as to protect the children of
the upper classes from the intrusion of those of the poor
and middle class."

A further *ukase* of May 15, 1891, dealt the finishing blow

to the better kind of schools connected with the *zemstvos*, which had already been gradually starved out of all practical efficiency.   By this decree they were handed over to the *popes*, a set of ignorant and frequently drunken men who, according to the repeated testimony of their own bishops, have neither the necessary time nor ability to look after the schools.   The consequence has been a complete transformation of popular education into a soul-destroying, ecclesiastical discipline, by which the rising generation is taught to make the sign of the Cross, to bow before the *eikons* of saints, to learn by heart portions of the Russian liturgy, and above all " for his earthly welfare and eternal salvation, to regard, honour, and obey the Tsar and the Government as a divine and holy authority."

I visited some of these priests' schools, so startling in their contrast to the district schools established under Alexander II. In these latter the classes were under the supervision of trained teachers, the walls were hung with maps, diagrams, &c., and there were materials for object-lessons for the younger classes. The school-houses I saw were ordinary peasants' cottages, and on the walls were merely saints' pictures, with a large portrait-group of the Imperial Family occupying the place of honour. At the age of seven or eight the children go to school to the *pomostchnik*, a kind of curate to the priest, who is, as a rule, seldom sober.   The lessons consist of psalms and liturgies *in the old Slavonic*, and are taught by the priest reading the portion word by word, while the child learns it parrot fashion, without understanding a syllable.   This kind of training is not compulsory by law, but it is by practice.   It is only "private" in the sense that the child's parents or guardians are permitted to pay for it.

The curriculum of the district schools themselves, arranged by the Holy Synod, and under the immediate supervision of the priest, is as follows :—

*First Year.*—Twelve prayers in Old Slavonic learnt by rote.

*Second Year.*—The Russian version of these prayers, also by rote.

*Third Year.*—Same as second year, with a little mental arithmetic on the four rules.

To teach the children to read forms no necessary part of the syllabus, and, as a matter of fact, the majority of children pass through these three years and are thoroughly illiterate at the end. It is only those children who push themselves forward, as it were, who get a knowledge of reading outside the regular course. The former schools used also to have libraries of serviceable books, which the children were allowed to take home with them, but now the only books allowed are such as belong to the Orthodox training, liturgies, legends of saints, &c. When

SCHOOL CHILDREN AT PLAY.

the schools are closed, the children soon forget the little knowledge they have acquired. They take their share of the hard work in the fields, &c., and have no books at home by which to keep up their scholarship (?).

Nor are private schools allowed to supply the deficiencies of the national system. A number of these had been established by private beneficence in Siberia—in Tomsk, Omsk, Krasnojarsk, Irkutsk, and Jenesseisk—and were making good progress. They were delared by a prominent Government newspaper (*Graschdanin*, Oct. 9, 1889) to be of revolutionary tendencies ;

the local authorities received the hint to hamper them as much as
possible, with the result that they have now come under the control of the purest obscurantism.  This device is a favourite one
with the Government, and most effectual.  A decree forbidding
the establishment of any private school *without special consent
of the priests,* and a hint to these gentlemen not to give it when
asked, has proved the most easy and thorough method of preventing the peasants from getting education that could be
invented.

I did, however, meet a young *mushik* of really good education.
Not only could he read and write, but he had read to some
purpose, and had acquired considerable information concerning
other lands.  When I spoke of America and the help sent from
there to the starving peasants, he said, with tears in his eyes,
" I love the republic."  He had also taught himself arithmetic,
and was now practising drawing, using the pictures in a book
he had as copies.  I found out the reason of his unusual
acquirements: he had been brought up in Siberia, and had
learnt from the educated political exiles.  Other ardent spirits,
thirsting for the light of truth, receive help from the sectaries,
who include in their number almost all who have any education
at all among the peasants.  This young man had got his
knowledge in Siberia, and it was pretty certain to be the means
of sending him back there.

To say that it was a crime in the eyes of Government to ac-
quire a better education than is common in one's own class might
seem an exaggeration if it were not amply proved by many
instances.  Here is one.  In the government of Ufa, a man
named Semjanoff held a position in the mines.  He was the
son of a poor miner, but by his exceptional industry and self-
devotion had passed through all seven classes at the gymnasium,
and, consequently, obtained a fairly good post in the direction
of the mines.  His superior never had any fault to find with
him in any way, and all was going well, when there was a change
of governors in the province.  The new governor, a man after
Pobiedanostseff's own heart, at once sent for Semjanoff.

" Now, you rascal, what are you doing here? " he roared, as
soon as Semjanoff entered the room.

" I beg your pardon, I——" began the startled man.

" What have *you* to do with 'beg your pardon,' you scum?" cried the governor, without allowing him to speak.

" Why do you insult me like this?" exclaimed Semjanoff.

" On my word, just listen to him," fumed the governor. " To the guard with him, put him in fetters! I'll teach you! Three days of gaol for the fellow!"

" But he is a man of education," whispered the former governor, who was present.

" So he has had an education, has he? Then he shall have *three weeks!* I always give double or treble to educated folks! I'll soon show you rascals how I'll deal with you!"

Semjanoff lost his position, and was degraded to the rank of simple clerk. Soon after he was sent with a sealed order to the chief of the police. The order ran " Give the bearer fifty lashes." It was performed with punctuality and despatch. Two days later he was sent with the same order, with the same result. It then became the established rule for this unfortunate man to take an order to the police and be flogged three times a-week.

Brought at length to the verge of insanity, so that he was hardly responsible for his actions, he tried once to escape, but was soon brought back, and received more of the same treatment. A second attempt was attended by like results, and at last nature took her revenge, and he became completely insane. Even then his persecutors were not satisfied. " They lashed the poor lunatic with the knout, just as they had flogged the sane man," says our authority, and adds "there are legions of Semjanoffs here."* What was the cause of all this ghastly brutality? There was not the slightest fault to be found with him, as commonly understood. But he had committed an unpardonable offence: he had set the bad example of getting an education superior to that of the class from which he sprang.

A few figures, taken from official sources, and referring to the first years of the present decade, will throw considerable light on this matter of popular education in Russia. About

* " Kama und Ural" by Nemirovitch-Wantschenko (1890).

200,000 recruits are yearly enlisted in the army, and of these only about 50,000 can read. Among the peasants proper the percentage of illiterates rises to 95 PER CENT.! In some parts, *e.g.*, the district of Novorzhcvsk, Kholm, and Tovopetz, in the neighbourhood of St. Petersburg, there is only one school to each 200 villages. In these places one finds only from 5 down to 1 per cent. of children of school age in the schools in consequence of deficient school space. If Russia had the same proportion as her neighbour Sweden, for example, she would have about 250,000 schools, while she actually has only 18,000.

Again, take Russia's enormous budget of 1,000,000,000 roubles; of this only 500,000 are devoted to popular education. That is one-eleventh part of what is devoted to the maintenance of the Imperial Court ; one six-hundredth part of the cost of the army, and one two-thousandth part of the whole. At about the same time Great Britain was spending about £9,000,000 for elementary education, &c., with a population little more than a third that of Russia. Moreover, about two-thirds of this paltry sum of 500,000 roubles goes in salaries of inspectors.

In fact, Russia stands behind China in point of popular education, for in the latter country 2·6 per cent. of the population goes to school, in the former only 2·3 per cent.

In the government of Cherson, by a recent *ukase* of the Holy Synod, Stundist peasants are plainly forbidden to allow their children to be taught to read, and other districts are said to be threatened with the same treatment because of the spread of heresy within their borders. Truly the present Russian Government may fairly be classed among the powers of darkness.

Not long ago the leaders of the Liberal party sent out circulars to the local authorities in order to ascertain the exact facts about education in Russia, or as nearly exact as the character of the said local authorities would allow. This would have given too intense a light for the bat-like vision of the Holy Synod. Pobiedanostseff at once sent his circular, too, to the same authorities, reminding them that they were under no obligation to reply to these questions, and this was followed

AN IMPROVISED TYPHUS HOSPITAL.

up by a third from the Minister of the Interior absolutely forbidding any answer being sent. At the same time Pobiedanostseff appropriated a sum of money devoted to popular education and placed it in the hands of a "committee" with *purely arbitrary powers*.

A sharp struggle is going on at the present time in Siberia, where the Liberal party is somewhat stronger, between the friends of education and the priests, but, of course, the Government is siding with the latter.

One great and wide-reaching consequence of this priest-ridden "education" is the ignorance and superstition in all sanitary matters. Talk to a peasant about the connection between dirt and disease, the destruction of forests and bad seasons, and he will not understand what you are driving at. For instance, I once told some peasants who were using dirty water for drinking purposes, that they were drinking disease and perhaps death. They simply gaped at me. Then I tried them on another tack and said, "No doubt the famine and the plague have fallen on you because you have neglected to pray to God and the saints." "Yes, Lord have mercy upon us," they cried in chorus, crossing themselves, "we have not worshipped God and the saints devoutly enough; that is the cause of all our troubles!"

To the Orthodox famine and pestilence are not effects of causes, but are sent by God or the devil either to punish or torment them. To get rid of them one must first try redoubled piety, prayers, cross processions in the field, pilgrimages, &c. If that is no good they try the other shop, and consult their sorcerers about means to pacify or outwit the powers of evil. Many of these sorcerers are maintained by communities, and are far more powerful than the priests. If neither piety nor black magic is of use, there is nothing further to be done. Any precautions of man's own devising are not only useless but positively dangerous, since they may irritate still further God or the devil who sent the plague upon the land.

Whether the authorities themselves really believe the same things, or simply use the superstition as a means of holding the peasants in deeper subjection, it is difficult to say. At any

rate, they play their part exceedingly well, and give no sign
that they have any faith in pure water and cleanliness. While
the people were dying by the tens of thousands, the officials,
who were careful not to set their sacred feet within the pre-
cincts of a plague-stricken village, busied themselves with
devising and issuing most sapient orders by which to counter-
act the ravages of hunger and disease. While I was in
Samara the children were forbidden to play in the streets or
fields so as not to offend the Great Powers. The poor little
starving mites were truly in no mood for play. Probably it
was for the same cause that parents of the Orthodox faith
were forbidden to give their children Jewish names, and *vice
versâ*, and all peasants were commanded to uncover their heads
before every one of higher rank, on pain of flogging and
imprisonment.

As a consequence there is absolutely *no* sanitation in most
villages, and when the thaw came after the terrible winter our
worst fears were realised. The village streets were turned into
canals, along which flowed streams of dirty, yellowish-green
water, setting the heaps of excrement, from men and beasts,
that had accumulated through the winter, in a ferment. From
these streams the women got their water for drinking, cooking,
&c., and from the heaps of refuse themselves there rose continual vapours, spreading in the atmosphere; an incense that
might fitly rise in worship of the great powers enthroned at
Petersburg.

Look at this village street awhile. Here comes one of the
doctors belonging to the expedition I have mentioned—*not* sent
out by the Government. He is riding on a horse whose legs
sink deep into the muck and filth. Soon after comes one of the
"sisters," shod with high boots, one hand engaged in holding
up her skirts, the other carrying medicine and food for the
patients; from *izba* to *izba* she goes on her errand of mercy,
wading through the liquid mud.

We will go with her awhile on her rounds, approaching her
with deepest respect. She belongs to no religious order; there
is nothing of the nun or "saint" about her. She is of high
rank, and has received a superior education. It is the inward

prompting of her own nature that has impelled her, like so many other young ladies of gentle nurture, to "go to the people," and risk her health and life in tending her suffering fellows. There is nothing theatrical, no touch of the stage heroine about her. Like her other sisters, she seems perfectly unconscious both of the dangers to which she is exposed, and of anything heroic in her occupation. It is the most natural thing in the world to help her needy neighbours.

We go first to the temporary typhus hospital—a peasant's cottage fitted up for the purpose. Above the door is the grim inscription: "No admittance! Infectious diseases!" Outside is a group of men and women waiting for news of their relatives, stricken by "the sickness," as the peasants call all kinds of disease. Two rows of beds are ranged along the length and breadth of the cottage, filled with patients of both sexes, about thirty in number. Sighs, groans, rapid breathing, prayers, delirious ravings fill the air, and though everything is scrupulously clean, it is impossible to keep the air pure in an unventilated *izba* full of typhus patients.

After this we visit some of the houses where patients are lying ill—and it is a difficult matter to find a place where they are not. Some of these cottages have great pools of water on the earthen floor, making it simply a mudflat, but here, too, are fever-stricken patients. In one cottage we visit one of the doctors, who has himself fallen a victim to the spotted typhus.

The members of the expedition told me that the state of things throughout the villages was frightful. Prince Dolgorukov himself came across a family of nine members, *all down with disease, mostly spotted typhus*. It was simply impossible to carry out any method of isolation. One doctor reported 351 cases, of which 155 were typhus, in a few days. In the village of Gavriulki half the population was down, and with the inset of the thaw matters were growing rapidly worse.

All this was simply the result of the Government's policy of keeping the peasants in ignorance and superstition. The pestilence was the result of the famine and the insanitary conditions of the villages. Of these the last is directly trace-

able to the mischievous teaching of the priests, made clear
above, that ecclesiastical jugglery, and not common sense, is
the remedy for disease.   As for the former, the example of the
Mennonites, who, in the severest times of famine, not only
escaped suffering themselves but were able to give large help
to others, clearly proves that the famine was not the effect of
bad seasons, but of the wicked exploitation of the mass of the
people by the officials and "upper classes."   For all these evils
the Court of Petersburg and the Holy Synod are directly
responsible; they stand guilty of the murder of the bodies and
souls of millions of their fellow men.

# CHAPTER VIII.

## A DAY IN A FAMINE-STRICKEN VILLAGE.

(SPECIALLY CONTRIBUTED BY P. VON BIRUKOFF.)

Early Dawn—Starved Horses—Applicants for Relief—A Terrible Story—In the Eating Room—Simplicity of Human Wants—A Hidden *Izba*—A Scorbutine Farming—More Applicants—Weariness and Its Effects—A Tangle of Thoughts.

It is a fresh spring morning. The sun is not yet risen, but the "*morgenroth*" stretches over half the sky. I go out into the streets to breathe the pure morning air. There is a breeze springing up from the east, and the village folk are beginning to stir. As the peasant women light the fires in their ovens slender columns of smoke ascend. The church bells are ringing for matins, and a number of old men and women are going, single file, into the church. Half-wakened, uncombed *mushik*-youths crawl slowly from the low *izbas* to harness the horses and fetch water. From other huts come peasant men and women with yokes on their shoulders.

The earth is hard in the morning frost. From a distance comes the ring of a horse's hoofs striking the frozen ground. It is most likely someone riding out on the steppes to relieve the horsekeeper, who has been tending the village horses on the hills where the snow has melted, and the poor beasts munch the sparse and short stubble left from last year's harvest, or the dried old grassroots. "They may find something," think the *mushiks;* so they keep one horse at home, to fetch water and for other household purposes, while they take it in turns to watch the others out on the steppes. However poor the feeding is out there it is better than at home, where everything is devoured, even to the rotten straw on the roofs of the outhouses, and in many places of the *izbas* also.

The sun's rays now break forth from behind a distant hill, illuming with its golden touch first the wreaths of smoke, then the housetops, and gradually spreading over all the village, throwing long blue shadows behind the buildings, while the snowfields, blinding in their intense whiteness, glitter as with diamonds. Now the smell of burning *"kisjack"* (fuel made from manure and straw) from the ovens is borne upon the breeze. Day has come.

CATTLE GRAZING ON THE STEPPE.

I return home, and sit down to the perusal of lists and accounts in connection with the different branches of our relief work among the starving folk. The most pressing need of the day is for seedcorn. The people begin to bring their different wants. A peasant enters, makes the usual sign of the cross and bows as he turns to the "holy corner."

"What do you want?"

"To see your grace."

"What is your need?"

"Please put down my name for sowing-corn."

"But will you not get it from the official committee?"

"I have no horse, little father. They gave me no rye in the autumn, and I could not sow. They frighten me by saying I shall get nothing. What shall I do—perish? We are eight in family. Don't forsake me, little *kormiletz*" (one who gives food), adds the peasant, with quivering voice. I see him sink upon his knees. I get him up with difficulty, inquire into his case, write down his need, and send him away.

The same moment comes another peasant with rolling gait, clumsy, rough, pale, and exhausted.

"I come to your worthiness—I beg your pardon; I don't know by what title to address you—to ask your grace for seedcorn."

"Do you get anything from the committee?"

"Your worship, what can I get from that quarter? We are seven in family; my wife, four girls, and the boy one year old, who is not yet registered on the committee's books, and I hear they are to give two *pud* (80 pounds) for each 'male soul.' So I shall only get two *pud*. How can I keep my family on that? Everything is sold and eaten up. I have no horse nor cow. I have hired myself out to a rich peasant to plough his field, and for this I shall plough my own little plot with his oxen, but I have no seed to sow with." I write his name on the list for further consideration.

A fresh applicant enters. He holds himself upright like a soldier, looks with a frightened and vacant stare before him, with one hand at his side in military fashion, while the other holds his cap.

"What have you to say?"

"I come to your high nobility to ask for——"

"Seed-corn?"

"Just so, your high nobility, because our family is—so to speak—large; and because I served as a soldier after—so to speak—we had been on the other side of the Danube."

"How much do you get from the *Zemstvo*?" I interrupt him.

"I am not aware, your high nobility, because when they sent me on military service my wife did not understand how to obtain help from the Government for her sustenance"—and for

9

a long time he tries to use the most difficult words in the hope of winning my favour. I write down his name and dismiss him.

A woman comes in sobbing. "My little father—I come to you——"

"What do you want?"

"My husband is very ill—his body is beginning to swell—he cannot climb down from the oven. Yesterday I heard that your grace gives medicine. Help us, little father, for Christ's sake! I have tried everything already; I have covered him with cow-dung, given him cherry-balsam, sprinkled him with holy water. Some time ago, little father, I had a visit from the monks of Athon monastery, who went through the villages with holy pictures, and I begged a small bottle of holy water from them. I got half a *mera* of rye from them, hardly worth a thank-you, but nothing is any good."

"Where do you live?"

"Little father, I live near the small stream, in the narrow lane, the third hut. First, there is an izba, with a board roof, then a wattled fence, and our little *zemlianka* (earthen hut), with a small window towards the yard, very poor. Come, little good-giver."

I promise I will, and enter her name.

Then come several others, each with a special request.

I go for a while to get tea with my landlady, and then go out. The sun is already high, and it is nearly noon. The frozen earth has thawed, small brooklets are purling along, beginning their day's work, carrying the dirty, melted snow to larger streams, which here and there are making their way beneath the snow. The pools in the village streets are still sheeted with thin layers of ice, with small openings here and there from which cracks radiate in all directions. I walk by the side of a wide brook that rushes down a hill until it loses itself in a pool; this has already overflowed its banks, over which it foams along in a small cataract. Across it are seen two small huts, and beyond the boundless steppe, rising with gentle slope until in the far distance it meets the infinite heavens. As I gaze over the plains I discover some black spots moving. Looking more closely I see that they are people, but what they are doing out there in the deep snow I cannot understand. I approach an *isba*, where two peasant women have stopped on their way to fetch water. They seem to have forgotten their errand, and have put their yokes and buckets on the ground, while with expressive gestures, pointing out on the steppes, they are telling each other some story. I draw near and ask what is going on out on the steppe.

"They are looking for him."

"Which him?"

"Jegor Michaelovitch, of course."

"What Jegor Michaelovitch?"

"Why, Jegor Michaelovitch Schupikoff who lives in the roofless cottage at the end of the street. Do you know Lukeria Ivanovna? Well, his brother is her godfather—they have been sponsors together at the psalm-singer's, and it is that child that is dead; it would have been of the same age as my Vasjutka, only it was dark-haired and mine is fair."

"Well, what has happened to Jegor Michaelovitch?"

Then the woman tells of a terrible accident. Jegor Schupikoff, a peasant with a family, who had been reduced to the greatest misery, and had sold and eaten up his horse, and fed his last cow with everything that the not-too-particular stomach of a Russian cow can digest down to the rotten straw of his cottage roof, had gone to his prosperous brother to borrow a load of straw. The brother had refused. The peasant came home crying, sat down to think awhile, talked it over with his wife, and as a last resort decided to go out on the steppe and try to dig out of the snow some remains of haystacks.

There were still three hours before sunset. "I shall go and try," he said. "Perhaps I may scrape together a small armful. It will last a couple of days, and then I will trust for what God gives."

Taking a rope and spade he set out. Towards evening a storm came on and it grew dark. His wife got a light and put a little food on the table for supper, expecting every moment that her husband would return with fodder for the cow. She

waited on; the children ate their thin water-soup and bread.
All night she sat up until the morning broke. Her heart began
to ache, but still she thought, "Perhaps he will come."

In the morning her neighbours came with wailing and
lamentation to console her, but made her only more sorrowful.
Yet she still thought, "Perhaps he has wandered too far, gone
to another village, and was afraid to return home at night.
Maybe he will return about noon, or he will come with some of
the peasants to the village—it is market day to-day."

People came from all neighbouring villages, but he was not
among them, nor had any one heard of him. She had at last
to acknowledge the terrible fact that Jegor was lost.

So another day passed; a snowstorm raged through the
night. Towards morning the storm ceased, the sky cleared,
and the *starosta* sent a number of peasants out on the steppe to
search for the lost man.

Full of sad thoughts aroused by this story I go on my way.
The noon bell is ringing. I turn my steps to the *izba* in which
one of the five free eating-rooms is established. As I enter I
hear the *molitva* (grace) being sung, and as the door opens,
I catch the words, "Thou precious treasure and giver of life,
come and dwell within us." The last word is slowly sung as
I come in, and I feel somewhat soothed.

The guests salute each other, take their spoons, and sit down
at three tables, set along the walls of the *izba* at right angles
to each other. There are only forty persons present. The
servers pour the soup into the large wooden bowls, and distribute equal-sized pieces of bread to each guest. As I look at
them a strange feeling comes over me. On the faces of most
I see satisfaction; in one corner is heard subdued laughing
and jesting. All sit down in quiet orderliness and begin to eat.
Within the *izba* was a spirit of content; no heartrending wailing that betrayed hopeless want.

"Here is no famine," I said to myself. "Is it such a simple
thing to satisfy the wants of men, to give them a piece of bread
and a bowl of warm soup—is this all? Can it possibly be so
simple? A horse needs 30lb., and a man 2lb. of bread and
warm soup, and all are happy! Then why do we not make

every one happy? Why is there so much suffering?" And thoughts crowd one upon another, like links of a chain, through my brain, carrying me far away.

I say "simple"; is it really so simple? I remember a story, read long ago when a boy, of a teacher asking if any one knew where salt was obtained. All were silent, till a little girl stood up and said, "I know." "Where, then?" asked the teacher, not expecting, though he had asked the question, that any child could answer it correctly. "They buy it at the shop," said the girl, perfectly convinced that nothing could be more simple. "What can be simpler?" she thought; "to get salt, when the jar is empty, one has only to throw a handkerchief over the head, get a penny from mother, run to the shop, and one has salt again." She does not think of the intricate process of procuring the salt; or the still more intricate process of transporting it to the shop, and, most intricate of all, getting the penny with which to buy it.

All this I remember, and begin to understand how intricate also is the process by which 2lb. of bread and warm soup come to the mouth of a starving man. Long rows of carts, freight trains, Vendrich*, flour merchants, &c., rush through my imagination.

But what seemed to me a moment has evidently been minutes to others, and when my attention is recalled to present facts, I notice an expression of curiosity on the faces of all present, as if expecting me to speak, and wondering why I was silent. The manager of the kitchen has been holding out a spoon for a good while, for me to taste the soup. I make haste to do so, say something meaningless, and, spite of my strange behaviour, go out of the *izba* with a vague feeling of satisfaction and consciousness of an effort that has been crowned with some success.

I return home to dinner. Several peasants are already gathered there. I inquire into their needs, write down their names, and dismiss them. In the afternoon I go out once more, and recollect the woman with the sick husband. I make for her home, and, with great difficulty, try to find her earth-hut

* The railroad inspector, since dismissed.

from her somewhat mixed description. At last I am clearly at the lane spoken of. The hut must be there, as I think, but beyond the fence I see only a snowdrift, darkened a little under the warmth of the spring sun; further out on the steppe are some outhouses and heaps of "*kisjack*"; it is evidently not here. "I must have taken the wrong lane," I say to myself, and go back to the main street to get information. At the corner a *mushik* is sitting at his door, and I apply to him.

"Where do the Koroljoffs live?" "Koroljoffs?" "Yes." "*Aah*," he drawls out, and points down the lane from which I had just come. Without hope of further information from that quarter I turn back down the lane.

Out of the gate of the first *izba* a little girl is running, but, seeing me, she hides behind it. I go into the yard after her; she looks at me with a shy glance, but does not hide again. I see that timidity has changed to curiosity.

"Do you know where the Koroljoffs live?" I ask.

The little girl looks at me attentively for a moment, and then says "Come," beckoning and running down the street in the direction of the snowdrift, where I had been already. I follow her. She turns round the drift and disappears, as if swallowed up by the earth. I also turn, and to my great surprise find an opening in the drift, at the end of which is the door.

Down the opening I go, and find that the drift is really the clay hut buried in snow; in this the family Koroljoff lives, eight persons. Stooping down, I creep through the low door, and enter the hut. A damp and suffocating air, polluted with the stench from the excreta of a sick person, not yet removed, meet me, so that I am near fainting. A few rays of light struggle with difficulty through a small window, for which an opening has been dug in the snow. The dim light prevents my seeing things inside the hut, but by an effort I get gradually used to the darkness.

The woman who had come to me is at the oven, busy with a stone jar in her hand. Behind her two little children, covered with rags, pale and dirty, are sitting on a bench, sucking a hard crust. In another corner something is lying on a bench, covered with a battered sheepskin cloak. A little girl, about ten years old, sits at the side, nursing a small child.

" Where is your husband? " I ask, after greeting.

" On the oven, little father. He will come down by-and-by."

" And who is that lying sick on the bench over there."

" It is a young girl. She has been ill a long time—it does not matter; perhaps God will take her away. We dare not trouble you with her. But that my husband is lying sick—what shall we do without him? " The woman burst into sobs, wiping her eyes with her apron.

At the same time the sick man comes scrambling down from the oven, moaning as he totters with great difficulty to the bench, and by the aid of his wife sits down by the table, resting his head on both his hands so that he almost lies across it. His swollen and pallid face shows extreme weakness. I ask about his illness. " Sick—all—through," he says, pausing between each word. " First my limbs ached—my gums pained me—my whole body began to swell."

Here is a bad case of scorbutus. I approach the sick girl on the bench to look at her legs. Blue spots on the calves, under the knees, and on the soles of the feet—here, too, scorbutus.

" How about the little ones, are they well? "

" Yes, pretty well; they only complain of pain in the gums, which bleed. I have a bigger boy, who is out begging; he is well."

" How have you got into such a bad plight? What do you eat? Do you get anything from the committee? "

" We get something, little father, but it is not enough. It was too little from the first. Then we borrowed. When we got more from the committee we had first to pay back what we had borrowed, so that there remained still less than before. The first week of the month we have enough to still our hunger, but the other weeks we have to starve. My husband is counted among the " rabotniki,"* and for the little ones they give nothing. What have we not eaten! We dug clay, which we

---

* " Labourers "—i.e., such as were considered able to work, and did not get help from the Government.

mixed with a little flour, but all kinds of clay are not suitable. One kind stops hunger a little, but once when we tried another sort our stomachs swelled, and we recovered with much difficulty."

I listen to this story in silence. What can I say? I, who am satisfied with nourishing food, what can I say to these people, who have been reduced to such a condition that they discriminate between two kinds of clay—eatable and non-eatable?

I go out into the fresh air, which I inhale in deep draughts. I feel as if my body, unaccustomed to this polluted, suffocating atmosphere, was poisoned; yet in this air a whole family is living and growing up! I know, too, that there are many such families; I have seen numbers of them myself. I recognise a fresh need, developing a new branch of relief work necessary—to fight the *scorbutus*. In my mind rise combinations of more eating rooms and nourishing food. So pondering I make my way home.

It is growing late. The impressions of the day are surging up in my brain. With a certain feeling of satisfaction I begin to think of rest. But the time for that is not yet come. Approaching the house I see at the door of my room a group of peasant men and women who have clearly been waiting some time, as some of them have sat down on stones outside. With humiliation I detect in myself a feeling of antipathy to these people who come and spoil my plans of rest. I have no courage to turn them away, and begin mechanically to inquire into their needs. I do not succeed, and begin to get impatient. Ten or fifteen peasants stand before me, each with one or more requests. Either because there are too many of them, or because I am tired out, I am no longer able to recognise in each a human being with his or her own personal dignity; I see only *numbers* of men who are expecting something from me that is either difficult or unpleasant.

According to my habit of trying to meet the requests of my fellows, I will not at once send them away, but choose a middle course—something absurd, in the usefulness of which I do not myself believe. I begin to make out a list, write down their

INSIDE AN IZBA.

names and those of their families, jot down some remarks and dismiss them, dissatisfied, of course. Yet they bow, thank me for my sympathy, make some further requests and finally go. I breathe more freely. But suddenly a woman leaves the retreating group, comes back to me, bows low, and with sobs and cries begins a long story about the misfortune that has overtaken them. I try to listen, but soon lose my patience, and ask, in a stern tone, " What do you want? " She tells me. I then find that it is already written down. With a sharp answer I show my displeasure, turn from her impatiently, go out and slam the door behind me. I am ashamed of myself. I walk to and fro, sit down and get up and sit down again; look vaguely at the papers on the table, and with much trouble compose my excited nerves.

I go to my landlady ; she has the boiling *samovar* all ready, and the sight of it soothes my disturbed mind, but the same thoughts haunt me all through the meal, and afterwards, when, alone in my room, I put my papers in order and prepare for rest. The same thoughts, sometimes bright, sometimes gloomy, but always the same subject. What must be done ? How help, and what will be the result? Will there be another year like this ? Sometimes, as if in the magic-lantern, the pictures change; my thoughts wander off to my far away home, and I begin to converse with my dear ones; these images vanish, and again my brain is busy with the questions of the day.

Before retiring to rest I again go out. It is dark and bitingly cold. The village is asleep, and overhead the dark blue heavens sparkle with myriads of stars; all is quiet. harmonious, majestic, beautiful. Where are all the sufferings? Why is it not on earth as it is up yonder ? We are only an insignificant part of this beautiful, harmonious nature. Can all the parts be of one nature? How can such a crowd of sufferings come from out a beautiful whole? Or are there, perhaps, no sufferings ? Do they exist only in our consciousness ?

I return to my room, throw myself on my bed, and deep and heavy sleep breaks off the current of my thoughts.

# CHAPTER IX.

## ON THE VOLGA.

WHEN I stepped on board the magnificent steamer *Puschkin*, that was to take me a five days' journey up the Volga from Saratov to Nishni Novgorod, I could easily have imagined myself on board an American steamer on the Hudson or the Mississippi. But this first impression was soon dispelled; the ugly saints' pictures hanging in the saloon, and the ragged, miserable-looking beings in the steerage reminded me forcibly that I was not in America.

A large number of soldiers were on board, and on the first two days they enlivened our passage with singing, lasting late into the night. Their strikingly original folk-songs, or rounds, were deeply impressive. Their weird strains, passing from tender melancholy into outbursts of almost wild savagery, seemed the musical expression both of the national character and the Nature-spirit of the country. In the transition from the softest *pianissimo* through *crescendo* to the wildest *fortissimo*, mingled with sharp whistling and shouting, and again through *diminuendo* until they died away in almost inaudible tones, one could hear the winds of the steppes rising from gentlest breezes to raging storms, or the soft rustle of the wind in the deep and sombre forests growing into the fierce gale that sways the tall crowns of the strongest pines, whistles through the branches of the birch trees, and again subsides in softest murmurs.

For the first part of the journey the weather is warm, and

all the passengers are out in the open, forming many a picturesque group. Let us walk round the lower deck, among the steerage passengers. The wind has free play, but the smell is very " thick." We are at once surrounded by a crowd of peasants, clamouring in chorus for bread. We buy some for them, and proceed on our tour. Behind a barrel, one of the ship's crew is sitting, singing a jovial song, with a fat and buxom lass in his lap. Further on, two small groups are on their knees, round some object spread on the deck. What are they doing? Praying? No. A nearer approach shows that they are peasants—*hunting*. They have laid out their sheepskin coats with the wool towards the sun, to entice the numerous inhabitants out of their remoter haunts into the light and warmth; when the unwary population, not suspecting any evil, migrate to the outer regions merciless hands pounce down and hurl the victims into Volga's depths. So intent on their hunting are the peasants that they do not utter a sound, or pay the slightest attention to the ring of spectators around them. When will all the Russian peasants take to this excellent hunting business, and clear out *all the vermin* that are eating into their very bones?

Leaving them to their engrossing business and going forward, we see a decently clad young man, of sympathetic appearance, distributing New Testaments among the peasants, who receive them with bowed heads, making the while the sign of the cross. He is a colporteur in the service of the British and Foreign Bible Society, which has been and still is doing a grand work in Russia. It reflects some credit on the Russian Church that the circulation of the Bible has been allowed in the Orthodox empire, however limited. The clergy have often been antagonistic to Bible distribution, and several depôts have been closed, but still the work goes on. It was in 1812 that the Russian branch of the British and Foreign Bible Society was established, through the untiring exertions of the English clergymen Paterson, Pinkerton, and Henderson. At first a parallel edition of the New Testament in Russian and Slavonic was distributed, then from 1818 an entirely Russian translation, while in 1824 the New Testament was issued in

no less than forty-one different languages, to meet the needs
of the many half-wild races in the distant parts of this vast
empire. Two years later, the Russian branch was suppressed
by Nicholas I., on the ground that it was "a revolutionary
society, which aimed at subverting thrones, churches, law,
order, and religion, throughout the whole world, with the
object of establishing a universal republic." All its property
was confiscated and the new translations put under lock and
key. The distribution of the New Testament was allowed only
under most hampering regulations. The Society sprang up
again under Alexander II. under the modest title, "Society for
the Promotion of Moral and Religious Reading," which, in its
turn, was suppressed in 1884 by Alexander III. The British
and Foreign Bible Society has, however, received permission to
distribute the New Testament, under the control of the Holy
Synod, but not the Old, unless bound up with the Apocryphal
Books.

It is scarcely possible to exaggerate the influence exerted on
the Russian peasants by the Bible. The widespread and
increasing religious movement of to-day undoubtedly owes its
origin and spread very largely to it. It is for the most part the
only book to be found in a Russian *mushik's* home, where, with the
exception, perhaps, of a collection of silly legends, is no literature nor any newspaper. The testimonies, whether written or
oral, given by the peasants as to their conversion to evangelical
religion almost always go back to Bible-reading as the means.

Among the steerage passengers on our journey was a peasant
in poor but tidy dress, with a pensive and intelligent look.
Getting into conversation with him we found him to be an
earnest, evangelical Christian ; at our request he gave us a
sketch of his life, which I put here into connected form.

"I am, as you see, a simple peasant. My parents were very
poor, owning but three *hectares* of land. A large family and
crushing taxes reduced my father to destitution, so that he had
to work for a *kulack* in our village as a *batrak* (*i.e.*, as a slave,
for debts incurred). Every day my mother was working away
from home to keep us from starving, until she also became a
*batrak* to one of our creditors. We children were seven in

number, my eldest sister, who had charge of us, being only nine years old. Of course, as happened with other children, too, we lived like cattle and pigs. I was the youngest, and went with my mother where she was working, generally lying on rags or the bare earth, exposed to mosquitoes and frequently an object of curiosity to a dog or a calf.

" My entrance into this world took place in an open field during hay harvest, and almost the entire summer I was hung in a *ljulku* (a kind of suspended cradle) in the heat of the sun or exposed to the rain, out in the fields where my mother was working.

" 1 was not baptized on the eighth day after my birth, according to Orthodox custom, but nearly six months afterwards. This was partly because I was born in the busiest season of the year, when my parents had to work every day for the *kulacks*, and partly because they were so poor that they had nothing to pay for the ceremony, though the priest cut down the price to forty copecks. At last the police compelled him to do it, but this made him so angry that he dipped me three times in icy cold water; I fell very ill and was near death, but at last recovered.

" When I was six years old the most severe calamity befell us. My father in despair took to drink, leaving the entire care of the large family to my mother. Soon the last traces of our belongings disappeared; my mother had to go out begging to keep us from starvation, and often we got no food before noon, when she returned with a morsel or two.

" After a few years I was sent to my sister, who had been married into a very Orthodox family. There I was taught to repeat prayers and sing psalms, but of a living faith I heard nothing. I learnt to stand before the picture of a saint and repeat prayers which I did not understand. When I was ten I had an irresistible desire to learn to read, but there was no school in our village, and had there been one I was too poor to have attended it.

" A soldier in our village, however, who could read, had some liking for me, and undertook to teach me. He used the old method, giving the letters the old Slavonic names, which made

it very hard for me, but thanks to my strong desire to read, I
got over that difficulty. In summer, when I had to take my
share of field work, I forgot almost all I had learnt, but in
autumn I began to teach myself again, and by spring could
read moderately well. No more could be expected of me, as
my opportunities were so limited. My education remained at
that point till I was sixteen. Then I had a great desire to read
better, and with much trouble got a church calendar and a
psalm-book, in which I read with diligence. My efforts were
rewarded with progress, and I could at last read so well that I
was often asked by the people to read the prayers over the dead.
(In Russia it is usual to read prayers over the dead for the
first three days after death.)

"Soon I had a great wish to learn to write, but was met with
the difficulty that I had no ink. I made some by boiling elder-
tree bark in water. Then I bought two goose quills at the
market for three copecks. I found in my father's chest a
small piece of paper, on which something was written, and
copied this out, though scarcely understanding a single letter.
When my father noticed my industry he asked the village
scribe to write out a copy and show me how to write. So I
learnt, but I cannot say that my style was beautiful.

"Then I began to take special pleasure in the church music,
and in service went into the choir. I was not driven away, so
began to join in the singing. Then I was asked to read psalms
before the service began (a Russian custom; it may be done by
a layman). The villagers began to think much of me, and
the psalmsinger, after I had helped him gratis, would give me
money from the bowl on the altar that is used in the service.

"The priest, too, began to notice me, and at weddings,
funerals, and Eastertide processions I went next to him,
holding the sacred pictures. Soon I became intimate with
the priest. I had thought before that the clergy were more
moral than laymen, but I soon changed my mind as I saw that
they allowed themselves every gratification and indulged in
spirit-drinking outside mealtimes. I, too, got into the same
habit, but my conscience began to reproach me, and I saw
that my spiritual pastor, instead of guiding me in the right

way, was leading me to eternal perdition. Such was the way in which the Lord called me to Himself."

After describing his agony of mind, and the effect produced upon him by a picture of the Last Judgment, he went on to tell of his coming into the possession of a New Testament, through a man who had been working in the city and had associated with the Stundists. By reading this he found rest and satisfaction in the truth.

" From that moment all was new for me ; I knew that I was beginning to live. My past life seemed like a black dream. All things round me, heaven and earth alike, were transformed. It was with me as with the blind man, I received my spiritual sight."

Of course his relatives and friends, the priest at their head, began to persecute him, and he came at one time very near banishment to Siberia. But he escaped the danger, and became the means of converting many others.

At one station where we stopped we saw one of those " Cross-processions " out on the fields that are so common, their object being to implore the Deity to send rain and avert hunger.

The scenery on the Volga becomes more and more picturesque the farther we push up its stream. North of the city of Samara it flows through the beautiful Shibulovski Mountains, and the treeless steppes are replaced by forest-clad heights. Here and there, surrounded by the dark pine woods, is seen a white monastery, nestling amid rocks, or standing on some hillside slope, while little villages of grey and red houses slumber in the valleys.

On the fourth day of our journey up the Volga we passed one of its tributaries, the Kama, which rises in the Ural Mountains, on the Siberian frontier, and joins the main stream sixty miles below Kasan. It is the great waterway to Siberia, along which prisoners are conveyed in floating prisons ; we saw one of these as we steamed by.

Kasan itself lies hidden from view, with the exception of its many gilded church towers and minarets. At this place a score of Mohammedan priests, called *mooli*, of the Tatar tribe,

10

came on board, proceeding as far as Nishni Novgorod. They all sat round a table, conversing in their strangely soft language; suddenly they would put their thumbs to their ears to shut out the world while praying.

These Tatars are, as a rule, excellent people. They call the orthodox "idolaters," because they worship the pictures of the saints; the orthodox retort the term on the Tatars because they do not worship Christ. In Kasan the Tatars have much the best hotels, which are clean and orderly. In the orthodox hotels, on the other hand, are women of bad character, drunkenness, dirt, and dishonesty.

Early on the fifth day we arrived at the picturesquely-situated and interesting city of Nishni Novgorod, the end of the steamboat journey. We stayed for a few hours only, walking through the streets, as it was the dull season; it is during the great fair that the city wakes up to full activity and life. Here and there we found traces of the frequent fires that occur in the wood-built houses in spite of the ingenious and far-sighted command said to be issued by the governor of the place, that the inhabitants must always report to the police at least two hours before the outbreak of fire!

On our way by train from Nishni Novgorod to Moscow we fell in with a liberal professor of theology in one of the southern universities, with whom we had a most interesting conversation.

Speaking of the terrible famine and its causes, the Professor remarked: "The priests, also, are a very heavy burden on the people's shoulders, keeping them down by ignorance and poverty. If I had the power, I would exterminate all this miserable missionary work among the masses, which is only intended to hinder the spread of light among our people. I believe firmly in the principles of religious liberty, and no progress can be made in our country before we have it."

My companion, an earnest evangelical Christian, remarked that there was an essential difference between the Orthodox and evangelical missions, to which he replied:

"May be, but so far I have not found, either in the Greek, Roman, or Protestant Churches, any mission which has not more or less been intolerant, and attempted compulsion of conscience in the name of Christ. In His name even war is carried on, and God's blessing is invoked on wholesale murder. Not only during war, but at all times they pray that God will give us victory over our enemies and trample them under our feet, as it stands in our Russian church prayers. There is much besides from which I have to dissent, and therefore I have of late come to the conclusion that it is best to leave the people without forcing upon them anything that contradicts their beliefs, and allow them to develop naturally."

To my question how, with such views, he could retain his position as Professor in an Orthodox University, he replied:

"It is quite natural. I teach religion as I would any other subject. I find it very interesting to study the different religions and compare them, and it is just through these researches that I have arrived at my present views."

"What! do you say we do not need our Orthodox faith?" here struck in, in half-astonished, half-insulted tone, a fat and ruddy youth who was sitting opposite my companion, and had listened to the conversation, evidently understanding no more than that the Professor had spoken against the Orthodox religion.

"What fault do you find with our Orthodox faith? Is it so difficult for you to make the sign of the Cross before a picture? Nothing else is required." And he broke out into a self-satisfied chuckle as he threw himself back in his seat and closed his little eyes, almost buried in fat, while his whole jovial and well-fed figure shook with laughter.

"And when the Great Lent comes on we eat in the last week cabbage and onions, and drink *kvass* as much as the soul requires; then go to the pope and leave our sins with him for twenty copecks, take the Holy Sacrament" (here he made a pious grimace), "and after the midnight service on Easter Eve we make up for the fasting by eating eggs, lamb, pork, butter, and cheese, and on Easter morning go a-feasting and have a jolly time till next Lent. No! there is no better religion in the world than our Orthodox faith! Is it not so, grandfather?" he said, turning to an aged citizen, one of the "old believers," who was sitting opposite him, and who, with a paternal smile, looked at the self-satisfied youth, saying half to himself,

"Youth, youth! If youth only had understanding, and age strength," quoting a Russian proverb.

"Do you know, grandfather," the young fellow chattered on, "my mother has a little shop of her own, but I have charge of the business, you know. My father died when I was just a little brat; it is only three years since I became master of the house, as it were. Heigho! how this business life bores me, grandfather! But then I sleep like a dead man when I come home at night at nine o'clock. Then I eat my fill of sweet cakes and pastry, which mother bakes for me, wash it down with a little tea, and so throw myself into bed and sleep until eleven or twelve o'clock next morning. It's no use trying to wake me before then. Is it a sin to sleep so much, grandfather? I can't help it! it's no use trying. I don't like it myself, but I can't help it."

"Sleep, sleep, my child," replied the old man. "When age comes on and conscience begins to accuse us of the faults and thoughtlessness of youth, sleep will flee."

"Well, grandfather, is it a sin to make the sign of the Cross with three fingers?" he asked, with a roguish smile, jesting with the old believer, who makes the sign with only two fingers.

"It is not ours to decide upon that matter, my child," said the old gentleman. "We have to love Jesus Christ our God, and believe His Word, and leave the rest with God. 'In every nation he that feareth Him and doeth righteousness is acceptable to Him.'"

"You are right," chimed in a middle-aged Tatar, in a mild voice, who had been sitting on a bench behind us, and now came forward. "I also believe that. But allow me to ask where it is written that Christ is God? In our Koran it stands that He was only a prophet, and that God is only One."

"I don't care about your Koran," cried the young man, flushed with rage. "That is no law to me; our Orthodox faith is better than yours!"

Now my companion interposed, and directed the conversation

into other channels; otherwise ignorance and fanaticism might have made the dispute too hot.

On our arrival in Moscow the following morning we found all the shops closed, and the whole city decorated to celebrate the birthday of the Crown Prince. I have said elsewhere that there are seven of these festival days, which by Imperial decree must be celebrated by the suspension of all useful work and business. Suppose that only one-half of the Russian people are engaged in any kind of useful work, these Imperial festivals mean the loss of over a million years of one person's labour, and if we take all the 133 festival days in the year (including Sundays) they represent about twenty millions of years of one labourer's time, not to speak of the moral loss to the people by enforced systematic idleness.

Between Moscow and St. Petersburg I met a highly-placed Russian official from the government of Kursk, who was an unusually sympathetic and liberal-minded man for his caste. He told me about the terrible distress of the peasants in his province, and was deeply interested in my account of the relief work of the Tolstoi family.

"The state of things is desperate," he remarked. "The peasants are not only unable to pay the taxes and the redemption money for the land, but the State must now support them, and there are about 35 millions of these destitute and helpless people. . . . Even in the most favourable circumstances it must be many years before there can be any change for the better.

When I asked him what he considered the best means of bettering the conditions of the people, he said that practical schools were indispensable, and spoke of a rational system of migration.

"But," he added, "there is no possibility under present circumstances of carrying either of these into effect." Then he reminded me of what I knew before, that several public-spirited and wealthy gentlemen had offered to establish practical schools of different kinds at their own cost, but had not been permitted to do it. A conspicuous case in point was the offer of one Sibiriakoff to build an agricultural academy in Samara, and

endow it with one million of roubles. For a whole year his
application lay unanswered at St. Petersburg, and was at last
met with a point-blank refusal. The Governor of Samara had
explained to the authorities that such an institution was not
needed in his province, and besides, would probably only become
a centre of political propaganda.

# CHAPTER X.

## AMONG GERMAN COLONISTS.

Skilful Boatmen—Adventures in a Row-boat—The German Colonies—Their
Prospering—and Decay—Mennonite Colonies—Their Principles—A Visit
—An Oasis in the Desert—Peace and Plenty—A Miracle of Co-operation—
Land for All—Successful Prohibition—A Wonderful Record of "Crime"
—"No Priests, Policemen, Publicans, or Paupers"—Co-operation and
Competition.

To get to some of the so-called German Colonies, where my
business led me, I took one of the great Volga steamers from
Samara to Volsk, having to complete the journey, some twenty-
four miles, in a row-boat.  I first took note of the great relief-
work organised by Countess Schouvaloff on her large estate close
by, and then went to a "contractor" to order a boat and two
oarsmen to take me to the village of Basel, in the German
Colonies.  I had often heard of the skill of these Volga boatmen, and was looking forward with considerable anticipation
to seeing it for myself during a pleasant ride on the bosom of
"Mother Volga."  When I came to the river I was unpleas-
antly surprised by finding a wretched-looking, half-rotten,
wooden box of a boat, manned by two rowers whose looks
inspired me with anything but confidence.  I returned to the
" contractor " and remonstrated, but was met with the eternal,
ambiguous Russian expression "*Nitchevo*"! I had no time
to try elsewhere, so decided to run the risk and trust to my
swimming abilities if any calamity should occur.

On leaving the shore one of the rowers at once gave evidence
of his incapacity ; probably he had never touched an oar before.
At every stroke he plunged his oars perpendicularly into the
deep, at the same time half rising from his seat.  The other,
who plainly considered himself the "captain," gave up rowing
altogether, took his seat opposite his " crew," and issued

orders in terms more forcible than polite, smoking the while
one cigarette after another. I should have lost all patience,
had not the unusually strong current carried us of itself out
into the open river, where it became almost imperceptible.
Here a small breeze sprang up, and the captain dived under a
seat and produced a bundle of rags. I asked what he was
going to do, and he replied " Sail ! "

An old oar was put up as a mast, with the boathook as sprit-
sail yard. Amid much fuss and shouting the sail was hoisted,
and, with another old oar the " captain " sat down aft to steer
his craft. It was the most picturesque sail I have ever seen.
Part of it reminded me strongly of the maps sometimes
exhibited at missionary meetings, with " Darkest Africa " and
other heathen lands coloured black in irregular patches; for
the rest, it resembled the loud " checks " favoured by a certain
class of tourists more than anything else.

But my observations and comparisons were suddenly cut
short, as an infant cyclone swept sail, mast, and all into the
water. The " captain " now took the oars, and we managed to
get to the other side of the stream, where the strong current
had eaten away the sand bank; the miserable rowers not being
able to keep the boat from the shore, we had a narrow escape
of being sent to " Davy Jones's locker " by a landslip. I took
the oars myself and pulled to our destination. Here the
rowers wanted an extra rouble for their "hard work." I
discovered that the " contractor " had given these poor men
only a few copecks apiece, keeping the larger part of what I
had paid him for his own share.

I visited almost every village in the German Colonies on the
Volga. These have had a very interesting history. They
date from the time of the Empress Catherine II., who invited
German immigrants to make settlements, and endowed them
with considerable privileges, her object being to erect a
strong barrier of defence against the half-savage hordes then
roaming over the steppes beyond the Volga. The colonists
built their villages near one another on the fertile shores of
the river, and soon entered upon a period of prosperity.
Before the great famine they numbered about 350,000. Their

large schoolhouses and churches, their well-built dwelling-
houses, surrounded by trim gardens, all spoke of a considerable
degree of thriving civilisation.

Unhappily, however, this prosperity must already be spoken
of in the past tense. For one thing, their well-being had, as
usual, attracted the hostile attention of a suspicious Government, and of late years every expedient has been employed to
hamper their development. At one time tobacco-growing was
a flourishing industry in these colonies; the authorities made
the sale of this commodity a monopoly, with the result that
their market was practically destroyed, and the industry
killed. Nor have they been proof against the wiles of
capitalism, both from without and within.

The consequence of this was that they were unable to stand
against a succession of bad years, and famine broke out in
their midst. I found, during my investigations, that these
colonists of German extraction, being accustomed to a higher
standard of living than the *mushiks*, fell much easier victims
to starvation than the latter. Typhus, also, had made terrible
havoc among them; the death-rate had in some villages gone
up as high as 180-200 per 1,000. From these causes, and
especially on account of the hostile attitude of the Government,
emigration to America has set in on a large scale.

The Mennonite Colonies, usually included by name among
the "German" colonies, but really of Dutch origin, form a
very pleasing and instructive exception to the general misery
and starvation. During the famine, not only have they not
suffered themselves, but they have been both able and willing
to give much aid to the needy round about their borders.

The ancestors of the present colonists shared in the invitation
of the Empress Catherine II. mentioned above, and received
from her the privilege of maintaining both their religious faith
and practice, and their communal ownership of land. They
were also exempted from military service, as contrary to their
religious belief, and received instead the obligation to plant
trees; a most excellent substitution. After overcoming the
natural difficulties, which occupied them some years, they
flourished greatly, and have continued to do so ever since. At

one time the sapient authorities attempted to curtail their
privileges, and large numbers emigrated to America, both to
the United States and the Southern Continent, but of late they
have been comparatively free from molestation.

The cause of the wonderful success of these colonists in
the face of considerable disadvantages is undoubtedly their
practical Christianity, *i.e.*, the steadily applied principles of
brotherly love in their communal life.

To give the reader a clear idea of these colonies we invite
him to share our visit to one of them. .

It is a very hot summer day, and we have a covered carriage
to protect us against the scorching rays of the sun. A few
hours' ride over the treeless, waterless steppe brings us within
view of an oasis in the desert, conspicuously green. It is the
Mennonite Colony of Halfstaal, in Southern Russia, which we
are about to visit. The nearer we approach the more vivid is
the contrast between it and the surrounding country. All
round is the dreary, flat, and sun-scorched steppe, unrelieved by
a single tree. Here, in the midst, is a tract of charming
verdure, grassy meadows, and luxuriant foliage. At one of the
outskirts rises a three-storied building of handsome dimensions; it is the school for deaf and dumb, supported by all the
Mennonite Colonies in common, and used for the instruction of
their deaf-mutes of both sexes. The methods of teaching and
all the arrangements are in accordance with the latest improvements in Europe. There is perfect order in the school, as in
the colony generally, testifying to the high moral and intellectual development of the inhabitants. Snug and roomy
houses on both sides the broad street peep cosily out from the
green gardens, which always form an essential part of a
Mennonite home. Here are no abominations of terraced
houses, in which, as Maarten Maartens somewhere observes,
the central inhabitant has only to read the newspaper aloud,
and all the others in the street may save their pennies; each
home is surrounded by a spacious plot of land of its own, with
separate well for both drinking and irrigating purposes.
Behind the house is always a kitchen-garden, beyond a well-
built cowshed and storehouse. Scrupulous cleanliness and

order is a conspicuous feature of all within the borders of these demesnes. The large common well is in an open spot on one of the outskirts of the village, supplied with a spacious cattle-trough.

The Mennonite colonies are, as a rule, of moderate size only, mostly consisting of from fifteen to fifty farms. The land is owned by the community, and each member has a right to cultivate 65 *hectares* (about 160 acres) of this communal land. He may, of course, if he please, purchase more land outside the bounds, but this happens very seldom. On marriage, a young couple is provided, if they desire, with these sixty-five *hectares*, a house, implements, and stock from the communal fund; in return, they must cultivate the land properly, keep it in good condition, and pay their yearly quota to the communal fund. Every farm is a small agricultural centre, perfectly independent as regards the use made of it, just as an owner of the soil would be, except that it is not permissible to let it run to waste or in other ways become impoverished.

The Mennonite Colonies of Russia are standing miracles of the triumph of human co-operation. Out of the dry, treeless steppes there have arisen, as if by occult forces, flourishing groups of homesteads, with fresh spring water in abundance; large plantations of fruit and the common forest trees; fields made fruitful by laborious culture; numerous herds of splendid cattle and horses. In this village district alone the number of trees amounts to about twelve millions. Each colony has its own school and a large storehouse for cereals, kept filled in case of failure of crops. Besides these, the Mennonite denomination as a whole has several high-schools. Out of the common fund they also support physicians, midwives, and hospitals. They also form their own fire insurance company, independent of all Government control. No premium besides the ordinary contribution is paid, but in each case the loss is borne by the entire community, and payment made from the common fund without delay.

The quota paid by each colonist to this communal exchequer is proportional to his income, and the burdens of taxation (to the Government) are divided among all able-bodied persons of both sexes between the ages of fourteen and sixty. Their own common fund is administered by responsible trustees, who receive no pay for their services, but regard it as a position of honour and trust. No defalcations have been known among them.

It very rarely happens that anyone neglects his duty of contributing his annual share to the common fund, or of cultivating the land he occupies. If such a case should occur, the delinquent is put under discipline, mostly of a moral kind ; they have the power of expulsion, in the worst cases.

Each colonist has his land adjoining his house, and not in different parts of the settlement, as frequently happens under the bad system of the Russian Government. It is not compulsory to take up this portion of land. Some prefer to work for others, or engage in some industrial occupation. They have a few manufactures, but obtain most articles of this description in exchange for their farm produce. They practise co-operation very largely in the disposition of such goods as are destined for the market, and not for home consumption. It is obvious that the right to become farm-holders on their own account entirely prevents that mischievous, unequal pressure, resulting in the forced sale of one's labour for a miserably inadequate return, that is lauded among Western nations as a " beneficent freedom of competition." The members of the community who live outside the colonies, *e.g.*, teachers, many of whom find positions in large cities, retain their rights of membership by the annual payment of their due quota, reckoned on their income. These duly qualified persons can always take refuge from the competitive storm of the capitalistic world, should they find its buffetings too severe, in these havens of co-operative helpfulness, and either take up their portion of land or fill any other position for which they are qualified, at their option.

When the Government grants of land were found insufficient, the community bought other tracts, so as to provide the minimum holdings guaranteed to each member.

The Mennonites are not communists in the complete sense of the word, but recognise private property in all but the land, and even there only that is communal that belongs to the community and is used for the guarantee described above. All buildings, trees planted, and improvements generally made on a farm by the occupier rank as private property, which is inherited by his heirs, who must be paid a just value by the new occupant of the farm. In this inheritance women share equally with men, as they have an equal responsibility for the Government taxes.

It was one of the privileges granted to the Mennonites, when they first arrived in 1789, that no one should be allowed to open liquor shops within their borders. This practice is maintained, and here at least the advocates of Prohibition may find an instance of its success. The police authorities have light work so far as the Mennonites are concerned, even with the manufactured crimes so dear to the hearts of Russian officials. Here are some figures giving the complete list of misdemeanours and crimes as recorded in police archives, in one case for a population of 12,121 during thirty-seven years, in the other in a population of 6,000 during ten years :—

|  | 37 YEARS. | 10 YEARS. |
|---|---|---|
| Disobedience and impertinence ... | 6 | — |
| Abetting escape of prisoners ... | 2 | — |
| Disobedience to parents ... ... | 11 | — |
| Calumny, slander, and untrue reports | 10 | 1 |
| Adultery ... ... ... ... | 41 | 24 |
| Neglect in quenching fires ... ... | 1 | — |
| Theft and roguery ... ... | 9 | 5 |
| Neglect of agriculture ... ... | 16 | 4 |
| Quarrelling and strife ... ... | 4 | 1 |
| Drunkenness ... ... ... ... | 1 | 7 |
| Offences against the faith ... ... | — | 2 |
| Keeping a tavern ... ... ... | 5 | — |
| Non-fulfilment of official orders ... | 3 | 17 |
| Non-fulfilment of agreements ... | 1 | 1 |
| Non-payment of bills and loans ... | 1 | 1 |

It will be seen that many of these would disappear altogether from English police-lists, and others would be transferred to the civil branch of the law. But did all these figures represent real crimes it would be a wonderful record, considering the number of years and the population. It is a testimony as to the efficacy of good economic conditions in the reduction of crime that cannot be gainsaid, for other communities have had as much religious faith as the Mennonites, but cannot show so clear a

record from roguery and theft.    Moreover the children born to
religious parents are not necessarily religious; at least, it is
not generally found so in other lands.    But all born into these
communities are allowed to remain, if they think fit, with
privileges independent of religious confession.    It is surely
because the religion of these people is logically applied to
their economic and social arrangements that we find this most
extraordinary freedom from crime.

We therefore sum up this brief sketch of the Mennonite
Colonies by repeating that, on the testimony of every impartial
observer, they practise the gospel of brotherly love in truth
and reality, not simply in word and doctrine.    They do not
seek to eat up, but to help each other and the neighbouring
people.    Usury is unknown.    Their religious concerns are
under the care of unpaid elders ; the only clergy they support
being of the missionary order.    In a word, co-operation is the
keynote of their life, not competition, and it is allowed to govern
their economic and social as well as their religious relations.
As a result they have no need of priests, prisons, policemen,
publicans, or paupers.

The contrast between these communities and the Orthodox
Russian villages in their neighbourhood, on the steppes, is the
sharpest imaginable.    In the latter are no trees—("they don't
grow," say the *mushiks*.    "Because you do not plant them," I
used to add)—no schoolhouses, no hospitals, no decent dwellings, but plenty of ignorance, drunkenness, dirt, poverty,
disease, and misery of every kind.    The fundamental cause
is the absence of true, practical Christianity in the relations
between man and man.

The same contrast is also to be found, although not so
glaring, between the Mennonite Colonies of other lands and
their neighbours, *e.g.*, in the United States and South America.
In the last-named, for instance, the Mennonites are on one side
of the River La Plata, and the Swiss, with a large sprinkling
of Italian, on the other.    Prosperity and happiness are to be
found among the former; with the latter, who practise competition and its resulting forms of cheating and jugglery, there
is poverty and misery.

# CHAPTER XI.

## IN THE CITY OF SARATOV.

The City—General Ustimovitch—A Stundist Meeting—A Prison-Evangelist
—Detectives—A Notable Picnic—Consecration of the Volga—Calumny
against Stundists—An Orthodox Missionary—Holy Water.

FROM the German Colonies I went to the city of Saratov, beautifully situated on the Volga, with a population of about 125,000. Looked at from the river it would easily be taken for a modern Western town, were it not for the large number of churches, whose Byzantine cupolas, so different from our Gothic spires, gave their unmistakably Eastern aspect to the place.

In the government of Saratov the famine had not reached such a fearful intensity as in Samara, yet the suffering had been very great, and the city itself was swarming with the starving peasants. Among those who devoted themselves to relieving the destitute General Ustimovitch held a prominent place. This noble man also gave much time and labour to editing a monthly periodical, called *Brotherly Help*, devoted exclusively to philanthropic topics.

I give the following entry from my diary, as illustrating my experiences and observations in Saratov.

On Sunday I was asked to address a meeting of Stundists, and accepted the invitation. The morning meeting was held in a private house consisting of three rooms and a kitchen. After singing and prayer by several of the brothers and sisters, a tall, fine-looking man stood up and read Hebrews xi., adding some practical and sensible comments. He spoke with deep feeling and conviction, which both attested his own earnestness and enlisted the sympathetic attention of his hearers. His dialect and dress told me that he was a simple peasant. While he was speaking a friend whispered to me, "The speaker is a prisoner. He has been sentenced to one year's imprisonment, but the governor of the prison, having great confidence in this man, has allowed him one month's liberty in which to visit his friends and do as he pleases. The reason for the governor's action was an outbreak of typhus in the overcrowded prison."

I asked what crime he had committed, and was told, "He has been preaching the Gospel in the villages, and hundreds of orthodox peasants have been converted, become sober, and left the worship of saints' pictures. For this he has been sentenced to imprisonment."

At the request of my friends I addressed a few words to the meeting, telling them of the sympathy felt by Christians in all lands with the persecuted Christians in Russia.

The evening meeting, at which I had promised to give a longer address, was held in the same room, and was much more largely attended. Before I rose to speak a slip of paper was put into my hand, on which was written in pencil, "*Detectives are present. Be careful!*"

With this unexpected stimulus I rose and told the audience that I was not going to preach, but simply to tell them something of my experience in the famine-stricken provinces of Russia. I thought this would be suitable matter for the detectives to report to their chiefs.

Starting with the magnificent gifts from America for the relief of the starving Russians, I told them how these contributions had come from all classes of the people, and took advantage of the opportunity to describe, in passing, the homes and lives of American "*mushiks.*" Then I described the relief work organised and carried out by Count Tolstoi's family, and the sufferings I had witnessed among the peasants of Samara. I added some remarks on the duty of brotherly kindness towards each other, and the prospect of better times when men shall watch for opportunities of mutual service instead of accusing and exploiting one another, and closed with the humble request that all present should take this friendly exhortation to their families and friends, and try themselves to put it into practice."

After having supped with a friend, I returned to my

GENERAL USTIMOVITCH AND HIS PAPER, "BROTHERLY HELP."

lodgings, where I was told that a gentleman had been inquiring for me. From the description and other attendant circumstances it was more than probable that this " gentleman " belonged to the police. I at once concealed some important documents and photographs, taken in the famine districts, and went to bed, sleeping soundly.

Among other visits next day I called on General Ustimovitch, who received me very kindly and invited me to a drive through the city. Sitting at his side in his elegant equipage, respectfully saluted by the soldiers and police and gazed at admiringly by the great multitude, I could not help contrasting the experience with that of the previous night, when I was hiding my papers, &c., from too great a curiosity on the part of the police. I endeavoured to adopt a mien worthy of the occasion, such as might have distinguished a Prince of the Blood or the Procureur-General himself !

At the General's proposal we made a picnic next morning at 6 a.m. to a height on the shores of the Volga. It was a curiously mixed party, including a peasant, a Tatar, and two Bible colporteurs. I took a Kodak picture of this interesting group, making a kind of silhouette against the sky. The General is in the middle with a Russian lady who has done and suffered much for her people ; to the right and left a Bible colporteur is handing the New Testament, the one to a *mushik*, the other to a Tatar. When we had had some tea, &c., a small choir went to the top of the hill and sang some songs in Russian, among them a translation of the beautiful hymn, " The Morning Light is Breaking, and Darkness Disappears." The General and myself stood at a distance listening. There was moisture in the General's eyes as he turned to me saying, as he pointed to the choir, " And such people are persecuted in Russia ! " " That is sad," I said. " Yes," he replied, " but the morning light is breaking."

When we returned to the town a number of small processions were going through the streets, and the church bells were pealing. I inquired the reason of this, and was told that it was a prominent saint's day, and that at noon there was to be a solemn " *vodoosvjastsstchenje*," or " consecration of the water " of the Volga; the Governor of the city and all the prominent inhabitants were to be present at the ceremony. I have before mentioned the great number of days on which all work must be suspended. There are 111 saints' days in the calendar to be celebrated, of which 76 are compulsory everywhere, and some of the remainder in different parts. Then there are the seven Imperial festivals, besides Sundays.

It was now, or should have been, the busiest time of the whole year. In the country there was the year's sowing to be done, and the Volga was but newly opened for traffic. Yet

A PICNIC PARTY.

the shops in the city were closed, and large numbers of people from the country had come up to take part in the festivities.

I started out myself to swell the crowd of idle onlookers. As I walked through the streets some peculiar-looking placards on the wall of a square attracted my attention. On closer acquaintance they proved to be compilations of the coarsest lies and slanders against the Stundists; some of them made up of extracts from the Russian newspapers. They were, of course, placed thus conspicuously to excite the fanaticism of the Orthodox mob. The Stundists themselves have no possibility of redress or defence allowed them, and interference

CONSECRATING THE VOLGA.

with these placards in any way would bring on the offender the direst penalties.

Long before noon the streets through which the procession was to pass were closed to the public by *gendarmes*. With my Kodak under my cloak I managed to elbow my way down to the magnificent river, whose waters, discoloured and swollen by the melting of the winter snows, were to be consecrated, and secured a place on a large steamer, from which I had a good view of the "holy" pavilion, where the ceremony was to be enacted. In the middle of the pavilion floor was an opening to the water, draped round with a white cloth, on which "holy" vessels were placed. The bridges, the steamers, the banks of the stream, and the roofs of the houses were all covered with onlookers.

Nearly an hour passed before the procession appeared, but as harbinger there came to the pavilion an important personage in the shape of an "Orthodox missionary." This is a new order of the Church, created to help the police exterminate the sectarians under pretence of "converting" them. There was a sanctimonious effulgence about his face that accorded well with his sleek appearance. I had seen this holy man before, and knew that he was a shining light within the fold of the Orthodox Church; I knew with what unctuous eloquence he could address the orthodox masses, and kindle their orthodox passions to such a degree that they would assault and rob the heretics, both in the streets and in their own homes. I knew how, through his holy zeal, many a sectarian had been thrown into prison, or exiled to Siberia or Trans-Caucasia, leaving their destitute families in misery and despair. I knew, too, how that holy man would be humility itself, could even go so far in his condescension as to hold intimate intercourse with the lowliest—of the fairer sex. I therefore watched him with the greater interest and attention.

With grave and solemn step he passed to the bridge leading to the holy pavilion, which none of the common or vulgar dared to tread. Here he stopped, and gazed on the masses with superior mien. He passed in review the quays and the

shore, half turned, threw his head back, and regarded the
people in the windows and on the housetops. Solemnly he
turned again towards the river, and, lowering his eyes,
surveyed the rowing-boats round the pavilion. His face
darkened as among these he discovered a boat-load of
irreverent youths, whose ribald grimaces and gestures were
not calculated to deepen the solemnity of the scene.

"Here they come!" A forest of standards and crosses is
seen above the crowd, slowly moving down the street, while the
bells are ringing in rapid time. Now the procession is fairly
within sight. In front is the Archbishop of Saratov, a saint
of ample dimensions, with golden mitre, glittering with its precious stones in the sun, upon his head, a *felonj* of "*partscha*"
(or long robe of white silk, shot with gold and silver) hanging
from his broad shoulders, and a staff in his hand. After him
follow monks, priests, nuns, deacons, and singers galore, carrying pictures of the saints, and behind them the notable civilians.
Suddenly the procession stops ; the archdeacon begins to sing
in a tremendous bass voice, the other singers soon joining in.
The Orthodox multitudes cross themselves again and again,
bowing deeply each time. Then the procession proceeds. Bowing and crossing himself, the Archbishop enters the "holy
pavilion," followed by the chief members of the procession.
First a *maleben* (prayer) is sung, followed by mass. After this
the climax is reached. The Archbishop steps to the opening in
the floor of the pavilion referred to before, and makes the sign
of the Cross above the water, the singers meanwhile singing a
hymn.

After the water has thus been consecrated, and obtained the
necessary miraculous power, the Archbishop approaches the
fence round the holy place, and with a kind of broom sprinkles
holy water on the masses of the people, some of the peasants having waded knee-deep into the stream in pious hope of
receiving a few of the sacred drops.

At this point I bring out my unholy Kodak, and manage to
get three snap-shots. One of these has been reproduced by the
artist, showing the "holy pavilion" and other details of the
Orthodox tomfoolery.

# CHAPTER XII.

## PRINCE DMITRI KHILKOV.

His Questionings—Abandonment of Property—Life as a *Mushik*—Influence on the Peasants—Conflict with Landowners—with the Church—"The Damned Stundist"—Banishment by "Administrative Process"—Journey into Exile—A Well-meant Offer—Settlement at Baschkitchet—Activity during a Cholera Epidemic—An Official Medical Commission—Imperial Persecution—His Confession.

WE shall give in this chapter an account in detail of the life of one of Tolstoi's followers, which will serve as an example of the difficulties under which he and his disciples live, and the manner in which they put in practice what they believe.

It is now some years since Prince Dmitri Khilkov, who is still in the prime of manhood, gave his earnest attention to the deep realities of life. He had inherited large estates in the province of Kharkov, and enjoyed all the advantages, usually so considered, that such a position entails. But when he came to examine the grounds on which that position rested, and put questions to himself with the intention of getting a satisfactory answer, he came to the conclusion, as Tolstoi had done, that the life of a privileged and wealthy person, surrounded by a peasant population plunged in degradation and misery, was opposed to reason, conscience, and the teaching of Christ.

Once arrived at this conclusion, he proceeded to carry out its logical results. He was not one to rest content with holding a high ideal, while making "the prevailing system" the excuse for a lower standard of actual life. The word "doctrinaire" was not in his vocabulary. He at once distributed his estate among the peasants, with the exception of even hectares (about seventeen or eighteen acres), which he

kept to cultivate himself.   On this he worked, paid taxes, and
lived with his wife and children.   " I kept bees," he says, in a
letter to a friend, " and a piece of land, and my seven hectares
supplied my needs for the support of my family.   I ploughed
the fields, cultivated grass and root crops, and generally got a
good harvest.   I had one horse and two cows."   In dress and
everything but personal character he shared the *mushik's* life
completely.   One who knew the Prince intimately, and on whose
veracity I  can implicitly rely, gave me in St. Petersburg the
following account of his influence on them.

   " Such a degree of savagery prevailed among the peasants in
that district of South Russia where Prince Khilkov lived that
it was even dangerous for a stranger to pass through it.   After
the great change in the Prince's life, he began to go among
them, New Testament in hand, talking with them in brotherly
fashion, showing them a better way, a happier mode of life, ready
with advice and help on all occasions, just as he had already
given up all his property for their sake.   And what was the
consequence ?   The whole region is transformed, drunkenness
and crime rarely occur, and the people live in mutual peace
and goodwill."

   Of  course, in the  eyes  of official wisdom all  this  was
" dangerous," and could only escape interference for a few
years.   It was, besides, impossible for one of Khilkov's
character and conviction to avoid collision with the authorities
of such a Church and State.   The landowners and ecclesiastics
were foremost in transgressing the nominal laws, and oppressed
the peasants in every way.   These looked for help to the
Prince, who never refused his aid, either of word or deed, to
those who asked him.   The story of his first collision with
these gentry will illustrate the impossibility of peaceful
relations between them.

   It is a favourite device to obtain the lands of the peasants
by goading them to revolt by some unusually flagrant injustice,
and then confiscating their holdings.   It happened that a
certain Count desired to enlarge his estates in this way, and
he received the aid of his fellows.   But Prince Khilkov
explained the plot to the peasants, and when they were

summoned by the authorities, with the purpose of bringing about the outbreak, they resolutely refrained from furnishing any pretext whatever.

His rupture with the ecclesiastics, also, could not long be delayed, and occurred in this way. The Archbishop of Kharhov was greatly troubled about the spread of the Stundists, and devised various means for combating this heresy. He adopted the practice, increasingly common of late, of arranging public meetings for discussion of religious questions. An order of "Orthodox missionaries" has been created whose business it is to conduct these discussions on the side of the Church. But instead of giving opportunity for free discussion, they are simply traps for unwary Stundists. The "missionaries" have free licence to heap all manner of lying calumnies on the heretics, but if the latter dare to attempt any refutation, they are silenced, and are marked by the police, with banishment to Siberia as a result.

In Prince Khilkov's district, when these meetings were held in the villages, large numbers of the peasants would attend, and, before the discussion began, would hand to the priests the pictures of saints from their homes, declaring that they had no further need of them. Sometimes they would ask him to read to the people such passages as Matthew xxiii., xxiv., Isaiah xliv., &c. The Orthodox who came and heard these things out of the Bible were astonished, and many joined the Stundists.

Another plan of the Archbishop was the distribution of a shameful pamphlet he had edited, written in verse, and called "The Damned Stundist." Prince Khilkov bought up several hundred copies, and provided each verse with a Biblical commentary, and a selection of Scripture passages on the back page of the pamphlet. All these he wrote with his own hand, distributed them among the peasants, and sent a copy to the Archbishop himself.

We give a *facsimile* of the title-page of this remarkable *brochure*, with the Prince's comments in his own handwriting, and a translation of the text and annotations.

Remember the word that I said unto you, A servant is not greater than his lord. (John xv. 20.) And these things will they do, because they have not known the Father, nor me. (John xvi. 3.) Blessed are ye when men shall reproach you, and persecute you, and say all manner of evil against you falsely, for my sake. (Matt. v. 11.)

AND IF HE REFUSE TO HEAR THE CHURCH ALSO, LET HIM BE UNTO THEE AS THE GENTILE AND THE PUBLICAN. (Matt. xviii. 17.)

IF HE REFUSE TO HEAR THEM, TELL IT UNTO THE CHURCH;

HOWBEIT THE MOST HIGH DWELLETH NOT IN HOUSES MADE WITH HANDS. (Acts vii. 48.)

## THE DAMNED STUNDIST.

If the world hate you, you know that it hated me before it hated you. (John xv. 18.) Blessed are ye, when men shall hate you, and when they shall separate you from their company, and shall reproach you, and cast out your name as evil, for the Son of man. (Luke vi. 22.)

*Printed at the Imperial Printing Office, Kharkov.*

Bless them that curse you. (Matt. v. 44.) Not that which entereth into the mouth defileth the man; but that which proceedeth out of the mouth, this defileth the man. (Matt. xv. 11; Mark vii. 15, 18-23.)

## THE DAMNED STUNDIST.

Out of the same mouth proceedeth blessing and cursing (James iii. 10).

### I.

*Roar, ye thunders of the church!*
*Arise, ye fulminations of the councils!*
*Crush with eternal anathemas*
*The accursed set of Stundists!*

But I say unto you, that every one who is angry with his brother without a cause, shall be in danger of the judgment (Matt. v. 22).

### II.

*The Stundist demolishes our dogmas;*
*The Stundist rejects our traditions;*
*The Stundist scoffs at our ceremonies;*
*The heretic, the accursed Stundist!*

And He said unto them, full well do ye reject the commandment of God, that ye may keep your traditions (Mark vii. 9).

### III.

*God hath honoured our Russian church*
*With great renown and glory:—*
*Her, our mother dear,*
*Slanders the accursed Stundist.*

For where two or three are gathered together in My Name, there am I in the midst of them.

### IV.

*Like stars in the firmament*
*The holy temples*
*Shine throughout our native land:*
*Shunned are they by the accursed Stundist.*

The temple of God is holy, which temple ye are (1 Cor. 3-17). Know ye not that ye are a temple of God, and that the Spirit of God dwelleth in you? (1 Cor. iii. 16).

### V.

*We offer prayer in the temples,*
*We sing the hymns of our church,*
*Or we perform the holy sacraments :*
*All is blasphemed by the accursed Stundist.*

And why call ye me Lord, Lord, and do not the things which I say? (Luke vi. 46). But go ye and learn what this meaneth, I desire mercy, and not sacrifice (Mat. ix. 13).

### VI.

*Our great and holy thaumaturgi,*
*Defenders of the Russian land,*
*And our spiritual shepherds :*
*Defamed are all by the accursed Stundist.*

For there is one God, one mediator also between God and men, himself man, Christ Jesus (1 Tim. ii. 5).

### VII.

*The relics of the men of God,*
*Our holy images of saints*
*And our processions of the Cross*
*Are loathed by the accursed Stundist.*

Are ye so foolish, having begun in the Spirit, are ye now perfected in the flesh? (Gal. iii. 3).

It is the Spirit that quickeneth; the flesh profiteth nothing : the words that I have spoken unto you are spirit, and are life (John vi. 63).

### VIII.

*When we sing Te Deums in the fields,*
*Or consecrate our brooks and springs,*
*Yea, when we kiss God's holy Cross,*
*Then gibes the accursed Stundist.*

Ye hypocrites, well did Isaiah prophesy of you, saying, This people honoureth me with their lips, but their heart is far from me. But in vain do they worship me, teaching as their doctrines the precepts of men (Matt. xv. 7, 8, 9).

## IX.

*Harsh an l gloomy like a demon,*
*Shunning people Orthodox,*
*In obscure dens he skulks,*
*God's foe, the accursed Stundist.*

How can ye, being evil, speak good things ? for out of the abundance of the heart the mouth speaketh (Matt. xii. 34).

## X.

*But if a simple sheep but casts an eye*
*Into the den of this wild beast,*
*By mockery, slander, and flattery,*
*Entraps him the accursed Stundist.*

For with what judgment ye judge, ye shall be judged (Matt. vii. 2). As the sparrow in her wandering, as the swallow in her flying, so the curse that is causeless lighteth not (Prov. xxvi. 2).

To the above commentaries Prince Khilkov has added the following Bible quotations, written on the back leaf of the above pamphlet under the heading :—

### LIFE'S POWER AND MEANING.

Fear not little flock (Luke xii. 32). Ye are my friends, if ye do whatsoever I command you (John xv. 14). A new commandment I give unto you, that ye love one another. By this shall all men know that ye are my disciples (John xiii. 34, 35). I say unto you, my friends, Be not afraid of them that kill the body, and after that have no more that they can do. But I will warn you whom you shall fear. Fear Him which after He hath killed hath power to cast into hell; yea, I say unto you, Fear Him (Luke xii. 4, 5). Beware of false prophets, which come to you in sheep's clothing, but inwardly are ravening wolves (Matt. vii. 15). Beware of the scribes, which desire to walk in long robes (Luke xx. 46). I am the Good Shepherd (John x. 11). But he that is a hireling is not a shepherd (John x. 12), because he is a hireling (John x. 13). But woe unto you, scribes and Pharisees, hypocrites, because ye shut the Kingdom of Heaven against men! For ye enter not in yourselves, neither suffer ye them that are entering in to enter (Matt. xxiii. 13). Woe unto you, lawyers! for ye took away the key of knowledge. Ye entered not in yourselves, and them that were entering in, ye hindered (Luke xi. 52). The Spirit of the Lord is upon me, because He anointed me to preach good tidings to the poor; He hath sent me to proclaim release to the captives and recovering of sight to the blind, to set at liberty them that are bruised (Luke iv. 18). Come unto me, all ye that labour and are heavy laden, and I will give you rest. Take my yoke upon you and learn of me, for I am meek and lowly in heart, and ye shall find rest unto your souls, for my yoke is easy and my burden is light (Matt. xi. 28-30). For I come not to judge the world, but to save the world (John xii. 47). The Son of Man came not to be ministered unto, but to minister, and to give his life a ransom for many (Matt. xx. 28). The Son of Man is come to save that which was lost (Matt. xviii. 11). I come to cast fire (of the truth) upon the earth, and what will I if it is already kindled? (Luke xii. 49). If ye abide in my word, then are ye truly my disciples. And ye shall know the truth, and the truth shall make you free (John viii. 31, 32). This is my commandment, that ye love one another (John xv. 12). Greater love hath no man than this, that a man lay down his life for his friends (John xv. 13). And as ye would that men should do to you, do ye also to them likewise (Luke vi. 31). (And therefore, love not only those that love you) but love your enemies (Matt. v. 44). Be not angry (Matt. v. 22). Judge not (Matt. vii. 1). Resist not evil (Matt. v. 39). In your patience ye shall win your souls (Luke xxi. 19). And if any man will go to law with thee and take away thy coat, let him take thy cloak also (Matt. v. 40). Then render unto Cæsar the things that are Cæsar's, and unto God the things that are God's. (Therefore, if they that rule and have the power demand your property, or even your life, let them take it without resistance. But give to no one your will, which is to be guided only by the will of your Heavenly Father, who has given it unto you. That which is not God's, give to the Cæsar, and to every one that demands it; but that which is the Lord's—the keeping of truth in your lives, according to His command—you must never render to any one, whosoever may demand it) (Luke xx. 25). For what shall a man be profited, if he shall gain the whole world, and forfeit his life? (Matt. xvi. 26). Be not therefore anxious for the morrow (Matt. vi. 34), saying, What shall we eat or what shall we drink, or wherewithal shall we be clothed? (Matt. vi. 31). But seek ye first His Kingdom and His righteousness, and all these things shall be added unto you (Matt. vi. 33). (If ye seek the Kingdom of

God, then observe) Neither shall they say, Lo, there! Or then! For lo! the Kingdom of God is within you (Luke xvii. 21). (The Kingdom of God is the perfecting of your spirit, the conformity of your life with His will, for the Lord is perfect and good.) First of all, beware ye of the leaven of the Pharisees, which is hypocrisy (Luke xii. 1). For I say unto you, that except your righteousness shall exceed the righteousness of the Scribes and Pharisees, ye shall in no wise enter into the Kingdom of Heaven (Matt. v. 20). And when ye pray, ye shall not be as the hypocrites, for they love to stand and pray in the synagogues; but thou, when thou prayest, enter into thine inner chamber, and having shut the door, pray to the Father, which is in secret (thy inmost heart) (Matt. vi. 5, 6). Worship God in spirit and truth (John iv. 24) (but serve Him not in temples, not with such spiritual songs, which have pleased yourselves, or by not keeping God's commandments, and by vain sacrifices). But when thou doest alms, let not thy left hand know what thy right hand doeth (Matt. vi. 3). Swear not at all (Matt. v. 34). Look not after a woman to lust after her (not even in your heart) (Matt. v. 28). Do not exalt yourself (Matt. xxiii. 12). Do not lord it over each other (Luke xxii. 24). For that which is exalted among men is an abomination in the sight of God (Luke xvi. 15). Not so shall it be among you, but whosoever would become great among you, shall be your minister (servant) (Matt. xx. 26). My peace I give unto you; not as the world giveth give I unto you (not by compulsion, but voluntarily); let not your heart be troubled, neither let it be fearful (John xiv. 27). Verily, verily, I say unto you, if any man keep my word, he shall never see death (John viii. 51). The words I have spoken unto you are spirit and are life (John vi. 63).

These things could be allowed no longer by the authorities. The Procureur-General of the Holy Synod, Pobiedanostseff, and his party concocted a scheme of getting Prince Khilkov out of the way by giving him living burial in the monastery of Sola-vetsky, which is on the White Sea, in the government of Archangel. But by the intervention of prominent friends this was altered to banisishment to Trans-Caucasia.

It is easy to make a legal pretext in Russia. In 1890 the Governor of Kharkov ordered the Prince to move to that city. He refused. In 1892 the *ispravnik* (chief of police) in the city of Sovini summoned him to receive an order from the Minister of the Interior concerning his person. The Prince did not obey, but gathered the peasants of his village together, explained matters to them, and bade them farewell. Soon the *ispravnik*, with ten armed policemen and an officer, came with a ministerial order of banishment to Trans-Caucasia for five years "by administrative process," *i.e.*, without trial or opportunity of defence. The Prince refused the privilege that members of the nobility have of travelling in comfort at their own expense, though accompanied by *gendarmes*. On the one hand, he refused to contribute in any way to the expenses of his deportation, and on the other he claimed no rank above that of a *mushik*, and desired to be treated as such.

On February 13, 1892 (O.S.), two officers, with fifteen armed soldiers, escorted the Prince from his village, who was then sent by common *étape* to Trans-Caucasia.

At Tiflis he was allowed to lodge among his friends, under strict police surveillance. This city is the first stopping-place of all exiled sectarians, who have reason to remember well the dark, damp, and overcrowded prison, Castle Metjesch, which few escape. The Prince was detained a good while before being forwarded to his final destination, and during that time an official of high standing attempted to save him from exile by procuring him a situation in Caucasia. When Khilkov called by request at his house, the valet, taking him for an ordinary *mushik*, rated him for coming to see his Excellency in so poor a dress, and would not let him in for a time. The Prince replied, "I am accustomed to go to my Heavenly Father in this dress, and his Excellency can hardly be of loftier rank than God." He refused the well-meant offer, declaring that he would abide by the "administrative order."

Finally, he was sent to the village of Baschkitchet, district Bortochali, in the government of Tiflis, inhabited by Mohammedans and banished sectarians, such as Dukhobortsi, Chalaputi, Stundists, &c. I saw an extract from one of his letters to a friend in St. Petersburg:—

"I am fairly well, although suffering just now from a severe cold. It has been very cold here this winter. I have a place

as servant to one of the banished sectaries, and my sleeping-
place is near the door, so I have been exposed to draught
and got a severe chill."

In the following spring the Dukhobortsi gave him a small
holding, which he cultivated as a kitchen-garden.   His wife
and children joined him in July, 1892, in voluntary partici-
pation of his exile.

Cholera broke out in the late summer.   Khilkov had a little
store of medicine, and the Dukhobortsi collected forty roubles,
with which they asked him to purchase the most necessary
drugs.   Both Prince and Princess Khilkov threw themselves
into the work of tending the cholera patients with untiring
assiduity, and had the satisfaction of keeping down the deaths
to a comparatively small number.   Besides this small stock of
medicines, procured by the exiles themselves, there was no
other in the district, nor any physicians.   It is true a " medical
commission " did come from official quarters, *but they had no
remedies with them*, and even wanted to take what they found in
Baschkitchet.   This was, however, refused them.   My trust-
worthy informant told me that " these gentlemen do not visit
the patients, but hunt the cholera, which they wish to frighten
away, carefully avoiding all cholera-stricken people who could
infect them."

Prince Khilkov and his wife were not married according to
the rites of the Orthodox Church.   Hence, as another blow at
the heretic, the authorities have declared their children illegitimate.   By the Russian *law*, they should be therefore under
the care of the Princess, who belongs to the Lutheran Church ;
but by order of the late Tsar, Alexander III., they were taken
from their parents altogether and placed under guardians in St.
Petersburg, to be brought up in the " Orthodox " faith.   To an
appeal made to him by the Princess the Tsar vouchsafed no
reply.   Letters from Russia received at the moment of writing
bring the information that the present Tsar has treated
another appeal sent to him personally in the like courteous
fashion.   Their infant girl, not yet one year old, they have,
however, so far been permitted to keep.

By request Khilkov wrote out for circulation among his

friends the main points of his faith.   We can hardly do better
than end the account with an extract.

## MY  CONFESSION.

The principles of our faith are common to all men, since, as
Tertullian said of old, "The soul of man is by nature
Christian."   In its broad aspect, stated for a circle of
intimate friends, my confession is as follows:—

We look upon it as our duty to sow around us in our daily
life the good seed, and to do loving deeds, even though that
should necessitate the giving of our lives for our neighbours,
our brothers.

We reckon as our brothers all who have anything in common
with us, without regard to creed, sex, or age, and without
recognising any privilege whatever which power, custom, or
culture may have conferred on us in the eyes of the world.

By good works we understand every kind of helpfulness that
we can show our fellows, by setting them free from spiritual
or bodily sufferings, lightening their severe toil, and spreading
among them the light of reason that illumines the path of our
life.

We observe no ceremonial rites, introduced and established
by Church, State, or ancient usage, since all these customs,
which are either outworn or have lost all significance, bedim
the light of life to reason.   They often aid in quieting the
restless conscience by affording it a satisfaction in the per-
formance of certain outward deeds, intended to appease the
gods for past sins.   Instead, we leave our conscience to be
plagued, without seeking to satisfy it with outer ceremonies,
until it becomes purged by repentance and renewed to
goodness.

We pass no judgments, have no law-suits, because the New
Testament enjoins that "if anyone smite thee on one cheek,
turn to him the other," and that we return good for evil.   If
any of our number sin, his conscience should punish him more
severely and justly than the courts and hangmen of this world.

We recognise no obligation to human Governments, because

we have no king besides God, who dwells in us and guides our life, if we love Him and keep His commands.

Since we acknowledge no responsibility whatever to earthly Governments, so we do not ask from them any rights and gladly renounce all kinds of honour, all riches and so-called privileges. While, however, we reject Governments, we have no illwill towards state officials, but love them as brothers, and are always ready to serve them by word or deed provided that they ask nothing of us that is contrary to God's will.

Our renunciation of the so-called privileges necessarily places us in the same position as the labourer, the mechanic, and the tiller of the soil. We do not own the land we till, for private property was established by violence, which is a conflict with the law of love, the command of our God, who dwells in us. We work where we are allowed, and use the implements of industry so long as they are not taken from us. If they hunt us away from one place, we flee to another.

Having for our life's aim the service of God and our fellow men, we know that, as poisoned water flows from a polluted source, so no good work can come from man so long as he is full of vices. Therefore our endeavours are specially directed to making ourselves perfect.

We are thoroughly convinced that if we ourselves grow better, in however small a degree, the good we can thereby do to our fellows becomes of correspondingly greater worth. This perfection of self involves striving after purity of body and spirit. While we follow after this purity we fear the temptations of pride, and seek lowliness. Only as we fulfil these conditions can we do the work of love. Purity, lowliness, and love—there you have the three ground principles of our life.

We allow perfect liberty to others, and set no bounds to the search after truth. So our profession may be to-day very different from what it was yesterday and may be to-morrow, but we have all one and the same way, the unchangeable and eternal way, that Christ has shown us. To maintain the spirit's freedom we give no pledges, take no oaths, institute or acknowledge no creeds, and introduce no outward ecclesiastical

ceremonies.  The doctrine about the Church or the gathering
of believers is included in Christ's saying, "Where two or
three are gathered in My Name, there am I in the midst of
them."  Such is our faith, such our hope.

Our kingdom is not of this world; that is, although we are
in the world, we serve not the world, but the God of Truth.
Serving this one and only King, Lawgiver, and Judge, we know
that He only can save or destroy us.

# CHAPTER XIII.

## A RUINED FAMILY.

Wealth and Rank—A Good Landowner and His Clever Son—Schooldays—
Liberal Opinions and Their Dangers—Disorder in the Schools—Accession
to the Estate—Scientific Research and Police Suspicion—At Moscow—A
Cruel Plot—Solitary Confinement Uncondemned—The Sentence—Exile to
Siberia—Destitution—Better Things—" No Rights "—Police and Love
Affairs—Fate of a Refugee—Waste of Human Life—Loss of the Estate
—A Young Girl's Religious Experiences—Education—Good Prospects—
Struggle after Truth—Reading the New Testament—Persecution by
Priests and Police—Exile—A Generous Revenge—Another Sister's
Fate—And a Brother's—Mammon and Priestcraft.

THERE is no lack of ruined families in Russia. Not merely
those who by reckless and vicious living have worked their
own destruction, but families of the highest repute and blameless life, who owe their misfortunes entirely to the machinations
of a " paternal " Government. They could be counted by the
thousand, these householders whose happiness has been crushed
by the Juggernaut of a cruel despotism, but we will here
content ourselves with one specimen. *Ex uno disce omnes.*

I met in different parts of Russia the *débris*, as one may say,
of this scattered family, whose reputation stood very high in
the eyes of wide and influential circles. One of the daughters,
who is well known to the authors, has supplied the following
facts concerning the origin and growth of their misfortunes,
chiefly centring round the history of her brother, whom we
will call Alexander.

This young man is the son of a rich estate owner, who
possessed 1,400 hectares (about $2\frac{1}{2}$ acres each) of land in two
provinces, with large herds of cattle and very many serfs, and
surrounded himself and family with all the comforts of life
usually enjoyed by the wealthy members of the nobility. He
was not, however, one of the many who spent all their means

and time in luxurious dissipation, such as costly wines,
gambling, hunting, and epicurean feasts ; he rather held aloof
from all society of that description.  Possessing considerable
skill as an engineer, he spent large sums in procuring different
kinds of agricultural machinery, and attempted to introduce
more rational methods of cultivating the land.

Alexander was born in 1860.  Even in his earliest years he
gave signs of mechanical and mathematical ability, and was
never so happy as when engaged with machines.  Whenever
his father was occupied on work of this description, either on
the repair of old or the construction of new machinery, Alexander would be at his side.  At twelve years of age he could
himself turn out excellent locksmith's work, which he practised
with great assiduity in the few spare hours left to him from
his other school studies, and so developed his mechanical
talents very remarkably.

His father was at this time occupied with improvements in
railroad construction, when a great misfortune befell him ; he
lost the use of his right arm by a paralytic stroke.  This
threw all the responsibility for the finer mechanical work on
his young son.  A model of a locomotive and a railroad, made
by Alexander, exhibited such skill and finish that even
specialists were astonished at his workmanship, and predicted
for him a brilliant career.  It was not only in mechanics that
he shone.  Teachers and schoolmasters joined in awarding
him the palm of distinction above all his comrades in his
school studies.

But this keenness of intellect led him into dangerous paths.
As early as his fifteenth year he began to look at things
with a critical eye ; fond of learning and devouring all the
information within his reach, he naturally began to make
comparisons, and analyse the conditions of life he found around
him.  He became the centre of a large circle of youths of his
own age, some of them thoughtful and earnest in their own
characters, others attracted simply by the example of their
fellows, and swayed by more powerful natures than theirs.
While under the magnetic influence of their nobler comrades,
these seemed to themselves and others to burn with unselfish

love for mankind and an earnest desire for its improved welfare, but as soon as the charm was broken by their removal to another sphere, they lost their ardour and pursued their own career, straining after their personal interests in carelessness of the sufferings of others.

This group used to meet at leisure hours for the reading and discussion of such works as would throw light on the problems that perplexed them, above all, the social questions that forced themselves upon their attention; for example, the "Political Economy of John Stuart Mill." They also had a paper for private circulation, in which they expressed their own ideas upon the burning topics of the day.

All this, of course, was done in secret, without the knowledge of the school and other authorities, who might report them to the police. For the Government of the Tsar does not love brilliant geniuses. Instead of using them for the good of the nation, for conquering the obstacles that Nature puts in the way of human welfare, that when overcome they may confer a richer blessing on mankind, the Great Autocrat and his satellites pounce upon them in their early years, and condemn them to prison and to exile. Many die a premature death, others lose their reason in the terrible torture of prison life; those that endure to the end come out of their fiery trial as strong eagles whose eyes have been dimmed and their pinions singed, so that for them soaring flight has become for ever impossible. In this way Russia is deprived of her greatest wealth, the talent and genius of the flower of her youth. Happily, fresh young lives take up the tasks from which their predecessors have been violently removed, and with indomitable energy and courage push on their work for freedom of life and thought, until death or Siberia cuts them off. The cause for which they perish is undying, and in time it will overthrow all obstacles; tyranny and official despotism shall give way to liberty and brotherhood, both here and in the other countries of the world.

In these studies Alexander and his companions passed three years of their school life, but they were not left in peace. The authorities had learned by experience that the fermentation of liberal ideas among students usually begins in the upper classes of the schools. Fearing the outbreak of disorder, the Minister of Instruction ordered all teachers to keep strict watch over their senior pupils. The result was what might have been foreseen ; these stringent measures only provoked the outbreak they were designed to prevent. The students, losing all patience under the continual harassment of petty interference on the part of the authorities, and supported as a rule in their liberal views by their relations and acquaintances, broke out in many schools into serious disturbances, in some instances proceeding even to violence. Many were expelled as incorrigible, and others were severely punished and threatened with the same fate if they did not mend their ways.

Owing to Alexander's prominent position in his school he escaped expulsion, but the watch upon all his movements was redoubled in stringency. His præpositor and others of his fellow-pupils were engaged as spies upon his private life. These had orders to report all visits paid or received by him, with the hours of departure, &c., duly noted.

Under this constant interference of strangers with his personal life his nervous system and health generally suffered such a strain that he decided to leave the school and return home for a rest. Just at this time, too, his father died, leaving a large family behind, and on him, as eldest son, the management of the estate and family affairs devolved.

While in the country he made an attempt at putting his liberal ideas into practice. Laying aside all prejudices of rank, he dressed in a simple national costume, worked with the peasants at all kinds of agricultural labour, and altogether eschewed those habits of the upper classes that are both exceedingly costly and serve merely to erect a kind of moral Chinese Wall between the privileged and the oppressed. His one aim was to uplift the standard of the peasant's life, both in material and moral respects, and he knew with how much suspicion they regarded all meddling with their personal affairs on the part of members of the nobility. It was for this cause that he removed all possible differences between them, and sought by unaffected friendliness and goodwill to gain their confidence. It was not difficult for him. He had been a child among them, and they considered him as one of their own. They gratefully received his counsels and tried to profit by them.

But not even on his ancestral estate could he be left in peace. The local police became inquisitive and put all manner of questions to his mother. Why did he dress so plainly? Why did he work as a common labourer in the fields? Why did he talk so much and so intimately with the peasants?

One thing especially aroused their liveliest suspicions. He had built a little house for himself at some distance from the family residence. Certainly this could have no other object than to serve as a centre for revolutionary meetings. Here they visited him at all hours of the night and day, searching for something compromising. They could, however, find nothing illegal, for the simple reason that he had built the place solely for the purpose of pursuing his mechanical studies and experiments without interruption or disturbance —a purpose they succeeded in effectually frustrating. Even this entire absence of anything on which to rest suspicion did not satisfy them, for they were, as a matter of fact, instigated by the *kulacks* or financial harpies of the district, who wanted to remove him so that they might have a hand in the administration of the estate—from purely benevolent motives, of course.

Life under these conditions of eternal police interference became unbearable; he resolved to leave the estate for a time, and entered the Technical Institute at Moscow. Here he won golden opinions from all: his teachers were proud of his splendid abilities and earnest application to his studies; his fellow-students loved him for his gentleness, and respected his stable character and firm convictions. Soon there gathered round him another circle of liberal-minded young men, as in his former schooldays, with the same results.

The authorities keep an especially strict watch over the students in large cities, and Alexander and his room-mate speedily became suspected persons. Private enmity supplied what was lacking in Government suspicion, and a diabolical plot was hatched against him.

One day, as he was leaving the Institute to return to his rooms, a fellow-student handed him a small packet and asked him to take it home. This student was the son of a priest who had been a bitter enemy of his father, but Alexander suspected no evil, and put the packet in his pocket. When he entered his lodgings he saw, to his consternation, that the police were in possession of the place, and had already arrested his room-mate. Thunderstruck, he stood still for a while, and was immediately seized. Conscious of his innocence, he attempted no escape, and the *gendarmes* continued to ransack the rooms for incriminating documents, &c. They found some verses containing liberal views, written by his comrade, and then proceeded to search Alexander personally. The traitorous packet was discovered, and proved to contain Nihilistic literature. "In the name of His August Imperial Majesty and because of criminal papers" found on him, they now made his formal arrest, and without any opportunity of explanation the two young men were hurried off to gaol and placed in separate cells.

The consternation of his mother, when she heard of her son's sudden imprisonment, may be more easily imagined than depicted in words. At once she hastened to Moscow to learn with what crime he was charged, and to try to procure his release. It was in vain. She could discover nothing but that the highest authorities had ordered that all suspected persons should be put in prison and detained there, until their case could be legally tried and sentence pronounced. All she could do was to strengthen herself and endure the inevitable. With much difficulty she did obtain permission to visit her son. When she entered his cell his appearance frightened her, so changed had he become in a short time. A settled melancholy was on his countenance, now pale and emaciated, and in his eyes she read despair.

More than a year passed before he was brought to trial, and all that time he suffered the tortures of solitary confinement. The agony of mind this means to a young man full of life and energy, deprived of all opportunity of exchanging the simplest thoughts with his fellows, forbidden also either to read books or touch pen and paper, can be only faintly imagined by those who have had no similar experience. In that year he suffered more than in all the previous trials of his life together, though even in these the worry and harassment of police stupidity and suspicion had not been inconsiderable. One thing only preserved his mind from becoming unhinged. He was allowed to learn shoemaking.

At last the day came on which his fate was to be decided. None but his mother and sisters were allowed to be present at the trial. The sentence pronounced on himself and his room-mate was fifteen years' penal servitude in the mines of Siberia, with loss of all civil rights. It was the refusal to betray the names of those students who belonged to their circle that induced the court to inflict this savage and barbarous sentence.

His mother and his two eldest sisters went to the Governor to intercede for some mitigation of this severity. After looking into the case, and finding that Alexander *was not yet of age*, he commuted the sentence to eight years in Siberia as a compulsory colonist. This was no doubt much milder than the penal servitude in the mines, which meant simply capital punishment by long-drawn-out and fiendish methods, but to a young man of his abilities, just on the threshold of life, and with great hopes for the future, the difference did not seem great. He must leave everything, his home, his relations and friends, his plans of self-devotion for the good of his fellows, the application of his genius to the welfare of mankind. All that opened in prospect before him was the cheerless life of an exile in a far-off desolate region, under the constant surveillance of the police, without whose permission he could not take a step beyond the bounds of a prescribed circle, nor even send a letter to his home.

One other privilege was won by the untiring efforts of his mother and sisters: he was allowed to travel at his own expense to his place of exile instead of going by the common *étape*. It was nothing much to look forward to, this tedious journey in a clumsy and open cart in the company of *gendarmes*, yet he was glad when the day of departure arrived.

He was to bid farewell to all that was dear to his heart,
but he was also to escape from the unendurable horrors
of his solitary cell.  He longed to see people, to hear
the sound of their voices, to watch their daily occupation,
and divert his painful thoughts by the study of Nature,
which in its cruellest moods is kinder than the savagery of
men.

It took him four months to reach his destination, a wretched
little village in the province of Irkutsk, about 200 kilometres
from the capital.  Here he must spend eight years without
going out of bounds.  By a great stroke of fortune his
former room-mate was sent to the same place, and they could
at least converse on matters of common interest to both, and
keep up each other's courage by the exchange of their most
intimate thoughts.  Otherwise their seclusion without books
or papers would have been but few removes from that of their
solitary cells.

A small portion of land was given them, which they
cultivated, and they began to make shoes, in order to earn
their living.  There were, however, two obstacles that proved
fatal to this occupation:  they could neither procure the
needful material nor sell their finished products.  One thing
after another they tried, but they were so fettered by restriction
that want and despair frequently stared them in the face.
Only twice a year or so could they receive news from home;
the mail took three months in winter-time, when the roads
were good, and in spring and autumn six months.  Not only
so, but all missives and packages addressed to prisoners had
to pass through the hands of the police.  So it happened that
things for winter use, despatched in time, would reach them
the following summer, when they were of no use.  Through
this delay and irregularity Alexander and his comrade
frequently suffered hunger and cold, for want of the money
and goods detained on the way.

They petitioned the authorities for permission to settle in
some place nearer a town, where they could, at least, earn
something for their support.  This was finally allowed them,
with increased stringency of police supervision.  Still they

were happier, in being able to procure by their labour the
necessaries of life.

After a time, Alexander managed to save sufficient to buy a
locksmith's shop and tools. His fame as a skilled workman
spread, and orders came in not only from his neighbours, but also
from people at a distance of 200 kilometres. The police,
however, would not allow him to go far from his house,
fearing that he would spread his liberal views among his
neighbours. He received a commission to build a church,
through his engineering abilities, but the authorities vetoed it.
They went so far that they would not allow him to marry,
because his *fiancée*, being also a political exile, was deprived of
her civil rights.

Alexander sent in an application to be registered as a
common peasant, that he might have, at least, some elementary
rights of living, but for a long time received no answer.
Growing wearied at the delay, he committed the enormous
crime of visiting his betrothed without the permission of the
police. They soon discovered his absence, raised a hue and
cry, and despatched messages in all directions about his
"escape." He was speedily captured by *gendarmes* and sent
to his former place of exile.

He would probably have had to drag on this weary existence
for many years, had not the Governor-General of Eastern
Siberia, a kind-hearted man, come to Irkutsk and visited all the
exiles. When he found that Alexander was of no common stamp,
and possessed such great skill in engineering and architecture,
and was besides of a quiet and gentle disposition, he ordered
him to be given a position in the workshop of one of the gold-
mines of Nerchinsk. Soon, too, he recovered his civil rights,
and his eight years of martyrdom closed. But it must not be
imagined that his position was restored to him. He will never
be free from the constant surveillance of the police, for all
Russian exiles have to endure this, even after their sentence is
worked out, if not of the regular police, of the secret spies,
which is still worse. But his life became comparatively bear-
able; he is married, and allowed to support his family by his
labour and skill.

As for his comrade in exile, he made several attempts at escape, but was recaptured and cruelly punished. Finally he disappeared, leaving no trace. None of his relatives and friends know of his whereabouts; his mother died several years back from grief at the unhappy lot of her son. It may be he succeeded at last in escaping from his tormentors, and found refuge in a more hospitable land, but it is equally probable that he is no longer to be numbered among the living.

Whatever his fate, this much is certain, that both these gifted young men are lost to the cause of human progress and liberty, through the brutal folly of a savage despotism, that is yet allowed the alliance and friendship of nations—or at least, their Governments and royal houses—that boast their own freedom of thought and action. It is not merely the material wealth of the empire that is criminally wasted by the stupidity and greed of the Russian Government and its horde of officials and secret police. The moral and spiritual resources that might uplift the nation in true well-being and prosperity are ruthlessly destroyed, and the most sacred things of human life trampled down in cynical savagery. Thousands of homes are desolated by the destruction of their most loved and gifted members; tens of thousands of lives are blasted in their dearest hopes. The Russian Government, that plants its steel-shod feet on human hearts, must answer to the damning indictment—

> Have ye founded your thrones and altars, then,
> On the bodies and souls of living men?

So far, we have given the facts concerning Alexander as supplied by the sister referred to above. We now turn to the other members of the family. When the eldest son had thus been successfully removed, the *kulacks*, with their allies the *tchinovniks* (officials), could proceed to their congenial task of getting the estate into their own clutches, under pretence of administering it as trustees, &c., and plunder to their hearts' content. This they did so effectually, that the helpless widow soon had to leave her home, with all its sacred associations with the lives of those who had been taken from her.

But this was but "the beginning of the sorrows." One of the daughters, because she was true to the dictates of her conscience, also fell under the ban of this enlightened Government, and has had to undergo a series of trials of great severity. We cannot do better than give her own account, as written in a letter, of her experiences.

"Like my brothers and sisters, I was brought up in the Orthodox faith, and was accustomed from my childhood to regard the Orthodox Church as the only true one. But all the prayers that my teachers taught me, which I repeated every morning before the *eikon* of a saint, could not satisfy my soul, although I was but a child. When I had ended these prayers, I would lay my wants before God in my own words, though I never heard any one else do so.

"In 1871, I was placed in a school for girls of noble families in the city of X., where I was instructed in languages, art, and the other subjects that form the curriculum of such institutions. Religion, of course, was treated merely as a matter of form. Yet in my inmost heart was an earnest and deep piety. Soon, however, the temptations of the world became too strong for me, who was so feeble, and my childish confidence in God began to disappear.

"In 1877, I was removed to the Grand Duke of Oldenburg's Seminary for young ladies of the nobility, in St. Petersburg. At that time I was sixteen years old. In this great city, with all its temptations, among worldly relatives and friends, I was completely conquered by the world. Still I continued to observe, in mechanical fashion, the ceremonies of the Church. During this period I was often invited to Court, but its splendour and magnificence never impressed me much.

"In the winter of '79 my father died and bitter trials befell our family; in the spring of the same year I finished my course at the seminary, and obtained a lucrative position as teacher in an Imperial school in the South of Russia. My salary was 1,500 roubles, with free rooms and attendance. I now tried to satisfy myself with worldly pleasures, but soon grew tired. Then I began to read philosophical works with great eagerness, hoping, in this way, to still my soul's hunger

13

for truth and happiness, but in vain. I was troubled with doubts concerning all the questions of life both here and hereafter. To my hunger for truth was added an intense fear of death. These inward struggles I carefully concealed from my friends and associates.

"In 1881, my eldest brother was exiled to Siberia, and shortly after we lost our estate. At the same time, one of my sisters was taken seriously ill. These and other trials induced me to begin to study the New Testament—a book I had for many years despised. In the summer I met my invalid sister at a health resort. She grew worse and worse every day, and I could clearly see that her end was near. From this time I began to think seriously of my own death.

"I had to accompany my sister to her home. She was thoroughly weak, and we resolved to stop a few days with our mother at X. The Volga steamer, on which we were travelling, arrived at midnight, so to avoid disturbing our mother, we stayed on board until morning. The night was still and beautiful. I went up on deck to watch the dawn. It was a morning never to be forgotten. For the first time I got a glimpse of the beautiful morning star. In my heart I resolved it should be my guiding star for life.

" Soon I had to leave my mother and sister, of whose recovery there was no longer any hope. When I bade her farewell I was almost disconsolate.

"I now studied the New Testament with great ardour, and soon found that I could no longer attend the Orthodox Church, kiss the *eikons* of the saints, &c. I then told the directress of the school that I must give up my post, and gave her my reasons for such a course. Both she and my fellow-teachers looked on it as folly, and asked me to stay on.

"It was late in the night, and they tried to persuade me at least to stay until next morning, but I felt an inward prompting, as if some one were saying, "Do not wait; to-morrow it may be too late." It was more than fortunate for me that I did not stay. It was immediately telegraphed to my relatives that I had become insane, and they wished to put me into an asylum. Others regarded me as a dangerous agitator against the Tsar-

and State, and at once reported me to the police. The whole
city was stirred. I had to escape secretly from the place by
night, and fled to another town. There, too, the priests soon
found me out, and wrote to the governor, persuading him to
set the police on my track; besides this they bribed a doctor to
give a false certificate against me, and in other ways tried to
get me exiled to Siberia.

" These plans were, however, frustrated. . . . Just as I
was leaving the city to escape from my persecutors another
misfortune befell me : all my money was stolen from me, so
that I was altogether destitute of means. But by a remarkable
providence I was helped out of this terrible difficulty."

So far her own account. This truly pious and quiet-natured
young lady was hounded from place to place by the police, until
at last she had to escape to a foreign country, and there remain
for some time. But she always yearned to return to her native
land. " However," she says, " I continually longed to come back
to Russia. The light and liberty that I found in Western countries, instead of weakening this longing, increased it still more.
My heart was full of deep compassion for my fatherland."

Finally she succeeded in crossing the frontier in a marvellous
way—she had no passport, but again was hunted about by the
priests and the police. With untiring devotion and courage,
she braved her persecutors, and cheerfully faced cold, hunger,
and pestilence, going from village to village to help and comfort
the poor, downtrodden peasants, both in material and spiritual
things. During the famine she bore her part in the relief
work among the starving until her health broke down.

The day of my arrival in St. Petersburg, another daughter
of the same family set out for Siberia as a volunteer to nurse
the sick in Tiumen, where spotted typhus and other terrible
diseases were making fearful havoc among the prisoners and
others. She had studied medicine in St. Petersburg, until this
was forbidden by the all-wise authorities. Then she applied
herself to the study of natural science, until a wealthy philan-
thropist in St. Petersburg enabled her to go to Siberia, there
to use her medical knowledge as a simple nurse.

After a few weeks of zealous work among the patients she

herself caught the spotted typhus; for some time all hope of her recovery was abandoned. The fever at last, however, abated, only to leave her a physical and nervous wreck; she had become insane.

In this condition she was sent home to her poor mother, whose bitter cup of sorrow was now surely full. But, no; her second son, who was at home, whose nervous system had already been strained almost to the breaking point, could not stand the shock of seeing his loved sister insane. His own mind was unhinged, and he, too, had to be removed to an asylum.

Such is the work of Mammon and priestcraft, but for which these innocent and truly patriotic men and women had been not merely happy in their own lives, but a means of inspiration and uplifting to the wretched peasants on their estate, who so sorely needed their help and teaching.

A STREET IN SAMARA.

# CHAPTER XIV.

## OLDER RUSSIAN SECTS.

Tsardom and Orthodoxy—Reforms of Nikon—The *Stanoveri*—*Popovtsi* and *Bespopovtsi*—The "Antichrist-Tsar"—Specimens of Hymns—Contempt of Suffering—*Stranniki* (Wanderers) and *Beguni* (Fugitives)—How They are Made—A Sectarian's Story—*Moltchalniki* (Dumb)—An Advocate's Experience—*Prugoni* (Dancers) and *Chlisti* (Flagellators)—Origin and Tenets—Initiation Ceremonies—Orgies—*Skoptsi* (Mutilators)—Mutilation—*Samonstrebitjeli* (Suicides)—*Nje Nashi* (Agnostics)—Their Behaviour towards Authorities.

Though Tsardom and the Orthodox Church in Russia are now so indissolubly associated, they are not exactly twin powers in the matter of age. It was in the eighth century that some Greek missionaries proclaimed Christianity throughout the land, and introduced, at the same time, a certain degree of that civilisation which then followed the Greek tongue. The Church thus established took firm root in the land, but Tsardom was of later growth by four or five centuries. Before Russian unity was won, a terrible scourge of Tartar rule had to be borne for three hundred years, just those three hundred years that saw the bowing of the English neck beneath the yoke of Dane, Norman, and Angevin, and left them at last a united nation. Under this reign of barbarism nearly all traces of the older culture were swept away; the Church remained as an institution, but the spirit was for the most part quenched. As regards the liturgy, many small departures from the usage of the Greek Catholic Church crept in, and a number of words were incorrectly spelled. Small matters these, but such as fasten with a firm hold upon a people of strong religious emotions and slight culture. The Tartars were subdued in the thirteenth century, and Tsardom triumphed, but the Church was unreformed until, at the instance of the patriarch Nikon, a revised liturgy was published in 1659. To us the reforms

seem trifling; for example, making the sign of the cross with
three fingers instead of two; writing the name of Jesus with
a J instead of an I; the use of the Swiss cross (arms of equal
length) instead of the Roman (with longer upright); turning
"against the sun," *i.e.*, eastward, instead of "with the sun,"
*i.e.*, westward.  But to the parties concerned these small things
were indications of momentous issues.  To the authorities they
meant marching in line with the Holy Catholic Church.  To
the malcontents they meant "adulteration of the pure Word
of God."  Here, then, was the beginning of the great separa-
tist movement of the *Raskolniki*, which has continued to the
present time, and given rise to countless sects.

Of course, there was persecution; the seceders were driven
away, carrying with them the old books in which they believed
(whence their name: *Staroveri*=Old Believers), to the vast
tracts of forest land on the upper courses of the Volga, that
are even now the chief haunts of the sectarians of modern
times.  After the secession, there developed two main parties :
those who retained the priesthood, and those who, when once
they found themselves at loggerheads with the holy officials,
asked what need there was of them at all, and decided the
question in the negative.  The former have remained practically unchanged; so little do they differ from the Established
Church that they are, for the most part, left in peace.  They
are, in fact, something like those good people at home who will
not use the Revised Version of the Bible, and in other matters
place the customary above the accurate in their esteem.  They
are known as *Popovtsi*.

The *Bespopovtsi*, those who have abolished the Holy Office,
are naturally more repugnant to the powers that be, and have
continually suffered persecution at their hands.  This has kept
alive the fire of fanaticism; according to the different conditions of time and place, or different impulses from individual
leaders, the energy has taken different forms, and many and
varied sects have, as a result, sprung into being.  To distinguish these from the Nonconformists, who owe their being
to causes of quite modern date, they are usually grouped under
the title of the Old Sects.  They are far too numerous to

describe in detail, but the chief, among which are the *Stranniki* (Wanderers), *Beguni* (Fugitives), *Moltchalniki* (Dumb), *Prugoni* (Dancers), *Chlisti* (Flagellators), *Skoptsi* (Mutilators), *Nje Nashi* (Agnostics), &c., deserve more than a passing notice, both on account of their own remarkable characteristics*, which throw vivid light on the Russian character, and also because they have been, for the most part, entirely misrepresented. This misrepresentation is not confined to the Russian official press, which contains, chiefly, gross caricatures of their teaching and conduct, but extends to those foreign accounts which have derived their materials from the turbid official sources.

The more these despised and persecuted sects are known, the more apparent it becomes how greatly they have been misjudged. The entire course of their behaviour, even in its most fantastic and fanatical forms, is just a conscious or unconscious protest against unbearable despotism and the miserable condition of things resulting therefrom. To avoid coming under the intolerable yoke of the "Antichrist-Tsar," and infection by the wickedness inherent in the whole system, the "Wanderers" and "Fugitives" leave their homes and become nomadic, or bury themselves in the primeval forest, or flee to the farthest steppes, in the face of the greatest dangers, in the certainty of severest toil and pain. Similarly, to avoid bringing more children into the hopelessly evil and corrupt world they see around them, to mortify their own flesh and save their own souls from this "City of Destruction," the "Mutilators," both men and women, endure the most ghastly operations on their bodies. Also the "Dumb," in opposition to what seems to them a cruel and arbitrary Inquisition, rather than a legitimate examination, shut their mouths and refuse to hold parley with the servants of the Evil One. Who can wonder that grotesque fanaticism abounds among these sectarians? Hunted and persecuted, powerless against the perpetual greed and oppression of those in authority, without resources against

---

* The most reliable and copious authority on the subject is Prugavin, a Russian writer, who devoted immense labour to the work of research. In the following descriptions, I have relied chiefly upon him for as much as has not come under my own observation, or been communicated to me by persons whom I could trust, though other authors have also been consulted.

hunger, cold, and misery of all kinds, and continually exposed
to new developments of evil fortune, these miserable folk are
subject to an unceasing strain, that naturally causes epidemics
of hysteria, especially in the northern and eastern districts; in
these ecstatic fits they see visions, receive revelations, and leap
and dance under the uncontrollable impulses that agitate them.
Their very songs, as well as their doctrines, are written in
pessimistic strains.   Here are two examples :—

> Evil years have fallen upon us; bitter times have come;
> Perished is the faith that's true; Christ's faith has disappeared;
> Unjust judges rule the land; the Church's pastors are
> Rough drunkards.  Crushed the people lie beneath oppression's yoke.

Again :

> I cannot keep myself from tears!
> Religion pines away and dies.
> Now godlessness blooms over all.
> Uprooted is the Spirit's law.
> The priestly place is girt with silver chains:
> We're ruled by lawless might instead of law.
> They who take bribes hold sway in all our towns.
> Corrupt officials rage in every place.
> The Spirit of Antichrist now lords it over us.
> I cannot keep myself from tears.

In their conduct towards each other, and, indeed, towards all
men, these sectaries are gentle and meek, and under the
severest persecution, which frequently overtakes them, they
display a fortitude that is almost superhuman.   In fact, one
might almost conclude from their demeanour under the most
terrible punishment, which they endure without a single sound
of complaint, that they find a certain satisfaction in suffering.
Take an instance.   Nearly twenty years ago, in the government of Volodga, a serf named Samarin entered a church
during the hour of worship.   Holding a lighted candle he rushed
up to the priest, snatched the chalice from his hand, emptied
the contents on the floor, and crushed the sacred vessel underfoot,
exclaiming, "I trample upon Satan's work."   Of course he was
instantly seized and brought to trial before the authorities.
Questioned as to his object, he replied with the utmost calmness

that he had done it to awaken the people from their godless slumber and to protest against the power of Antichrist. Under the fearful punishment to which he was sentenced he did not utter a murmur.

Let us see the special characteristics of some of these sects. First the " Wanderers " and " Fugitives." Their roots lie deep in Russian history. Long before the institution of serfdom, in the twelfth century, the semisavage free men betook themselves in large numbers to the forest depths and distant steppes to escape the newly-established Muscovite despotism. In later times they fled from slavery under the tyrannous landlords. At the present day they seek in flight refuge from oppressive taxation, forced military service, official rigour, police persecution, and other nameless miseries. Small wonder, then, that they are the most numerous of all the sects, and enjoy the reputation among the police of being the " most dangerous."

But it was only a little more than thirty years ago that they assumed the characteristics of a " sect," properly speaking. A certain Sovva took refuge from persecution in the village of Marosova, government Oloujetsk, and for a long time secretly taught the people that they should flee from the wickedness of the world and the tyranny of the officials into the forests, and gained many adherents. The authorities sought to arrest him, but he received timely warning and escaped to Archangel. The leader of the sect at the present day is said to be one Nikanov, who numbers many persons of repute among his adherents.

There are two divisions of this sect: the *skritniki,* who carefully conceal both themselves and their tenets, and the *pristano djershaljeteli,* or those posted near the steamboat stations on the Volga and other rivers, whose houses have secret doors, subterranean passages, &c. Their business is to receive and conceal wandering brothers, who mostly make their appearance by night. All who belong to this sect must destroy their passports and all documents that could give any information about any one. Such are held to be Satan's instruments. A new baptism is also necessary, and is performed as follows : A square enclosure is made by means of boards in the river. The candidate stands stark naked between his two godfathers, their faces turned to the east. The leader reads prayers, cursing Satan and spiritual and temporal authorities. The neophyte's passport is rent to pieces as a symbol that he has for ever broken "with the power of this world." He is then immersed in the water. After the ceremony he is clothed in a white garment that reaches to his feet, and receives a new name. A lengthy fast is prescribed for him, and he takes a solemn oath never to submit to spiritual or worldly authority, for they are the work of Satan; to regard all who live in the present system of society as Satan's servants; never to take up a passport, pay taxes, or fulfil any kind of official duty; to have no fixed home, but to live the life of a wanderer only.

Every new member must be instructed in the following tenets :— Antichrist is at the head of the present organisation of State, Church, and society. Tsar, governors, metropolitans, and all other officials are Satan's servants. The so-called Divine service, sacraments, religious ceremonies, &c., simply repress true and living Christianity. One must pray in secret without any forms whatever. Women are in every respect free and equal with men. Marriage is based on the most unrestrained freedom. Some say, "It is not a civil or religious ceremony that makes true marriage, but a mutual sympathy and harmony." "Marriage as a sacrament and civil act is out of date. Men and women must live together as they best please to preserve the human race," say others.

Among some groups marriage is celebrated in the following manner: Having received a promise of marriage from a woman or girl, the man goes to an appointed meeting-place, and there carries off his bride with some show of force,* either to his house, if he be of the *pristano djershdjeteli* referred to above, or somewhere in the forest. Then they live a wandering life from village to village, district to district, staying a longer or shorter time with their sisters and brothers. This union

---

* The student of anthropology will, of course, recognise in this a survival of ancient customs, a relic of the times when marriage by capture was a real and not merely a symbolical event.

endures so long as the consorts agree. Should strife arise, they go their several ways. The same freedom is allowed to the children, who are brought up to be "Wanderers" too.

In some places the free marriage is celebrated by the man and woman walking through a village side by side, each holding an end of the same handkerchief.

Among these and many other sectaries the Tsar is, for the most part, regarded as Antichrist personified. It is a common thing to find among them a curious picture, in which he is depicted in royal robe and crown, receiving a candle from Satan, who is saying, "Be thou the worker of my will." At the side of the Tsar the Orthodox Church is portrayed as a common strumpet. The sectaries continue to increase in number, but their mysticism is gradually giving place to rationalism, and instead of the ideas concerning Antichrist we find that the Tsar is simply looked upon as Despotism incarnate, beneath whose iron yoke the Russian people are crushed to the ground, and are in a perpetually perishing condition.

The way in which misery leads to religious fanaticism is well illustrated by the following evidence, given by a sectary before the tribunal that heard his case. "I lived in the government R., and was body-slave to a landlord, but, thanks to my ability to write and skill in reckoning, I was promoted to be bookkeeper on Prince B.'s estate. The Prince was of an altogether evil disposition; licentious, spendthrift, and tyrannical, he had ruined the *mushiks* without mercy. As bookkeeper I lived a happier life than the rest of the peasants, and had nothing to complain of, until misfortune suddenly overtook me. I loved Prasconia, the *starost's* daughter, and my love was returned. Our mutual passion was so strong that we could not live apart. She was a splendid girl—beautiful, high-spirited, and steadfast. All the lads contended for her favour, but she gave to none so much as a glance; to me alone was she gracious. We were already beginning to speak of the wedding day, when, to our ruin, the Prince, our master, came on the scene. The young girl took his fancy immensely; he desired to possess her.

"One day two of the Prince's men seized Paracha (her pet

name) in the street and carried her to him by force. The young girl struggled to break loose, entreated, wept, and shrieked for mercy—there was no help. Paracha was shut up in the Prince's house, and I do not know what happened to her there. What I do know is that I could not brook this injury. I cursed the life of a serf, and one dark night set fire to the Prince's house and made off to the forest. From forest to forest, from government to government I wandered, and knew no peace by night or day, like Cain who had killed his brother Abel. At every sound I heard in the forest I started and trembled like a leaf, fearful lest they should come and seize me and throw me into prison. Sometimes at evening I would come to an *izba* and peep in through the window. The whole family would be sitting round a *lutchina* (a lighted pine-splint, set on a stand, used to avoid the expense of tallow candles), the father making *lapti* (a kind of shoes), the mother spinning, the daughter sewing, the children building houses with bits of wood. Poverty was there, but they were all warm, they looked contented, and feared nothing. And I—I was alone, abandoned, and had not where to lay my head!

" At last I met an anchorite in the forest. The sun had set one evening when I saw an old man with snow-white hair come out of what might have been the cave of a bear, covered by the brushwood. He dipped himself three times in the stream, resumed his clothes, bowed to the four points of the compass, and turned again towards his cave. I sprang towards him. ' Holy man,' I cried, ' do not refuse me a kind word.'

" ' Who are you ? ' asked the old man.

" ' Fear nothing, I am only a peaceful fugitive.'

" ' You are not a robber ? '—' No.'

" ' What is your faith ? ' ' I know nothing about it myself,' I answered. ' I have not been taught.'

" ' Will you learn to know the true faith ? '—' Yes.'

" ' Well then, follow me ! '

" We entered an underground cavern. It was somewhat spacious, but gloomy. The walls were wooden, there was a stone table, and on the table a book lay open. There was no bed, but on the stone floor a hide was spread. The old man bade me sit on a stone, and began asking me questions. I told him everything without reserve. 'I see,' said the old man, 'that you are unfortunate, that you are in Satan's kingdom, and that there you are on the road to perdition. Will you find peace for your soul and gain the kingdom of heaven?' 'I will.' 'Well, then, listen to me. I, my son, have long sought the true faith. I have tried all religions, and have at last come to the conclusion that it cannot be found anywhere; the whole world is wandering in darkness. The authorities persecute us, because they are servants of Satan or Antichrist; the common people know not what to do. . . . I have therefore determined to win God's grace by prayer and fasting. Let men retire to the forests and deserts to escape lies, ruin, and Satan's kingdom! Do you also fly from the world, fast and pray. Then shall you understand the true faith, and peace shall descend upon you.'

" After the conversation with the old man I passed the whole night without a wink of sleep. He prayed all the time kneeling upon sharp stones and pieces of broken glass. When morning came he left his cave, dipped three times in the stream, and bowed to north, south, east, and west.

" The old man's speech, his long, white beard, his emaciated body, his mild expression, his long, flowing robe, girt about his waist by a coarse rope, his bleeding feet and knees, made so deep an impression upon me that I determined to become his disciple. 'I will forsake the world and retire to a desert place,' I exclaimed to myself. 'I will pray and fast; I shall at length find peace, and gain my soul's salvation." I dug out a cave in the forest, where I settled, and imposed on myself a strict fast, taking nothing but bread and water. Three years passed in this manner; my fame spread through the surrounding country, and many came to consult me concerning their soul's salvation. All were seeking for truth, for the true faith, for God. With one accord all declared that Antichrist ruled the whole world; that nowhere on earth could truth be found; that judges and authorities committed only unrighteousness and oppression, that they are the devil's servants.

"Yet I knew no more than they how to counsel them, how to help them. I could only weep with them, and fast till my strength gave out."

So runs his testimony before the court of justice. This man was afterwards led astray by one of those unscrupulous impostors who find these emotional religionists only too easy a prey. He was seized by the authorities and cast into prison. Having made his escape, he wandered from province to province throughout the land, from the Upper Volga to Caucasia, from Moscow to Siberia, hiding by day, and at night pursuing his journey, everywhere warning the people against the rule of Antichrist, and urging them to flee from the falsity and corruption of the world. Frequently arrested, he told the authorities he was God's servant, seeking to save his soul from the power of Satan, his servants, and sin.

These sectaries are most numerous in the governments of Petersburg, Vologda, Jaroslavl, Tver, Olonjetsk, Kastroma, Kasan, and Vjatka.

The *Moltchalniki*, or the Dumb, are closely connected with the *Beguni*, and share most of their opinions, with the addition that they persistently refuse to answer any of the official questions concerning their name, age, rank, &c., and before the judges at their trials maintain an unbroken silence. The sentences passed upon them, though for the most part entailing banishment to Eastern Siberia, they hear with the greatest unconcern, and leave the court without saying a word. Some of them not only refuse thus to parley with the ministers of Antichrist, but even eschew all speech among themselves as leading to sin.

An advocate, to whom had been allotted the duty of defending a *moltchalniki*, describes his experience in the following account.

"I had been entrusted with the defence of one of these sectaries. I went to the prison where he was confined, and asked permission to visit him. After a few minutes they brought me into the presence of a powerfully-built man of medium height; he wore trousers of ample size, over which were drawn boots that came up to his knees, and a *kaftan*, such as the Russian serfs are accustomed to use. Long hair and a long beard encircled his face, which wore a mild and resigned expression. His age must have been about forty. Silently he advanced to the table and gave me greeting.

"'The Court has confided your case to me,' I said, turning to him. He laid his right hand on his breast and bowed. 'Are you willing that I shall represent you before the Court?' He again bowed, shaking his head in dissent. 'Why do you not wish me to take up your cause?' The sectary pointed to the saint's picture in the corner of the room. 'You entrust your cause to Providence?' I asked. He nodded his head in affirmation. 'Yes, but you cannot deny that the intervention of an experienced advocate can present your case in the most favourable light and do much to bring about your release?' He smiled in an unconvinced manner and shrugged his shoulders. 'Do not forget that by obstinately keeping silence, and refusing to give your name, you render yourself liable to be treated as a vagabond, and run a great risk of being banished to the furthest parts of the empire.' He made a gesture to show that it was of no concern to him, and remained mute. 'Will you not speak? Ah well—perhaps you will consent to answer my questions in writing? I am not your judge, you know, but your advocate whom you can hardly regard as an enemy.' The sectary continued to gaze at me with the same look of mildness and resignation without opening his mouth. I found it useless to try to persuade him. 'Do as you please,' I said, 'but, believe me, I have no other interest in meddling with your affairs than my simple desire to help you.' He crossed his arms over his breast and bowed low.

"'Well, what do you think of him?' asked the warder, as he fetched me from the prisoner. 'The man has made a deep impression on me. He must have lost his senses.' 'I beg your pardon, he is simply a confirmed fanatic. There are many such in these parts. His behaviour in prison is blameless; he obeys all the rules, works diligently, never refuses to lend a hand to his comrades. He is thoroughly sober and religious; you can't pick a hole in him at all. There is only one

14

thing—he would sooner let himself be killed than speak a word.'

" Eight days later he was sentenced. To the end nothing of consequence had been brought against him. The whole trouble was this: An unknown man was found in the market-place of a little village by the village constable. Since he could get no answer to the questions he put to him, he brought him before the commissary, where he was searched and found to be without a passport. Refusing to give his name and occupation, he was treated according to Russian law as a vagabond, and handed over to justice. Despite all admonitions from the President of the Court he remained dumb, and although nothing else was brought against him but that he had no passport and would not speak, the Court was compelled to banish him to Eastern Siberia. In silence and deep calm he heard his sentence. Not a muscle moved in his face. ' Remove the prisoner,' cried the President. The sectary, maintaining continuously his expression of tranquillity and indifference, bowed himself to the judge and followed the warder."

Sometimes these "dumb" are found in large groups, but they mostly lead an isolated life in the remotest forests or on the distant steppes.

Still further advanced on the road of fanaticism are the Prugoni (Dancers) and Chlisti (Flagellators). The former believe in the descent of the Holy Spirit upon man, which only takes place as far as the majority are concerned during their religious assemblies, when by the exercise of dancing and prayer a sufficient degree of ecstasy has been induced. Still, there are two or three persons in each group who are believed to be continuously inspired. One great point in the doctrine of the founder of this sect was that the end of the world was at hand, so that all who would be saved must purify themselves by repentance, confession, ascetism, and the religious exercises above mentioned.

But it is among the *Chlisti* that this kind of fanaticism attains its most interesting development. A peasant named Danilo Filipovitch, an unusually pious man, of the province of Kostroma, gave the initial impulse to this sect. For many years he occupied a cave near the river Volga, and busied himself in prayer and reading holy books. But finally he stuffed all his books into a sack and threw it in the stream, declaring that "revelations come from the living God alone." This Danilo Filipovitch is said to have received the " indwelling of the Lord of Hosts " at a public meeting, while surrounded by his followers. Now his adherents are found in all parts of the empire, in the larger towns and many of the provinces. They call themselves " Christi," or Christs, for reasons that will be seen below, but the Orthodox call them in parody " *Chlisti*," or Flagellators, because this forms part of their religious exercise.

The distinctive doctrine of this sect is that the Godhead dwells, either latent or active, in every man. In fact, man, made in the image of God, is the only being we can see or imagine. This is, of course, closely connected with the Biblical account of the Divine Incarnation in Jesus Christ. According to the *Chlisti* Jesus was just a man like ourselves, but by His self-sacrifice and holiness He gave scope in His life for the indwelling and actualisation of the innate Deity and became God. This development is possible for every one. " Every man can become a Christ, and every woman a Holy Virgin." It simply depends on the quality and degree of our faith, our self-denial, and consequent spiritual ecstasy. When through hysteric leaping and dancing the ecstasy reaches its height, the Holy Spirit descends on men and transforms them into God-men.

The practical instructions given by Filipovitch to his disciples were of the following kind :—

" Young men, drink no intoxicants, neither marry.
Married men, live with your wives as with sisters.
Avoid all unrighteousness, live in peace with each other.
Carefully conceal your tenets and do not betray them even under the knout, fire, or axe."

It is a natural consequence of the doctrine of the indwelling of God in man that these sectaries highly value the worth of manhood, elevating the Divine in it to an object of worship. At their *radjenije*, or meetings, which are always held at night so as to escape the notice of the police, their leaders, both men

and women—for the different sexes are on a perfect equality—
sit in the midst. The other sectaries, with a view to Divine
revelations, betake themselves to such bodily and spiritual
exercises, e.g., prayer and dancing, leaping, &c., as will induce
the desired ecstasy.

The close connection between this kind of religious orgy and
the excitation of the sexual instincts has frequently brought
it about that these nocturnal assemblies terminated with a
svalni grech, or unrestrained promiscuous intercourse. Although
one cannot place implicit confidence in official gazettes nor in
the communications of Chlisti reconverted to the Orthodox
Church, there remains little doubt that these excesses have not
only taken place in the past, but also occur at times in the
present day. The seeming contradiction between this and
their tenets as described above is sometimes explained by the
assertion that what takes place under "inspiration" is quite
different in kind from ordinary marriage. Of course the real
explanation rests upon obvious physiological facts.

A Chlist who reverted to the Orthodox Church has given a
description of his initiation to the authorities. According to
him the Chlisti inculcate a life in accordance with God's law,
plain feeding, avoidance of all marriage or other feasts, total
abstinence, celibacy and prayer, and practical godliness. As
he was a seeker after truth and his soul's salvation, he applied
to be admitted to this sect. The leader explained to him how
he must live, held a long conversation with him, and read
prayers and the Gospel on his behalf. Satisfied with his
sincerity he consented to his admission, and appointed a day
for the ceremony. On the appointed day he was placed under
the care of a young girl, who acted as his godmother. Clad
in white robes, with a burning candle in his hand, he was led
by her into the room where the members were gathered in a
circle, each holding a lighted candle. Following her example
he bowed low before the assembly, whereon all stood up.
Approaching the leader the young girl bowed three times, and
said, pointing to the neophyte, "This slave of God seeks to
save his soul."

The leader thereupon addressed a long discourse to him, and

administered an oath that he would live according to the rules
of the denomination, devote himself body and soul to God and
holy things, and keep as a close secret all that he should see
and hear.

When the oath had been taken, the prayers and ceremonies
began. All commenced to spin round with giddying speed. At
first each one twirled round with increasing rapidity on the
heel of the right foot; then the company ranged themselves
along the walls and ran barefoot after each other in a circle,
stopped, danced, flogged each other, and made all kinds of
contortions, uttering an inconceivable outcry.

In the midst of the din could be distinguished these cries
above the rest: "O God! O King! Saviour! Spirit! Spirit!
O——" The long white robes of the sectaries over their
otherwise naked bodies, their pale faces, the wild outcry in the
semi-darkness—all made a weird scene that struck the new-
comer with terror.

The dance ended with a perfect orgy; men and women both
stripped off their garments, threw themselves on the ground,
went on all fours, leaped on one another, and abandoned all
restraint.

These excesses are, as has been said, the exact result one
would expect from the conditions. It is evident, however,
that here, too, as in the case of the simulated marriage by rape
among the *Begúni*, we have a survival of ancient customs. As
Dr. Dale once remarked, it is a mistake to speak of the
conversion of Europe to Christianity. Individuals have been
converted, but with the nations it is simply a case of a
Christian veneer being applied by State authority, and genuine
heathenism survives in much of our "Western civilisation."
So among these people, who are not of Indo-European race,
the customs described above are remnants of an older phallic
worship; there are many proofs of this in other practices of
theirs, which could be adduced if it were our present purpose
to enter at length into this branch of the subject.

The *Skoptsi* hold the same faith and practise the same
ceremonies as the *Chlisti*, but are far more thoroughgoing in
their measures to subdue the flesh. Believing that the only

way to give scope to the indwelling Deity is to thoroughly subdue
the flesh, and that the only way of accomplishing that is by
" cutting it off," they submit themselves to emasculation. The
psychical process which leads them to this is illustrated in the
case of the peasant Brumin, who told his story before the
judges. Asked how he came to undergo the operation, he told
how he began with an aversion to flesh meat, and lived solitary
in fasting and prayer. Strange visions troubled him by night
and day, angels and demons fighting for the possession of his
soul. He wanted to enter a monastery, but his parents were
opposed to it. Thoroughly preoccupied with the thought of
saving his soul, he dreamed only of religious sacrifices and pious
works. One day he met in the forest a wandering monk, who
asked him to put him on the highway. As they went Brumin
conversed with the monk about his spiritual needs and visions.
The latter listened attentively and said, " If you will save your
soul, you must kill the flesh." Brumin was quite ready to
make an end of that flesh which stood in the way of his
salvation. The monk then performed the operation on the
spot and disappeared, leaving the peasant senseless, and
bathed in blood. It was close upon morning when Brumin
returned to consciousness, and dragged himself home with
difficulty. It came out afterwards that this monk had
emasculated more than eighteen persons, children among the
number.

To avoid the observation of the police, these operations are
performed in as out-of-the-way places as possible. Men,
women, and children alike submit themselves to it; the
contagious enthusiasm being sufficiently powerful to overcome
the natural terror. The method used formerly to be by burning
with red-hot iron; cutting instruments are now for the most
part used, and it may be imagined that, with the rough instruments at their command and the not too careful handling, loss
of life is not unknown.

There is among the *Skoptsi* the same rapid spinning and
dancing as with the *Chlisti*, and the survival of the worship of
the generative force of Nature personified is even more marked.
The account of some of their ceremonies in connection with

the so-called " Communion " reads more like a description of Astarte worship than anything Christian.

Yet the members of both these sects whom I have met in Samara and other parts of Russia were distinguished from the surrounding Orthodox peasantry simply by their decent and intelligent appearance, and all with whom I conversed about them gave unanimous testimony that they were inoffensive, sober, and altogether exemplary in their behaviour to their fellow men.

One of my friends told me that he had a discussion with one of the leading *Skoptsi*, and attempted to refute their doctrine by referring to the command to " multiply and fill the earth." He replied, " Do you really believe that it is to fulfil that command that men and women live together ? Is it, moreover, your candid conviction that it can be your duty to bring any more human beings into this world to suffer all this misery we see about us—to perish both body and soul ? "

In later times, with the growth of the more rational inclinations before referred to, many of these people have abandoned the doctrine of outward emasculation, and inculcate in its place the slaying of the flesh by spiritual weapons and complete abstinence from all sexual intercourse. They are known as " spiritual *Skoptsi*."

The profound pessimism which characterises all these sects, and is the natural result of the miserable conditions of life from which they see no escape, finds its logical outcome in the extreme teaching of the *Samoistrebitjeli*, or self-destroyers. The vast forest tracts of the upper Volga have been the theatre of the most tragic dramas. Two centuries ago, more than ten thousand of these *raskolniki*, hunted and persecuted like wild beasts, sought to escape the tyranny of the " Antichrist Tsar," and enter the glories of the heavenly kingdom by martyrdom through the " baptism of fire." In many places, the spots are shown where these holocausts took place, and are visited in secret by troops of *raskolniki* pilgrims. No one who knows anything at all of what the Russian peasants generally, and the sectaries in particular, have to undergo, can wonder that self-destruction has become the special tenet of a sect,

whose preachers proclaim that the world is hopelessly corrupt and is on the point of perishing entirely; one must,
therefore, escape from this life of lies and sin; one must
die.

Their songs are characterised by a hopeless despair, a
burning hatred of life.

> There's no salvation in this world, nay, none at all!
> Here flattery rules, false flattery, o'er all, alone.
> Death, and death only, can to us salvation bring:
> There is no God in this dark world, none can be found;
> Folly and lies alone, whose tale no limit hath.

The Russian newspapers have, in late years, contained grim
descriptions of the manner in which the sectaries carry out the
dictates of their faith. Unreliable as these papers are in all
matters concerning these " heretics," we know from other
sources that in this case they base their descriptions upon
facts. Here is an extract:—

" The proselyte signifies his wish to die. He is brought to
an empty *izba*, into which the leader accompanies him, and
reads prayers. After a time, the door opens, and "Symbol of
Bloody Death " enters; it is a tall, powerfully-built man,
clothed in a red robe. He places a cushion over the head of
the seeker after death, sits on it, and remains there until the
unhappy fanatic is smothered."

The details in this account may not be altogether reliable,
but it is certain that ever since the beginning of this century
the preaching of these singular teachers has spread through
the region of the Upper Volga, urging the people to escape by
self-destruction the abominable rule of Antichrist. Among
these apostles a certain monk, named Falalei, had a great
reputation. In his forest home he devoted himself to prayer,
reading holy books and discussing religion with his visitors.
It was impossible, he said, to live a true and holy life in this
world of lies and sin; the only escape was suicide; one must
die for Christ.

·Many followers adopted this teaching. One night eighty
persons gathered in an underground resort, specially prepared
for this purpose, by the river Perevosinka. Great quantities

of straw and pitch had been stored there, that they might perish in the flames rather than fall into the hands of the police, if the alarm were given.

The proceedings began with prayer and fasting. Fortunately, a woman, who was not altogether sound on this matter of suicide, took advantage of the darkness to escape, and told the authorities what was going on. The villagers made for the place, but the sentinel, posted at the mouth of the cave, gave the alarm, "Antichrist comes! Save yourselves." "We will never fall into the enemy's hands alive," shrieked the fanatics, setting fire to the straw. The peasants and the police tried to extinguish the flames, and to snatch the brands from the suicides. They resisted, flung themselves into the fire, and slaughtered each other with axes, crying, "We die for Christ!" Some were saved, and the leaders either imprisoned or banished. But this gave no check to the spread of the doctrine. One of the prisoners, Sukhov, a peasant, escaped, and continued his preaching with such success, that in one village thirty-five people slaughtered each other, going from house to house, until only one was left, who fell by his own hand. The details were given by a woman who was the unwilling witness of the massacre, and called the police—but too late.

Belonging to the same general stock, but with an altogether rationalistic development, are the *Nje Nashi*, or Agnostics, a most interesting sect of more recent origin. They live a wandering life, and refuse all connection with the authorities of Church and State, as do the *Raskolniki* generally, but they go a step farther, and deny all religion as well. Vasili Shyshkov, of Saratov, now banished to Siberia, is considered their founder. He belonged to one sect after another, but found no peace for his spirit. Then he severed his connection with all communities, and began to study the sacred writings on his own account, to find the way to God. But, instead, he discovered all sorts of contradictions in the Bible, and after much inward struggle rejected everything, Bible, God, religion, and the life to come. There was no influence of "the exact sciences" in all this. To the question, "How was the world created ? " his answer was, "It has not been created; it has existed from all eternity."

The examination of one of these Deniers or Agnostics, a peasant trader, named Chichkin, before a magistrate will give a good idea of their attitude.

"Who are you ? " asked the judge.

"Don't you see that I am a man ?   Are you blind ? "

"What is your religion ? "—" I have none."

"What God do you believe in ? "

"I don't believe in any God at all.  God belongs to you. You discovered Him.  I don't want Him."

"Do you kneel to the devil, then, and pray to him ? " said the judge, with irritation.

"I kneel neither to God nor devil, because I have no need of either.  The devil is your discovery.  God and the devil, with Tsars, priests, and officials, are your affair.  You are all children of the same father; I don't belong to you, and I won't have anything to do with you."

These people naturally reject all ownership as now understood.  Their mode of "exchange" is exceedingly simple.  "If you want anything, and I give it you, take it.  When I want something from you, you shall give it me in return."  Chichkin would have given meat, clothes, money—anything whatever to the first comer, to satisfy a real need.  But he would not give a single kopek for tobacco, wine, &c.  "I would rather throw my money into the sea than help you to poison yourself with tobacco," he would say.  If anyone said, "Thank you," to him, he replied, "Stuff! you have what you want, you have eaten; go away content and happy."

In their efforts to be natural they neither shave nor cut their hair, and use no spirits or tobacco, so as to preserve bodily health and the force and beauty of the spirit.  They dream of a life in which every one works for himself, satisfies his needs out of the earth's produce, makes what goods he wants, and avoids all superfluity.  They are perfectly willing to help their neighbours, but altogether refuse to be compelled to work. When Chichkin was in prison he was shaved, and according to the rules, he should then have begun to work, but he wouldn't.

" You have brought me here by force; I didn't ask you to put me in prison," he said. " You must therefore feed me and work for me. Let me go, and I shall work for myself and never trouble you for aid." Though they beat him unmercifully, fastened him to a wheelbarrow, shut him in a solitary cell, gave him bread and water only—he was unmoved.

Women have complete equality with men, and their only union is that of free love. As a protest against the present form of marriage they have given up the terms man and wife, and say simply " friend." This is illustrated by the extract from a trial, where a man, a woman, and a little girl were before the magistrate.

" Is that your wife ? " said the judge. " No ; that is not my wife."

" But you live with her ? " " Yes ; but she is not *mine*, she belongs to herself."

" Is that your husband ? " he asked the woman. " No ; that is not my husband," she said.

" What is he, then ? " asked the astonished judge. " I need him, and he needs me; that is all. But we belong each to ourselves."

" What of the girl, does she belong to you ? " " No, she is of our blood, but she is not ours ; she belongs to herself."

" What fools you are ! " exclaimed the judge, impatiently. " Does that coat you are wearing belong to you ? " " No; it does not belong to me."

" What do you wear it for, then ? " " I wear it so long as you don't take it from me. This skin was once on a sheep's back, now it is on mine ; to-morrow it may, perhaps, be on yours. Why do you want me to know to whom it belongs ? Nothing belongs to me except my thoughts, my understanding, &c."

Pessimists and agnostics as they are, they yet have an ideal which they believe will be realised in the distant future. A last judgment shall come on the earth, a terrible struggle between the evil and the good, a kind of Battle of Armageddon, in which the good will triumph, and a kingdom founded on truth and justice will be established on the earth.

There is very little connected knowledge of this strange sect, since they naturally have no definite organisation or creed. They are found one here and one there, and always refuse to give any account whatever of themselves or their antecedents. This is illustrated by the account of an official who visited the prisons. After describing his experience with one of these folk, he goes on to say :—

"I came across another original of the same kind and sect, in prison also. In the prison rolls he had been described as Tchnochruistov, but no one knew his real name, or where he came from. I met him in a Siberian prison, where there were confined more than eight hundred prisoners.

"This man was of a milder and more communicative temperament than the former, so it was easier to get into conversation with him. He rejected God and all religion, chiefly because of the absence of all palpable or visible proof of God's presence or utility. He pointed out the contradiction between real life and religious teaching.

"'The priest tells you that God is good and just, and that not a hair of a man's head falls without God's will. That sounds beautiful. In this prison there are eight hundred of us at present, and we shall all go to penal servitude. At least fifty of these are entirely innocent. I know that from reliable sources, and many are banished just because of their faith in God and sincere piety. They are therefore unjustly condemned. I say nothing about myself; I don't belong to your lot, and your God has nothing to do with me. But why does He not protect and defend the innocent? They trust in Him, you know, and worship Him. Some of them pray all night and bow their heads to the ground while they cry to Him from on their knees; but all the same they are flogged and sent to the mines. How do you explain that?'

"This sectary recognised no authority. 'What do we want with them?' he asked. 'What use have the people for government by all these *tchinovniks?* How can one single person look after the needs of a hundred million men? No; Government is not for the people's benefit, but, as is clear today, the people are for the Government's benefit. But all that is no affair of mine.'

" After a few moments he went on, ' Suppose we take you as an example. You are not a bad sort of man, so far as I can see. You are, besides, very intelligent. Now then ! Can you conscientiously say, with your hand on your heart, that you fully discharge your duty to every one ? Can you keep an eye on everybody ? Yet your duties are not extraordinarily extensive. How, then, can you manage that a Government shall know everything, control everything, keep watch over everything ? The result is general disorder, general lying?—what the devil do you want with a Government then ? '

" ' But one can't get along without authorities. Disorder, crime, and theft would ensue. The strongest would always get his way, and lord it over everybody. Suppose that I' fancied your waistcoat. I am stronger than you, and simply take it from you. What will you do with me ? "

" What will I do with you? The waistcoat cost three roubles, and to get it back I spend ten. I ask you if that is worth while ? Moreover, to protect my waistcoat I have to pay you, inspector, and maintain police, warders, judges. The waistcoat is truly not worth all that.'

" ' How would you arrange life, then ? '

" ' In the first place, I shouldn't arrange life at all. I am by myself, I need nothing. That is all. As for the rest, if you are strong and will do me an injury, there are twenty others as weak as I, and we will handle you in such a fashion that you won't want to do an injury to any one else.'

" ' There would be endless quarrels.'

" ' Don't you worry ! We shall get on very well without you,' said the man, positively.

" His ideas on patriotism were cosmopolitan.

" ' For you,' he said, ' there are Russians, Germans, Tartars. For me there are only men and brothers. The only difference is that they speak a different language from mine. As for you others, you quarrel continually, you carry on war, you never have elbow-room enough. In my way of thinking there is enough land, water, and air for all. Give men freedom, leave them in peace, and there will be no more strife.'

" He was a mild and peaceable man, inoffensive in his conduct to his fellow-men. He never quarrelled nor did any one a bad turn; on the contrary, he came to every one's assistance if there were need, and while they regarded him as crazy, every one loved him.

"But his dislike to authority changed him into an altogether different man. He never lost an opportunity of showing them his contempt and protesting against their power. One day the governor of the place, a tyrannical kind of man, visited the prison. He inspected everything, and put the usual questions to the prisoners about their needs and desires. All stood cap in hand before him, except the sectary, who looked round him unconcernedly with his hat on. This conduct attracted the governor's notice.

"'Who's that fellow that doesn't take off his hat? Take off your hat,' said he to the prisoner.

"'The hat's yours, not mine. If you want it, you have only to take it off me,' said the man, composedly.

"'How dare you?' roared the governor.

"'Instead of yelling like that you had better inquire into the cause of the prisoners' wretched lot,' said the sectary, quietly.

"'Handcuff him! Flog him!' shrieked the governor, beside himself with rage.

"They seized the unhappy man and took him away. He was flogged so severely that the inspector found him the next day in hospital, unconscious. He was there a long while, but owing to his powerful constitution he recovered. Asked what made him behave like that to the governor, he replied, 'I had to.'

"Soon after he was transferred to another prison, and only vague rumours were heard of him. The whip, instead of subduing, only hardened and irritated him. He displayed an unheard-of force of character, and underwent terrible experiences. He was flogged and lashed times without number, deprived of food, confined for a whole year in a dark and damp cell. He bore all without giving way or renouncing his opinions. After a terrible scourging in one of the Siberian prisons, he was taken by force to the convict mines. All the time he was driven forward by a cudgel, but when he got to the place he lay on the ground, and the fiercest blows could not make him get up. The time came to return to the prison ; the military guard had to carry him in a wheel-barrow, as if he were celebrating a triumph, to the huge delight of all the prisoners. One way or another he always had the best of it."

It should be mentioned that there are some *Nje Nashi* who do believe in a God, but utterly deny the Orthodox God. In this they will probably have the sympathy of many. To reject the caricature of the All Father that is frequently put forward by those who arrogate to themselves the name of "Orthodox" is not to deny God, but the devil. But the care with which these *Nje Nashi* conceal their views makes it extremely difficult to discover what they do believe.

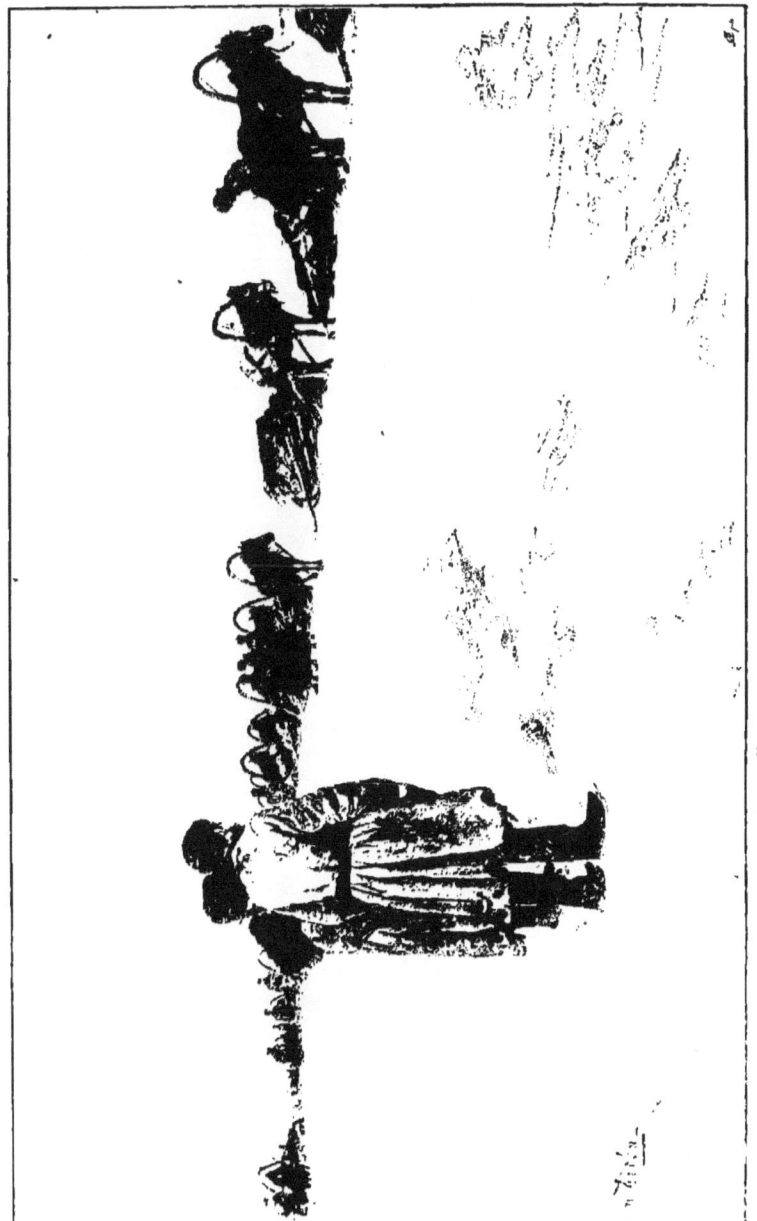

AN "OBOZ," OR TRAIN OF SLEDGES, BEARING FOOD.

15

# CHAPTER XV.

## LATER SECTS.

Close Connection between Social Conditions and Religious Development—
The Upper Classes and the People—The *Schalaputi*—Religious Tenets
—Communism—Conscience the Sole Lawgiver—*Molokhani* and *Du-
khobortsi*—The *Stundists;* their Origin—Letter from a Persecuted
Adherent—Testimonies to the Moral Life of *Stundists*—The Missionary
Gathering in St. Petersburg—Bishop Nikanor—Outrages in Kiev—
Prince Khilkov's Letters—General Ustimovitch's Protest—Character
Sketches—Ivan Tchaika—Ustim Dolgolenko—Panass Pantilimonovitch
Tolupa.

WHEN writing of the older sects, such as the *Nje Nashi,
Skoptsi,* and *Samoistrebitjeli,* we had occasion to remark on
the close connection between the social, economic, and
governmental conditions of Russia, and the rise and development of these persecuted religionists. The student of Russian
Nonconformity will find that this inter-relation holds good
with regard to the later sects also; this is made abundantly
clear by the great authorities such as Prugavin, Alvamov,
Livanov, and others, who have written on the sectarian
movement with painstaking research and great insight, and
whose pages we have largely consulted, both to correct
personal impressions and to study their history. On the one
hand is the emptiness and artificiality of upper-class life, with
all kinds of unnatural stimulants and consequent weariness
and *ennui,* and on the other, the crying inequality, oppression,
and injustice, with their consequent degradation, endured by
the masses. These are clearly mirrored in the various phases
of Russian sectarianism to-day, each of which is, in its way,
an attempt to remedy the evils of human life.

Among the devotees drawn from the upper classes, whether
belonging to the older and more or less fanatical "Flagellators" and "Mutilators" (many aristocratic persons are
known to have joined these), or to the modern "Paschko-

vites," there is mostly a strong emotionalism and earnest
endeavour to save the *individual soul* from the evils of this
world and that to come. The popular sectaries, on the other
hand, while by no means neglecting the purely spiritual
aspirations, are usually 'earnestly trying to remedy the *social*
evils of this life, *i.e.*, to inculcate and realise in all present
human relations the fundamental principle of practical
Christianity, brotherly love.

That is, among the upper classes there is weariness and
pessimism with regard to this present life, while among the
popular sectarians, spite of all the oppression and misery that
they suffer, there is undying hope and belief in the final
triumph of righteousness and love here below, and earnest
endeavours to fulfil the daily prayer—Thy kingdom come *on
earth* as it is in heaven. This is true of both the older and
later sects as regards the endeavours of brotherly love and
helpfulness, as it was of the earliest Christians; the Old
Believers at one time established prosperous colonies in the
most inhospitable wilds of the North, and others have been
formed in Eastern parts of the Empire by the *Molokhans*, &c.
It is true that in treating of the more fanatical sects we have
laid stress on a certain pessimistic hopelessness with regard
to this world, but it must be remembered both that many of
the · adherents of these extremists were drawn from the
upper classes, and that, in point of numbers, they do not
compare with the more moderate sectaries. Among many
divisions of Russian Nonconformity of the present day there
is not simply the practical brotherly helpfulness shown
to individuals, but also a strong faith in the efficacy of
righteous social relations to bring true happiness of life here
on earth.

Perhaps it is among the *Schalaputi*, or "spiritual Christians," as they call themselves, that this brotherly love has
found the most thoroughgoing expression in the relations of
everyday life. The origin of the name of this sect, which with
so many others sprang up about half-a-century ago, is not
known. Having its birthplace in the province of Tamboff, it
has, under different names and with changing theological

views, developed and spread very rapidly over the middle and southern provinces, especially in Caucasia, where its adherents are most numerous.

At first it seems to have resembled in its views the *Chlisti* and allied sects, but in later years it has abandoned the more negative tenets, such as abstinence from sexual intercourse, &c., for more positive and practical Christianity. A peasant named Avvakum Ivanovitch Kopylov, of Tamboff, was the principal representative of the former tendency; another peasant, Perfil Petrovitch Kutasonov, of the same government, was the leader of the latter.

It is impossible to sketch a system of their doctrines, because they cannot be said to have any, from the nature of their primary beliefs. Their chief source of religious knowledge and teaching is the "inner man," *i.e.*, the mind and conscience. They attach great value to the books of the Old and New Testaments, but do not believe in their literal inspiration. Miracles, the creation of the world, the Orthodox doctrine of the Trinity, &c., they do not accept literally, saying, "These are invented by the priests." "They are for the priests," &c. A logical consequence of these beliefs is unrestrained freedom of interpretation of the Bible, which naturally leads to great variety of individual opinion, preventing the adoption as a body of any scheme of doctrine. They are at one, however, in these fundamental principles and in the rejection of the Orthodox Church with its priesthood, *eikon*-worship, and ceremonies. Their meetings are held in private houses, or in secluded spots on the steppes, or within the forests, and consist of singing, prayer, reading from the Bible or other sacred book, and "conversation." There is no clerical caste.

But that which binds them together is not theory but practice. "All men are brothers," is the central doctrine on which their outer life is built. It is heard most frequently in their "conversations," and from it the duties of life are deduced.

The first duty of all is *to work*. It is immoral and sinful to eat the fruits of other people's labour, when able to work for oneself.

Hence all other means of getting a living are rejected. To lend out money on interest, to receive a salary for fulfilling social duties, or to trade for gain is wrong. None of these occupations are found among them ; all labour for the most part at agricultural work. They are very industrious, and set a notable example to the surrounding Orthodox population in all respects. In selling their products they never take advantage of competitive conditions to secure the highest possible price, but charge what, in their opinion, they are really worth.

They both own and cultivate their land in common. Their houses are also common property, and are mostly built in groups of five or six, with no fences between. Sometimes two or more families form one household, so that they have associated homes in the fullest sense.

All the produce of the land they divide into four parts : one is reserved for seed ; a second is stored up to guard against famine ; a third is for home consumption ; and the fourth for sale. The income of the community is distributed according to the wants of each family ; all are expected to work, and all are amply provided for. Besides looking after those within their community, they give as much help as possible to those outside—" because all men are brothers." If they lend out money, they receive no interest, and they never sue any one for debt nor for wrong done. In fact they carry out in practice the motto often heard upon the lips of would-be socialists in England—" From each according to ability, to each according to need."

When differences arise between them, they are settled by the community in the common meeting. No documents are kept and no rules followed. " Conscience " is the sole arbiter, and so strong is the collective conscience that all abide by its decision. These meetings, where all matters of common interest are discussed and decided, have a strong " family " character, and mostly end with a common social meal.

There are, besides, " meetings of the fathers "; that is, of the most prominent members of the different communities, which are united in an association. Here are discussed matters affecting the entire body, such as the needs of weaker communities, the aid of persecuted families, establishment of colonies, and so forth.

The *Schalaputi* have the distinguished honour of being branded by the authorities as "a very dangerous sect," and have suffered severe persecution. Yet they have many thriving communities scattered about the empire, and chiefly in Northern Caucasia, while there are great numbers of adherents in other places who are prevented from organising themselves into communities, but practise their principles of "brotherly love" as individuals.

The followers of the celebrated peasant Suttajeff, whose tenets so much resemble those of Tolstoi, also lead as far as possible a communistic life, and other sectaries of different names are Christian Socialists.

We have already described a meeting of the *Molokhani* (p. 79). The literal meaning of this term is "milk eaters," because they consume milk in Lent. They are, in fact, an evangelical sect who reject ecclesiastical authority and ceremonials, and apply their common - sense to religious matters. The *Dukhobortsi*, or "Spiritual Fighters," are another division of Evangelicals. Like most others, they are firmly opposed to all militarism and the use of violence, and are of much higher character than the Orthodox generally. They are at present suffering great persecution in some parts.

The *Stundists*, of whom much has been said and written of late, form one of the most prominent and influential Russian sects of the present day. The name of this sect, as is well known to many, is derived from the German word *Stunde*, an hour, because it received its principal impetus from German pietists who had settled in Southern Russia, and were in the habit of meeting for " an hour " of prayer, singing, reading and meditation on the Gospel.

A Russian peasant named Ratuschni, who had worked for these people, became converted at one of their meetings, and began to preach the " Stunda " among his countrymen, and quickly gained a large following. This was in 1864. Since then the denomination has spread very rapidly, especially in Southern Russia, so that at the present time its adherents may

be numbered by hundreds of thousands.   As a body the Stundists have no fixed creed, but hold what are usually known as
the evangelical doctrines common to Protestants in Western
Europe.

A large proportion hold Baptist views with regard to that
sacrament; the large majority adopt the Quaker's attitude to
military service and swearing, and all are much less formal-
istic and dogmatic than most Western Protestants.   They lay
the greatest emphasis on the practical side of Christianity.
Their services resemble those of the early Christians, and they
maintain no special clergy; " elders " are appointed instead.
They do, however, sometimes support missionaries.

The Stundists also have in many cases formed themselves
into communities for the purpose of putting into practice more
thoroughly the principle of Christian brotherhood, but they
retain the institution of private property.

They have been and are still persecuted by the Russian
Government in the most barbarous manner, on the flimsiest
and most absurd pretexts, such as "favouring the German
Emperor," "being Socialists," &c.   They are at present
"deprived of all rights," and treated accordingly.

To give some idea of the way in which these inoffensive
Christians are treated both by the authorities and the Orthodox
mob, we give some letters and documents out of a pile in our
possession that would in itself make a complete volume.
Mention has already been made of a letter from a Stundist
peasant which Count Tolstoi read to me (p. 63).   Here it is:—

" .   .   . You wish to hear from me, and I will now briefly
tell you some of my last experiences.  A few miles from the
city of Kursk lives a brother in Christ who owns a small
piece of land.   We wished to live together, and I therefore
moved to him, and got part of his land, about four acres; on
this I sowed different kinds of corn, which soon began to grow
and ripen.  We wished, as I said, to live together, and now
rejoiced over God's blessing on our labour ; but then a storm
broke over our heads.

" On July 15th we began very early to cut the corn.   After
breakfast my brother went to the house, and I began to sharpen

the scythe. As I was doing this a constable came up to me and roared out, 'Stop that!' took my scythe from me, and brought me to the police-station. Arrived there he called out, 'Where is the police?' After a time the chief of the police came in.

"'Here is the Apostle Mozdza,' the constable said to him.

"The chief of the police then began to shower on me the coarsest insults for being barefooted and with nothing on my head. 'What are you loafing about here for, you damned lazy loon?'

"'I am not lazy,' I replied. 'I always work when I am able.'

"'You scoundrel, you are without boots and a hat.'

"'It is hot, and I perspire when I work.'

"'An orderly worker dresses orderly.'

"'I have clothes, but was not allowed to put them on before I was taken from my home.'

"'Why do you not go to church?'

"'I follow Christ and His Word, and do not consider it either necessary or edifying to go to church. God bids us love our neighbour as ourselves, yea, even to love our enemies. Do you do this, Mr. Chief of the Police?'

"The chief of the police replied by drawing his sword and raising it over my head, roaring out to the constable, 'Beat him with the knout!'

"I answered with the words of Jesus, 'Blessed are ye when men persecute you.'

"The chief of the police then bellowed out, 'Thou Satan's ——!'*

"The conversation continued in the same strain. Afterwards I was left in charge of the people occupying the house. Later on the chief of the police came back and ordered the constable to do things that did not belong to his office, and with which the chief had no business to meddle.

"I was then sent nine miles further, having to walk barefooted and bareheaded in the scorching sun. Thanks to God, however, it soon began to rain, and my sunburnt head was cooled.

* The word here used is too coarse and blasphemous to be translated.

When we arrived at our destination I was again brought to the police.   Here I was asked,

"‘ Why do you not fulfil your duty as a *dizaski?*’ *

"‘ My father does it in my place.’

"‘ You must do it *yourself.*   If not, I will teach you *how.*’

"I replied that I could not do it.   I was then shut up in prison together with murderers and other criminals, who were awaiting their sentence.   Among these I found in the dense crowd amidst dirt and vermin my dear sister in Christ" (spoken of before).   "On the following day we were sent together to another place in a cold storm—I having still to walk with bare head and feet—marching fifteen miles, escorted by gendarmes.   Here I was again brought before the police, and they said to me,

"‘ You must go and do your duty as a *dizashi.*’

"‘ I cannot do it.’

"‘ Why ?’

"‘ Because I am a Christian.   I cannot serve in a way that compels me to occupy a position as policeman over my brothers.   Christ was the servant of all, and he that desires to be a follower of Christ cannot occupy any other position than that of a servant and a brother among brothers.’

"‘ Why, we are all Christians, as many as have the Orthodox faith.’

"‘ I do not know if, and to what extent, you are a Christian. For my own part my conscience at least tells me what a Christian ought to be.   We are Christians only so far as we follow after Christ in our lives.’

"‘ Do you make the sign of the cross ?’

"‘ Is that a proof of Christianity ?   Christ says that only those who do His will and keep His commandments are His true disciples.’

"The chief of the police again commanded me to perform this official service, that they were trying to compel me to fulfil.   I refused.   Then I was taken to the prison, and did not know what was going to become of me.

"Now, judge for yourselves if it can be a Christian act on the

* A kind of police service, filled by the peasants in turn.

part of the authorities to treat in such a manner those who with
all their heart desire to follow Christ, loving their neighbours
as they love themselves, and therefore refusing to occupy a
position that would imply a violation of their obedience to
Christ and their love to their fellow-men.

"While I was in this place the chief of the police again
came and commanded me to perform the above-mentioned
service, saying, ' Go and do your duty.'

"I answered, ' I cannot do a public service in which I shall
have to act as a police over my brothers.'

"Then a priest came in, accompanied by other persons,
among whom were some gentlemen. The priest said, ' Render
unto Cæsar the things that are Cæsar's.'

"I answered, ' This I do; but the things that are God's I
must not render unto Cæsar. The *body* I render unto Cæsar,
but the *will* unto God.'

"The priest asks, ' Are you Russian ? '*

" ' I am the Lord's.'

"The priest: ' We all belong to the Lord and are Christians,
if we have the true faith.'

"I answered, ' The true faith is to follow Christ and do His
will, and His will is that we should all and each of us love and
treat each other as brothers; yea, even love our enemies.'

"The Priest: ' Yes, we love our enemies, and we desire to
make them better in the prisons."

" ' Yes,' I replied, ' in former days the Church used to burn
people to death in order to save them.'

"The Priest: ' But we never do that.'

"I : ' No, in the present time they are slowly tormented to
death in prisons, or left to starve to death.'

"Although they loved me, yet they took my work from me,
and reduced me to misery" (referring to his former sufferings)
"and now, when I had found a refuge and got a small piece of
land of my own, I was torn away by violence from my home,
like a common criminal, although I have done no harm."

I have mentioned the placards that I saw in Saratov, vili-

* Russian in this sense is equivalent to " Orthodox."

fying the Stundists. For the better understanding of what
follows, it will be well to give more details of these. One of
them consisted of a newspaper extract, reporting the sermon
of an Archbishop, Ambrosius, in which he said : " The
Paschkovites and Stundists destroy the foundations of the
moral life of our people, because they deny the power of the
holy sacraments, they spoil the true believers' efforts for
righteousness and the experiences of their spiritual life. The
Stundists take everything from the true believer, and give him
nothing in return but denunciation and slander against the
Church ; and Paschkov's teaching altogether denies the efficacy
of good works towards salvation, and, in so doing, opens the
door to every possible crime. That this really is the case is
seen in the life of the young among the people, in the increasing
drunkenness, theft, murder, attempts at railroad robberies,
parricide, child murder, &c., which were formerly unheard of."

How unreasonable is this attempt to brand the evangelical
Christians as the cause of the increase of crime may be seen
from the fact that the Russian press has for twenty years
criticised the life and teaching of the sectarians, and continually condemned them for schism and rejection of the
Orthodox Church, but never for offences against morality.

Moreover, from the mouths of the Orthodox leaders themselves have come the most weighty testimonies to the strictly
moral life of the Nonconformists. In 1891, for example, the
great Orthodox missionary gathering in Moscow reported the
following :—

" We have examined the Stundists from the moral point of
view. They have no fixed creed, but endeavour to build on a
foundation of practical Christian morality. In their outer life
they try earnestly to fulfil the ethical commands. In contrast
to the surrounding people, the Stundists keep Sunday as holy,
drink no intoxicants, smoke no tobacco, use no foul language,
abuse no one, &c."

Still stronger is the following, from a sermon by an Orthodox
bishop, Nikanor, in the government of Odessa. Taking for
his text Deut. xxviii. 44, " He (the stranger in the land) shall
lend to thee, but not thou to him ; he shall be the head and

NONCONFORMIST EXILES IN TRANSCAUCASIA.

thou the tail," he said : "I once travelled through a village, and as soon as I entered it, I saw a gin-shop. I went in and asked the keeper if he were *Molokhan*, Stundist, or Orthodox, and got the answer that he was Orthodox. Then I asked him who were his chief customers, his neighbours, the Mennonites, the sects just named, or the Orthodox. 'Mennonites or sectarians!' he exclaimed, 'I assure your Excellency, that you could not get them inside a gin-shop for any money. The best customers I have, certainly, are the Orthodox.'

" I left the place greatly depressed, and thought within myself the Bible's saying, 'he shall be the head,' is true of the sectarians and Mennonites, and 'thou shalt be the tail,' of you, beloved Orthodox Christians. As I passed along the street, I saw a neat house, and went in. The owner received me very politely, and brought me into a poor but tidy room. There was no picture " (of a saint) "in the corner, but, instead, I saw, on a table that was covered with a white cloth, a Bible and New Testament. I asked the man what faith he professed, and learnt that he was a *Molokhan*.

" I could see from his conversation that he was a sober and orderly man, and, besides, well grounded in the Holy Scriptures. As I took leave of him I passed the same reflections as on coming out of the gin-shop. Not far from this I saw another neat and pleasing-looking house. I went in there also; the man was a Stundist, equally friendly, sober, and orderly as the *Molokhan*, and even better acquainted with the Bible. Besides the Bible I saw on his table 'Spiritual Songs and Psalms.' I had the same thoughts as when I left the *molokhan*. As I went further along the street I met a rabble of drunken fellows, shouting and singing obscene songs in harsh voices. I knew them for my own sheep, and was ready to weep. I thought once more of the Lord's word: ' Thou shalt be the tail.' "

Our readers will now be in a position to appreciate the following extracts from correspondence furnished by a Stundist lady well known to us, who is compelled herself by persecution to live outside Russia. The truth of the narrative given does not depend upon one but five different

correspondents, giving names and details of the monstrous
outrages perpetrated upon innocent victims in the name of
Orthodoxy.

"*September 8th*, 1892.—Permit us hereby to inform you
that in the villages of Kapustintsi and Skibentzi, in the
*volost* of Babenjetskaja, in the district of Skvirskij and the
province of Kiev, all the male members of evangelical or
Stundist households are taken every day by force, according
to the orders of the *ispravnik*" (chief of police) "and the
*natcholnik*" (official next to the Governor) " of the district, to the
public works of the village communities, where they are
forced to work under the guard of *gendarmes* until quite late.
Then they are again taken out to serve as night watchers, the
women and children being left at home at night. While the
men are thus kept away from their homes by force, the
*starosta* and *starshina*" (heads of the town and village), "in
their official capacity, and wearing the badges of authority
on their breasts, get together a band of drunken villains
and break into the homes of the defenceless women and
children, maltreating the latter, and committing the most
heinous outrages on the former, smashing the windows and
destroying everything they come across. In some *izbas* they
set fire to refuse and rags, and shut the doors on the poor
inmates, thus tormenting them through the whole night. At
sunrise the men are again sent to work at one place, the
women and children at another.

"If any of these Stundists have horses, even they are taken
to the works of the village communities, where they are kept
working all day, and left without food in the night. As a rule,
it is impossible for these unhappy men and women to buy or
sell, or even to prepare food for themselves. In fact, they are
treated worse than if they were criminals sentenced to penal
servitude, and all this they suffer for the sake of the Gospel.

"When they work or serve as night-watchmen they are
always guarded by soldiers. '*All these sufferings are greater
than we can bear,*' they write ; '*even all our books are taken from
us. We are oppressed to such a degree that we cannot even make
our cries of distress heard by any.*' "

In another letter, written in pencil on a scrap of paper and handed furtively to a friend for fear of the police, the persecuted victims say :—

"Dear Brethren,—We beg of you warmly and with tears to take this paper, either you or someone else who can cry out loud. Maybe someone may hear this cry of distress in this time of despair. They grasp us at present by the throat, so that we

A TRANSCAUCASIA TOWN.

cannot even call out so as to be heard. . . . A terrible calamity has befallen us."

The report of these atrocious outrages reached Prince Khilkov in his exile, and he managed to despatch the following note both to the Governor of the province of Kiev and to the Minister of Justice in St. Petersburg :—

"Your Excellency,—I hereby enclose two letters which I have received from peasants in Kiev, who are persecuted for the sake of the Gospel. I send these letters to your

16

Excellency for this reason, that I find it hard to believe that all these monstrosities that are being perpetrated in these villages are done in accordance with your order.   I cannot understand how outrages committed by a band of drunkards upon defenceless women and children, this kerchief-pulling from the heads of women " (a great outrage in the eyes of Russians), " this filling of *izbas* with dirty water, &c., can be measures officially undertaken to put down Stundism in the government of Kiev.   It is disgraceful that such means of opposing Stundism and bringing back the apostate to the bosom of the Orthodox Church should be adopted at night and in drunkenness by the Church's own children.   Your Excellency will doubtless agree with me that the coarsest nocturnal outrages on women are hardly the measures calculated to inspire much respect for the faith of their perpetrators.

" Finally, I appeal to your Excellency to do your utmost to mitigate the sufferings of the persecuted Christians in those regions."

Kiev was by no means the only theatre of these outrages. Such pamphlets as " The Damned Stundist," the sermons and speeches of priests and " Orthodox missionaries," and other means of incitement still more despicable had their natural result.   Prince Khilkov sent the following letter to the Archbishop of Kharkov, dated February 3rd, 1893 :—

" Your High Holiness,—It is pleasant to every man, engaged in any kind of work, to see the fruits of his labour.   Admire then,  your  High  Holiness,  the  fruits  of  your  own.   The repeated appeals made by your Holiness and other like-minded spiritual  shepherds,  who  are  described  in  John  x.,  have found a ready response in the hearts of the village police in the province of Kiev.   Now rejoice !

" The placards which by your orders are being nailed to the church walls, and in which one part of the population is incited  to  hate  the  other;  the  pamphlet  'The  Damned Stundist,' which has been circulated by your High Holiness with  so  much  zeal ; your  own  and  your  helpers'  sermons delivered in the churches, have finally accomplished the aim for which they were written and pronounced (for should one think they had any other aim, he would deny to you and your accomplices the possession of common-sense).

" Houses are demolished, windows smashed, furniture and tools hacked to pieces, *izbas* are filled with smoke and water in order to still more torment their inmates, new zealots of 'the sign of the cross' invent a new and original means of compelling women to cross themselves . . . !

"At the judicial investigation of the matter, the lowest tools will, no doubt, alone be found guilty, just as in all railroad accidents the watchmen always are the guilty parties. But who are they who incite these blind tools?

"In the village of Pavlovka, in the district of Soomi, a police officer, accompanied by a dean and two priests, belonging to those parts, rebuked the peasants at a public meeting for tolerating Stundists among them. ' *In other places of Russia,*' they said, ' *such people are torn in pieces,*' probably alluding to the government of Kiev, and wishing to evoke the same disorders in their district as have occurred in the *volost* of Babinjetzkaja. Is not this *to incite*—to speak about ' *tearing to pieces,*' the Stundists in their midst, as is done in other places?

"Happily the community of Pavlovka, thanks to the awakening faith in the teachings of Christ, is no longer a suitable soil for such seed. Otherwise the Orthodox zealots would here, too, have been able to act in the same spirit as at Kiev.

" If it be denied that the atrocities on the *volost* of Babinjetzkaja have been committed through incitement, the following question arises: Where, then, were the spiritual shepherds of the same *volost* while these lowest 'servants of justice' committed their barbarities, which continued, not for one or two days, *but for several months?* Where, then, were the chiefs of the police?—these spiritual shepherds and chiefs of police, whose Argus eyes never overlook anything, not even the boiled chickens in the peasant's pot during Lent, and whose talons remove with striking success ' this evil ' (*i.e.,* the chicken) from the peasants' homes.

"These lowest of the blind tools of the police and priests will, no doubt, be punished, but the instigators? The hand of the

Minister of Justice does not reach them; but so much the more must their own consciences punish them—if they have any at all.

"I beg your High Holiness most earnestly to cease your incitements. You must see that no good will come of it, nor con it. Remember that to propagate one's faith is one thing; the circulation of a pamphlet like 'The Damned Stundist' is quite another. May the enormities of Babinjetzkaja be the last! At least see to it that none may have cause to reproach you for having had a share in evoking such wicked deeds. I think that a man may from such fruits unerringly judge of the tree that produces them."

We are permitted also to give an English translation of a protest, sent by General Ustimovitch to one of the highest officials standing near the late Tsar, enclosing a copy of an open letter sent to him as to other persons of rank concerning the persecutions.

"Permit me to call your attention to the enclosed open letter. It is impossible that your High Excellency should not have been filled with indignation at the atrocities which, in the name of Orthodoxy, have been perpetrated against the Stundists in the province of Kiev. If it really be the Tsar's wish to oppose the spread of Stundism, the felonious deeds described in the letter can certainly have nothing to do with the manner of fulfilling that desire. The heart of every Christian must be full of deepest indignation at all these fiendish acts, which have been committed against peaceable Stundists by barbarians who are counted as belonging to the Orthodox—and this at a time when so large a proportion of the children of the Church are almost drowned in drunkenness, sloth, ignorance, and wickedness. It is certainly gratifying to see how in the neighbourhood of Moscow—though there only—processions of the cross, with hundreds of thousands of followers, take place in honour of the purest and most praise-worthy Saint in Christ, the most holy Sergius, the wonder-worker and light-bearer. But it is sad to know that the same Christ, in whose name all saints are worshipped, is in other parts of Russia altogether forgotten, and even blasphemed and wickedly abused. It is sufficient to see that even in the cloisters there are found the most deplorable cases of treason against Christ and his Gospel on the part of the monks. It is unnecessary to speak of the type of the Russian *pope*, so repugnant to every true Russian, and so very far removed from the example of Jesus Christ's true disciples. Nor need I refer to the general absence of those good and illustrious examples of Christian piety and wisdom in high and notable circles, which ought to mark the true progress of civilisation. All this is more or less known, and also the fact that our theological seminaries are far from being nurseries in which to train true shepherds and servants under the sceptre of the loving Christ. But why increase the evil, which only encourages the masses and village authorities to commit such outrageous violence against the most peaceful part of the population? Such a system is hardly *politically* wise, because the oppressed and tormented, becoming martyrs in their own esteem and the eyes of those like-minded with them, gain in strength in their difficult position, which is more likely to increase than to diminish.

" There can be no doubt whatever that the Tsar knows nothing of the atrocities described in the enclosed letter. If they were known to His Majesty, then the methods of the opposition to the Stundist propaganda would be conceived in quite a different manner, at least on the part of the local authorities in those places where the persecutions are going on."

The following character sketches, *taken from life*, will both illustrate the Stundist character and throw light on many traits of Russian life. They were written by an Orthodox Russian.

## IVAN TCHAIKA.

Ivan Tchaika was always a very pious peasant. None of the villagers said prayers or crossed themselves so zealously as he did; none bought such expensive pictures of saints; none made so many pilgrimages to Kiev. In his own words, a spiritual fire burned within him. But in vain he said his

prayers and listened to the singing in the church, in vain he
knelt for hours, bowing his head repeatedly to the damp earth.
He was dissatisfied with himself, for it seemed as if he could
never fulfil his Christian duties, and he felt that his Heavenly
Father was dissatisfied with him too.

While yet a boy an incident occurred that made a deep and
lasting impression upon him. He was acquainted with a
young girl named Paraska, a poor orphan in the service of
a Jewish saloon-keeper in the village. According to
Tchaika's account, though handsome and clever, she was
yet "a little strange." Her look was always pensive, and
her eyes seemed ever filled with tears. She never laughed
loudly like the other village girls, but mildly, with a peculiar
silvery tone in her voice that at a distance would be taken
for sobbing rather than laughter. Often she would start
without a cause, and was always frightened if accosted from
behind. She disliked hard and coarse work, and in the
village was known as "the noble young girl," a reference
to her mother's intimacy with a nobleman.

Late one evening Ivan came to his Paraska. The moon
was shining, and the stars shed a pale twinkling light over
the calm sky. As Ivan approached the Jew's house he heard
Paraska's voice, as if talking with some one in the saloon.
Silently drawing near, he found Paraska kneeling before the
picture of the Holy Virgin, and her voice had in it the ring
of real conversation rather than of prayer. And how she
spoke! It seemed at first to Tchaika that every hair was
standing on end and his whole body tingled; but soon his
eyes filled with tears as he listened to her sincere confession,
her earnest prayers, her sad voice, and saw that beautiful
figure bathed in the pale light of the moon. The words he
heard remained engraven indelibly upon his heart: "O thou
most Holy Virgin, Mother of God, have mercy, have mercy
on me, poor orphan girl! Let me not perish, let me not be
ruined! O Lord! how shall I live in this world, without
parents, without relatives, without friends? O Mother of
God, see how weak I am!" Finally she burst out, "O Mother
of God! I am perishing—perishing!"

Ivan himself broke into sobbing, and ran forward to Paraska. . . .

Soon after this Paraska began to lead a bad life, and drink with drunkards in the saloon. But this moonlight night, this pure and innocent Paraska, who prayed so intensely to the Holy Virgin, could not be moved from Ivan's memory. Many a time afterwards he tried to pray in the same way, but however he tormented himself it was all no use. " If I could only pray as she did, if I could only feel as I did when I heard her pray!" But his strongest endeavour was in vain.

But the time was to come when Ivan would renew the experience of that memorable evening, and increase it. A well was opened to him, whence he could at all times draw the fervour of prayer.

His sister had married a certain Ustim Dolgolenko, and soon Ivan heard, to his unspeakable horror, that Ustim and his wife Alona had burnt their holy pictures, and left off going to the Orthodox Church. Tchaika, who was a staunch adherent of this Orthodox Church, burning with deep indignation at the conduct of his relatives, set out to bring them back to the true fold. Alas! he himself was led astray and became a Stundist.

This, however, cost him much inward struggle and pain. Convinced of the truth of the Gospel, the power of which he had experienced at a Stundist meeting, he threw away his holy pictures. But night and day the thought that he had done something terribly wrong tormented him. Several misfortunes befell his family, which added to his torment. He went again to Ustim, who read to him from the New Testament, explained the Gospel to him, and sent him home comforted and victorious out of his struggle. Ivan has now learnt to read himself, and knows the New Testament almost by heart.

Once a gentleman who knew of his past trials said in jest to him, "You were frightened at the first difficulties!" Ivan replied in solemn tone, "Sir, why do you sneer at us ignorant peasants? It was hard at first to leave the Church with all its ceremonies in which I had sincerely believed—but I have left it. You gentlemen, who are better than we, why do not you openly leave institutions and ceremonies. in which you do not believe? No, it is easier to keep silent. It is no use for you to come to us with your learning and wisdom. If you do not come with a warm faith we will not believe in your sincerity nor accept you."

### USTIM DOLGOLENKO.

Ustim Dolgolenko is a tall, broad-shouldered peasant, with expressive brown eyes, thick nose, spotted red, and such long moustaches as one hardly meets outside of fairy tales. He talks slightly through his nose. Ustim is the village poet, comedian, satirist, and singer. He can sing you verses about "The Pope and His Wife," "The Archbishop and the Nun," &c. He is the boldest and coarsest in the village, a gallant with women, a drinker, in short, a thorough prodigal—the most noted and strongest fighter, the most skilful mower, the best workman. He is of pliable disposition, soft-hearted, frank and honest, humorous, and razor-tongued. Ustim needs none to put him up to playing a trick on pope, *kulack*, or village elder, or to set going an anecdote, jest, or nickname that shall immortalise them in the village and neighbourhood. If he has money, he asks everyone to drink; if he has bread he gives to every one who is hungry. He will give his last rag to the first beggar that comes, and never refuses to help any one. Spite of his sharp tongue all the villagers love him. At festivals and other gatherings stories are told of his escapades, his sallies, his jokes, and his ditties are sung. The saloon-keeper makes money out of him. Ustim has already squandered his cow, his horse, his *izba* in drink. All he has left is the crop in his field. The land itself he has rented out for two years to come, and now must work as day labourer.

Such was Ustim Dolgolenko. His two years of service were spent with the German Colonists, who found him an excellent workman, and his wife (whom he often beat) a clever and industrious woman, and gave them good pay. Ustim worked hard, was sober and abstemious, and returned with a good sum of money to the village. There he bought a new *izba* and returned to his old work—and his old drinking habits.

Ustim had an "evangelical" neighbour, on whom he showered all possible scoffing and mockery. He could swear that at the religious meetings held in the house of this Stundist he had seen people with pigs' heads, who, nevertheless, howled ike dogs; he had seen it and heard it himself. He had also seen devils with curling locks like those of the Jewish saloon-keeper, coming to these meetings with small bags full of golden grain. Every time he passed the Stundist's house, returning from the saloon, he would shout, "Hallo, Stundist! Hallo, the devil's godfather! Give me a couple of your golden grains!"

One night very late, as Ustim was on his way home with a bottle of brandy in his hand and a considerable quantity of spirits in his head, he saw a light in his neighbour's house. In a twinkling he broke through the door and entered the *izba*, which was full of people. They were in the act of singing a hymn, but on his unceremonious entrance all became silent.

"Halt! Silence!" shouted Ustim, imitating the tones of a commanding officer. Then he began to sing one of his vulgar songs, and to dance.

One of the Stundist's sisters, a young woman with a pale face and great expressive eyes, gazed steadily at Ustim, and then glanced round the circle of those present. Her body began to shake as with an ague, her lips quivered, and the muscles of her face twitched. Suddenly she fell on her knees, all but Ustim following her example. "O Thou merciful God," cried the young woman, "O Jesus our Saviour, how long wilt Thou leave us weak without Thy help? How long shall we wander as sheep without a shepherd, as fatherless, motherless children? See, Lord, how we are scattered over the whole earth! See how weak and feeble, sinful and guilty we are before Thee. Lord, uphold us, give us power, make us able to fulfil Thy holy bidding; lead us, Saviour, in the narrow way, and not the broad! Oh, open our eyes that we may see in what darkness we are! Uplift our hearts that we may love

our neighbours!   Have mercy, Lord, on all sinners who are
here, for we are weak and feeble."   She broke down into
sobs; many of the women wept aloud.   Ustim turned pale
and crouched down, but the whole gathering began to sing
in solemn tones, " Come to Jesus as thou art," &c.

Ustim was sobered at once; he tingled all over, with a
feeling that was at once painful and pleasurable.   An
emotion hitherto unknown awoke within him.   His heart beat
violently, love and reverence took possession of his entire being.
At that moment a fresh visitor, one of the Stundists, entered
the room, and having saluted all the brethren, approached Ustim
and said, in heartiest, most cordial tone, " Good evening, brother,
peace be with thee also !" took him in his arms, and kissed
him affectionately.

Ustim trembled; he felt electrified; tears coursed down his
cheeks, and he fell on his knees, crying, "Dear brothers, dear
sisters, forgive, forgive me! I did not know—I thought——"

Ustim is now one of the most pious and staunchest Stundists.
He leads a sober and rational life; he has since taught himself
to read, and is considered one of the most gifted preachers.
He has composed music to several hymns.   No one sings at
meeting, so beautifully and expressively, no one prays so often
or so freely as Ustim.   His wife has regained her health and
happiness; they live together now like two doves.


### PANASS  PANTILIMONOVITCH  TOLUPA.

Panass Pantilimonovitch is a retired officer of the Black Sea
Fleet.   He took part in the Crimean War, and received many
medals.   His thin, long face looks still longer through his
thin, long, dark brown whiskers, that seem as if they were
glued to his meagre cheeks. His eyes are weak and readily water;
he is unusually tall.   Every Sunday P. P. regularly dons his
shabby uniform, with a mass of decorations on his arms and
shoulders, hangs all medals possible on his breast, and, leaning
on his plum-tree staff, with proud and stately steps proceeds to
God's temple.

P. P. cannot stand present-day soldiers; he has contemptuously nicknamed them "marmots." "What sort of soldier is that?" he will vehemently exclaim. "He has scarcely learnt to hold a rifle in his hand before they let him return to his old woman! No; if he had been drubbed as much as I, he would have known what military service is. True, it was very strict in our time, and at first it seemed very hard. I very nearly hanged myself from the yard-arm, through vexation and fright, but after they had cut me down, kept me in hospital, and given me some more of the necessary drubbing, I lost all my rustic foolishness."

The neighbours, who know P. P. as a hot-headed, ambitious man, often poke fun at him. He gets particularly angry when anyone jests at his war-medals and suchlike. Then he raves, shouts, and sometimes spits in his antagonist's face. Yet all this does not prevent them from highly respecting a man who leads a sober life, never takes anything that is not his, makes boots all winter and tends his kitchen garden all summer, asks nothing from anyone, lives happily with his wife, goes regularly to church on Sundays, and reads "Lives of the Saints" at home, owns a well-stocked library, consisting mostly of such works as "The Holy Theodora," "Description of Hell," "The Thirteen Sufferings after Death," &c. How can they help revering a man who never tells a lie—his tall stories of his naval exploits not counting as lies—never cheats, and enjoys such confidence that on saints' days the saloon-keeper hands over his entire stock of *vodka* to him without measuring the amount or counting the money paid? How can they do other than honour a man who, even when sitting in a dirty grogshop, retains the dignity of an admiral, and if anyone misbehaves commands "Silence! Out with you!" and order is restored? What else can they do but respect a man who always holds himself erect before the *stanavoj* (village police); who once called the elder of the village district "a venal rascal"; and, finally, is an intimate friend of Psalmsinger Agathon?

No one could help loving P. P.; he was an upright, benevolent man, who never refused to help the needy. He always stood up to defend the weak against the strong; he publicly withstood the *kulack* and "mir-eater" when he tried to

oppress some poor fellow.  No bully dared ill-use his wife,
nor cruel parents to maltreat their children in P. P.'s presence.
He had nothing against a moderate amount of corporal punishment.  "One must punish," he would say, "but it should be
done with discretion."

P. P. had no land, and this grieved him deeply.  "What!"
he used to exclaim, "an ignorant peasant, who has never
fought a Turk, never shed his blood for Tsar and country,
owns land and a house, while I, the officer Tolupa, who am
known by the higher authorities, whom the General Kornilov
himself has clapped on the shoulder more than once, who have
been wounded three times—Tolupa must in his old age suffer
want like a beggar, without land, without a home!"

At first Tolupa was ready to leave everything and walk on
foot to St. Petersburg to present his hard case in person, but
he thought better of it, and determined to treat the matter in
a more common-sense way.  "Here in Russia we have, of
course, holy laws," he would say; "I must treat this thing
according to law; then I shall surely gain my just cause."  In
general, he had a very deep reverence for law, and his opinions
in this respect were marked by the most childlike simplicity.

Tolupa took up the matter with great zeal.  He wanted not
only to get something for himself, but to unite all homeless
veterans in common effort for their cause.  But to convince
the other soldiers in his own and neighbouring villages, he had
to spend six months, and an immense amount of strength,
activity, and speech.  Provided at last with a petition signed
by a hundred men, and attested at the village office, and having
ordered a mass for the success of his enterprise, he set out on
foot for the district town, convinced that his cause must be
crowned with success; all he had to do was to keep to the law.
In town he fell in with a "gin-lawyer" (one of the lowest
kind), who drew up for ten roubles an application to the
authorities of the district.  His application was rejected, in
the first place, because it was so badly drafted that it was
impossible to understand what it was about.

Tolupa took a post as doorkeeper for a month or two, till he
earned sufficient to get a better lawyer, who wrote an intelli-

gible application for him. This time the district authorities discovered that it would not do, because it was not written according to legal form. Tolupa returned to the village, continued his work, called his co-applicants together, and provided himself with a legal application. One cannot give all the details ; it is enough to say that after two years Tolupa found that to gain his cause was not so easy.

When he found that he could get no satisfaction out of the district authorities, he bade farewell to his wife, and set off for the chief town of the government. At home he was accustomed to a few comforts, tended by the loving care of his wife, but on this tedious march he was soaked through and through, slept in the open air, ate dry bread, &c. His constitution, formerly as strong as iron, though worn, could not withstand all these privations. He reached the town with great difficulty, and had to spend five weeks in hospital. The Governor received his application, and returned it to the district authorities for further investigation. . . .

A year later saw P. P. again marching slowly, with a sack over his shoulders, to the government's chief town. He was older and more bowed, always restless and excited, both at work and at rest ever thinking of this one thing. He had had during this time to suffer many insults, sorrows, and disappointments, but these did not grieve him as much as the fact that those who were, in his opinion, appointed to look after the observance of the law themselves trampled it underfoot. " They are not servants of the Tsar," he cried, indignantly, " they defy his will."

When, at last, his case was forwarded to the authorities in St. Petersburg, P. P. breathed more freely. " Now our cause is won. It is no longer insignificant officials, who understand nothing of laws and statutes, but ministers ! " He would have preferred these ministers to have been military men. " A soldier," he said, " is always just, even if strict, and never flinches from the law." He particularly liked the military men of the Emperor Nicholas's time. " How is it to-day ? Now they take all kinds of liberties on themselves ! " referring to the Stundists. " Look at those ignorant peasants, who abjure the holy Christian faith, and openly worship idols, and they are tolerated! In my days they would have come into the executioner's hands, and, with nostrils slit, have been marched off to Siberia. But now? Now there are no laws—everyone does as he pleases!"

It must be acknowledged that as time went on his neighbours visited P. P. less frequently, and many avoided him altogether; in fact, they were all tired of him. As soon as anyone came to him, he began narrating all the details of this lawsuit, taking from his trunk a great pile of papers—copies, reports, letters, and different resolutions; if the visitor could read, he got him to read all through them; if not, he would do so himself, spelling his way very slowly, and sometimes muddling up the words in a very curious manner.

It was a severe blow to the old man when a document from St. Petersburg, having passed through all intermediate stages, finally reached him. It explained that his case could not be remitted to the Senate, because some of the documents were on unstamped paper.

"So the stamp is necessary! Is that what his wise law requires?" he exclaimed, excitedly, struck his breast with his fist, and coughed. When his wife begged him, with tears in her eyes, not to trouble about it, he answered, "Why should I live in this world? But, do you know, I can no longer walk in the street. Not only the stupid peasants, but even the children point their fingers at me and cry, 'Hullo, Pantilimonovitch! Have you won your lawsuit? You know the laws!'"

He grew calm, however, when the matter was finally remitted to the Senate. "Now, at last, I need not be anxious. It is not for nothing that the Senate is called holy," mixing up the Senate with the Synod.

It could hardly be expected that the old man, on losing his case in the Senate, could stand such a heavy blow, for his life was centred entirely in this issue, for which he had sacrificed so much time, strength, activity, and health. But the reverse happened. When, after two years' waiting, he received the final adverse resolution, he only grew a trifle pale, and said simply, with a half-ironical smile, "May God judge them!"

The explanation is simple. P. P. had, during the interval, become changed from a worldly warrior into a soldier of Christ. The story of his conversion is very brief. The principal part was played by a little book—the New Testament. Up to his 68th year, P. P. had never read this, although he could read fairly well. Once he travelled a few miles by rail from his village, and at a certain station had to wait a couple of hours. On the platform he met a man, who seemed a kind of pedlar, also waiting for the train. P. P. was a companionable and talkative old fellow, and went up to the stranger, saluted him, and sat down to a chat. How long they talked I do not know, but this much is certain, that the pedlar, who was a Bible colporteur, opened his satchel, took out a New Testament, and gave it him as a present, having marked a few passages with pencil.

P. P. began to read it with all the eagerness of youth. "How could I think myself a Christian without reading this book!" he exclaimed, and set about studying the Gospel with increasing fervour. All his sufferings from the lawsuit—insults, reproaches from his companions, and scoffing from others—drove him to seek solitude, in which he found in his newly-acquired book a never-failing well of consolation. There were many things he did not understand, but he read, thought, prayed, and compared its different parts, and without having met any Stundists arrived at views much like theirs. His lawsuit on behalf of destitute soldiers had supplied him with many instructive experiences, and trained him to look at things with a more critical eye; his childish simplicity had received severe blows. P. P. knew, for instance, before this that the priest Ivan never sealed a coffin (a Russian custom) before he had got two roubles. He knew, too, that "Father" Ivan compelled the peasants to work for him on Sundays, got dead drunk, and would abuse Agathon, the psalm-singer, in the coarsest terms. But he was used to all that, and gave it no attention; now it irritated and repelled him; our soldier began to analyse things.

Once, on hearing of an outrageous act by Father Ivan, he put on his uniform and went to him with the sincere purpose of converting him, and leading him into the way of truth and righteousness, but he was repulsed in a shameful manner. Soon P. P. stopped going to church, and began openly to preach a life according to the Gospel, and to criticise the immoral life of the surrounding people.

The Stundists now only needed to come and take him into their community. Five years have passed since then. P. P. has had during this time to sit in prison for his views, and once more to march into the town, this time as a prisoner, with the *étape* transport, to answer charges before the Archbishop. All, young and old, scoff at him now; his neighbours regard him as a peculiar man; the young fellows play him many disagreeable tricks, but he bears it all with the stoical calm of a philosopher. He has grown old and grey, his thin whiskers still hanging down from his wasted and wrinkled cheeks.

Though bowed with age somewhat, he still retains his stately gait and majestic bearing; only the sharp, commanding tone has disappeared. If you visit him in the morning you will hear him and his wife sing a morning hymn together, another before their meal, and at night an evensong. The military instinct is still strong within him, and he sings with special enthusiasm such hymns as are couched in martial strains, such as " Ho my comrades, see the signal, waving from the sky," &c.

In the Stundist community he is highly respected and even feared, for no one speaks out the truth in the face of everyone more boldly and sincerely than does our naval officer, Panars Pantilimonovitch.

# CHAPTER XVI.

## THE TWO WORLDS, PEASANT AND OFFICIAL.

Two Nations in One—Study of "the People"—The "*Mir*"—Peasants' Views on Land Tenure—On Jurisdiction Generally—Later Corruption by Officialism—*Tchinovniks* and the "*Mir*"—Examples of Official Oppression—"Uriadniks" or Rural Police—Their Misdeeds—Wickedness in High Places—The Logoschino Affair—Experiences of a Russian Friend—Tolstoi's Description of Russian "Justice."

THE student of Russian affairs must at the outset grasp this fact very firmly, if he would hope to understand the inner life of the nation—that the Russian people is not one but two. We are not speaking of the different *races* to be found in the Empire, but of the two worlds, the official and the popular, that meet each other at many points, yet remain distinct in kind. It is not simply a lateral division separating the " upper classes " from the mass of the people, for the ramifications of the official system are so wide and deep that there is not a village omitted from their lists, not an individual whose life is untouched by the ubiquitous *tchinovnik*. Yet this tremendous organisation of bureaus, registers, bye-laws, &c., this intricate and complex network of red tape, this all-penetrating and Argus-eyed system of police, remains completely outside the real life of the peasants, incomprehensible to them, because in its very nature opposed to their modes of thought and judgment; while in its turn the world in which the peasants live is as unintelligible to the genuine *tchinovnik* as the spirit-world is to a confirmed materialist. This will be illustrated by some account of the manners and customs of each.

It is now about half-a-century or more since such men as Dal, Jakushkin, Kirejevski, &c., began to study the life of the peasants, before then a *terra incognita* to the educated world,

17

and found there such traits of character and qualities of
sterling worth as awoke their wondering admiration. True,
beneath their nominal Christianity they retained many pagan
ideas and practices, and to the upper classes showed suspicion
and mistrust. But in their life with each other they displayed
an honesty, reliability, and devotion to the common good that
contrasted sharply with the corruption of the aristocracy.
The rise of the modern democratic movement in Russia dates
from the pioneer work of these explorers in the peasant world;
since then thousands of men and women belonging to the
upper classes have "gone to the people," to learn their life
and do their part in bridging the gulf that yawns between,
and many of these have made valuable contributions to our
knowledge of different sides of the *mushik's* life. It is of deep
significance that Count Tolstoi, with his extensive learning,
penetrating genius, and deep knowledge of men, points his
educated countrymen who are seeking for a religion of the
heart and conscience "*to the peasants*," whom he has learnt to
know better than any other man.

The centre of the peasant's life is the *mir*, or village community. The origin of this institution is obscure; according
to Tchitcherin and others it is not older than the sixteenth
century, and was instituted by a *ukase* of Tsar Fédor Ivanovitch; others recognise in it a survival of ancient usage, dating
from a time before the rise of autocracy. However that may
be, whether the *mir* in title and official connection is or is not
a thing of recent creation, it is certain that in its purest form
it embodies convictions and practices that lie so deep in the
Russian peasant's nature that they can only be explained as
the result of long ages of use.

The *mir* is the village community itself assembled to decide
all questions that affect the life of the community, where all
are equal and officialism is unknown. It has, indeed, a *starosta*,
or village elder, as president and executive agent, but his power
is not *over* the *mir*, but *from* it.

Of all the matters that occupy the *mir* naturally the land is
the chief, and it is here that its peculiar nature is most revealed.
The Russian peasant has no conception of land as private

property. The intellectual conception of land to be found among economists of every school, as the source of all material, without which no one can produce anything whatever, and which no one has produced, is with the *mushik* a deep-rooted moral conviction. It is not "my land" in his mouth, but "our land," and this refers not only to his own holding, the communal land, and what is rented from landlords, but also that on which he works for a master. Centuries of slavery, during which both they and the land became the private property of the great lords, could not beget in them any other idea than that private ownership of land was a mere accident of unrighteousness, destined, with other unnatural conditions, to pass away when the true state of things should become known to the "little father" in St. Petersburg. "We are yours, but the land is ours" *(mi vashi, zemlja nasha),* they said to their masters. The only ownership, in their eyes, is that of the actual cultivator, and he has no rights in it but that of cultivation.

. Under serfdom it was the function of the *mir* to allot the lands held for their own use under the lords. This, of course, did not apply to the "*barskije,*" or personal slaves, but to the serfs on the land, who in this respect occupied a position somewhat analogous to the English villani. After the abolition the *mir* became responsible as a whole to the Government for the regular payment of the redemption money, as explained in a former chapter. It then became its duty to allot the land to the several members, who received their share, and with it the proportional liabilities. The adult working male formed the unit of calculation, but if in a household the working power was increased by the presence of a number of women or boys able to assist, this was taken into account. The division was revised yearly, and any alteration of conditions allowed for. This is still the practice in connection with the lands thus held in common.

The jurisdiction of the *mir* is far-reaching, embracing all civil and a great many criminal matters. Ten village judges are elected by the *volost,* or group of villages; these must all be members of some *mir* or other in the group, and they decide all matters by their sense of right, without law-books, rules, or any other juridical apparatus, of which the peasant has a whole-some horror.  The *principles* on which they act are the strong convictions of all ; the application to special cases is made by their conscience and common-sense.

The principle they follow in relation to the land has been mentioned.  Equally unconventional and practical are those that relate to inheritance and property in general.  Although kinship is with them a most sacred tie, it is not of itself a sufficient claim to inheritance ; work only can assure this.  If an adopted son has taken his share of the family labour for a sufficiently long time—ten years or so—he enjoys equal rights with his foster-brothers, while a son by birth loses these if he separates himself from the family.  Neither blood-relationship nor the " will " of the deceased can be effectually pleaded before these village judges against the stronger claim of co-labour, though, of course, all this is in complete contradiction to the law of the land as understood by the official world.  It is interesting to note that a man only inherits his wife's property after about ten years of labour-partnership ; otherwise it reverts to her own family.  The Russian State law also limits the share of a woman considerably, but the *mir*-practice recognises no differ-ence in this respect.

The same principle is seen in operation in many directions. If, for example, one man sows a part of another's land, the matter is not settled by the whole becoming the property of the latter, as would happen under State law.  If it is a genuine mistake, the man who has sown the seed reaps the harvest, paying the other rent for the land and a little more ; if done intentionally, the owner reaps the harvest, but pays the other for the seed.

According to peasant conception, the authority of the *mir* extends to all matters concerning the life of its members ; hence it frequently acts in direct contravention of both State and Church law.  It has sometimes happened that entire communities have decided to adopt a new religion. At other times they have used their common-sense and declared a man and wife who are manifestly unfitted for each other to be no longer man and wife, and treat them accordingly, although divorce is not recognised by the Greek any more than by the Roman Church. In short, the peasant abhors documents and law-books, and applies his sense of right and wrong to every matter, either individually or communally. Of course, this is not to say that his resulting conduct is perfect; one can assert, however, that the consequence has been a brotherliness and mutual helpfulness that has preserved a sweet and wholesome spirit among the *mushiks*, in spite of all the ignorance, superstition, and degradation due to the miserable condition of life to which they have been condemned by human greed and lust of power. The *mushik* counts it an honour to work and suffer "for the *mir*," that is, for the common welfare of those with whom he lives in daily relation. He has a great pity for the weak, and even the debased, whom he calls by the all-inclusive term, "unfortunate." Nothing can be more touching than the practical compassion by which a peasant places a piece of bread outside his window, that the fugitives from prison or exile may find it in their need. At the same time, the *mir* can itself, on occasion, send one of its members to Siberia, if it judges him deserving of that punishment.

All this, however, refers more especially to the times before the misfortunes of later years began to break down the protection which the *mir* afforded its members against the official world. Yet much of it is still true, in spite of the ravages of Church and State, landlord and *kulack*, famine and pestilence; one would naturally expect these to beget in the harassed and poverty-stricken peasants a selfishness and demoralisation of the worst kind, but they still retain a rustic heroism, a lowly self-devotion to truth and right, that reminds one of the stories of the earliest Christian times. But the trail of the *tchinovnik* is found to-day even in the *mir* itself.

The official world is "much of a muchness" in every land, but in Russia it is to be studied in all its glory and excellence. "*Tchin*" is a word of general import, denoting all that belongs to rule and government and external authority, and a *tchinovnik* is a personal member of the huge army employed in enforcing that external authority. He is naturally incapable, like his brothers all over the world, of understanding how mankind could possibly avoid coming to grief, were it not for his quill-driving, his stamped paper, his big portfolio full of sealed documents, his red tape, and his carefully-drawn regulations. Such an institutitn as the *mir*, with its absence of bye-laws and dependence simply upon the common-sense and conscience of the present day, regardless of all codes and rules, is to him a monster of anarchy, and from the time of the abolition he has been trying to bring it into subjection and "order." Happily, the Liberal party was at first too strong to allow of its abolition, but a surer way has since been found of accomplishing the desired end. The official element has been introduced into its constitution, thus linking it on to the vast and complex State machinery of which it seems destined to become a mere cog-wheel in time, should no radical alteration be brought about by some upheaval of those democratic forces that are now held under by the military and police.

The method was simple in conception; the village elder, or *starosta*, must be made a *tchinovnik* himself; in practice this was not so easy, for as a rule the *starosta*, though a man of good intelligence and practical wisdom, could not read nor write, and a *tchinovnik* without those qualifications would be an unheard-of anomaly. The difficulty was overcome by providing him with a *pisar* or scribe, who kept the registers, &c., of the district, amounting to sixty-five in number for each *volost*. This scribe has really become the more powerful of the two, since the *starosta* is entirely dependent upon him. His authority is wide-reaching, and he generally uses it in a way that makes him anything but loved by the peasants. His character is usually none of the best, as seems to have been desired by the Government, for their regulations forbid any one who has been through a "gymnasium" to hold the post. The *starosta* himself, though, as just said, dependent on the *pisar*, has, under the new regulations, become invested with official powers over the community, in place of deriving his power from it; he summons and dismisses the *mir* at his discretion, and can inflict fines not exceeding one rouble at a time, or punishments of not more than twenty-four hours of forced labour or imprisonment.

To complete the slavery of the peasants under official despotism, a new order of country police was created in 1878, called *uriadniks*, chosen from the roughest, and invested with practically unlimited powers in their own sphere—two conditions that have inevitably made them, as a rule, into wild beasts in human shape. As proofs of this we give instances culled first from reports of proceedings in the police-courts, and accounts in the *Zemstvo* newspapers.

A certain *uriadnik* named Makoni came one day to a village in Samara, Vorony Kust, to attend a meeting at the local offices. There he met some friends, one of whom, a well-to-do peasant named Chaibol, invited him and others home "to take a glass." As they opened the gate to go, a big sow used the opportunity to run out, and took it into its head to follow the *uriadnik*. This he resented as a gross insult on the sow's part —and shot it dead. Coming back in a somewhat "elevated" condition they met the owner of the sow, a saloon-keeper, who asked for compensation. This enraged the *uriadnik* so much that he declared he had a legal right to shoot both sows and men, too, if he pleased. An old soldier who stood by observed that he, too, had served the Tsar, but had never heard of such a law. Without a word the *uriadnik* rushed at him and felled him to the ground, afterwards dragging him with much violence to the lock-up.

Another *uriadnik* entered a cottage and found a calf tied by its leg to a table. Without further ado he drew his sword and cut it to pieces.

In one place a *uriadnik* fired point-blank into a crowd of unarmed people, and in another he rushed into the midst of a number of peasants who were attempting to put out a fire, and slashed right and left with his naked sword.

In the district of Bogorodsk the *uriadnik* used to steal the peasants' oats at night. Caught once red-handed, he threatened to imprison the owner, declaring that he was "in the execution of his duty"; with revolver drawn he went his way in triumph through the crowd of enraged peasants. The matter was reported to the authorities, but the man was not even dismissed.

During my visit to Russia in 1886 the following incident occurred in the village of Borki, near St. Petersburg, and was also the subject of police-court proceedings. *Uriadnik* Geras-- simov subjected a peasant named Marakin and the brothers Antonov to the cruellest torture. The unhappy victims were taken to an ice-cellar, and there stripped naked; their arms were fastened behind their backs, and by a rope tied to their hands they were hoisted up until their toes just touched the floor. In this position they were left for several hours, the *uriadnik* coming in now and then to see if, by additional torture, he could induce them to agree to his desires. Evidence was also given that on the way Marakin was bound hand and foot, and, fastened by his heels to the back of a vehicle, dragged at a gallop through the mud.

In other places we have given examples of how the *kulacks*, the allies of the *tchinovniks*, handle the peasants, and the third party to this Unholy Alliance, the priests, make common cause with them in grinding the faces of the poor. We now tell the story of what is known as the Logoschino affair, which exemplifies the practice of many of the most highly-placed officials. It would, like other crimes of the same description, have passed without notice had not party interest in the highest Government circles made it the occasion of disgracing a rival. Even then it took seven years for justice to be done.

After the Polish rising was suppressed (1863-4), about 70,000 hectares of land belonging to the nobility who took part in the insurrection was confiscated, but this was not enough to satisfy the greed of the *tchinovniks*, who proceeded to plunder the peasants. One of these plunderers was General Tokarjev, Governor of Minsk, who received from Potapov, the Governor-General, an estate of 3,000 hectares, worth about 9,000 roubles yearly. But this land really belonged to the peasants in Logoschino, who had a well-attested claim, and sent a deputation to the Governor, with title-deeds, as soon as they heard that their land had been made over to him. But the deputation was refused a hearing, and the deeds of the peasants " disappeared " without any traces left. When the Minister of the Interior, to whom they had appealed, asked for explanations from Minsk, reply was sent that the land was State property without shadow of doubt, and the peasants' complaint groundless.

Meanwhile the Governor-General was not idle. When he learnt that five peasants were going as a deputation to St. Petersburg, he despatched an intimation to the Ministry that these men were revolutionists; result—they were thrown into prison without any trial, and banished to the White Sea coast. Everything being now clear in his favour, Tokarjev proceeded, in 1874, to take formal possession of the estate. Agents were employed to collect the rents, but the peasants refused to pay. Twenty-six of them were thrown into prison, and soldiers were sent to enforce obedience and the payment of rent. The peasants attempted to break through the ranks, but were beaten off with clubbed muskets and scared away with a volley of blank cartridge. *Four days before the news of this reached him*, Tokarjev had telegraphed to St. Petersburg that the inhabitants of Logoschino were in revolt, and had repulsed his soldiers. General Loschkarjev was immediately despatched, with a free hand. He took a battalion of soldiers and 250 Cossacks, and marched from Minsk against " the rebels."

Colonel Kapgar now comes upon the scene, a ready tool in the Governor's hand. His first act was to store several cartloads of birchrods in the police station at Logoschino ; then, escorted by two policemen, he summoned the villagers, abused them in the coarsest terms, and told them that " a general was coming with an army who had full power to bury them alive, flog them to death, in short, do as they pleased with them if they did not at once submit." The terror-stricken peasants at once gave way, and sent three of their number to pacify this terrible general. They met him some miles from the place, but did no good. At evening Loschkarjev with his troops entered the village, and at once commanded the Cossacks to keep watch all round and see that none escaped. A fresh deputation brought bread and salt as tokens of submission. But the General would have nothing to say to the "rebels" before they had paid 500 roubles rent for 1874, and 5,000 roubles for 1873—that is, the year before Tokarjev became possessed of the place! But they could do nothing in the presence of the armed soldiery but ask for time. They were allowed just forty hours, with the intimation that if the 5,500 roubles were not then forthcoming, the whole sum of 12,000 roubles would be exacted.

Then the General left matters in charge of the *ispravnik*, Colonel Kapgar. He at once refused to allow them even until the next morning, and insisted on immediate payment. When they represented that they had no ready cash for such a large amount he rushed about like a madman, swearing, striking, and kicking at them all, and shouting commands for their punishment. He ordered each of the 233 families to pay him twenty-five roubles on the spot, and they had at once to sell their goods to the "Jews" for absurdly trifling sums, or to borrow at a rate of 3 per cent. *per week*.

An eye-witness gives the following samples of the treatment meted out to these unfortunate people, whose only crime had been refusal to pay rent to a robber for land that was their own. The peasant Korolevitch was so roughly handled that he never recovered. Lukashevitch, an old man of sixty-nine years, asked the *ispravnik* for some days' grace, but he gave him two violent blows in the face, felling him to the ground, and thereupon ordered him to be flogged; this was done under Kapgar's own supervision, and so effectually that the old man had to be carried from the spot. Kapgar even demanded money from an old blind beggar, and when he declared he had none, hit him in the face and threatened to flog him, but the old man went round the village and begged ten roubles.

The soldiers also, as was small wonder, behaved like brigands. One of them came to a peasant's hut to take him in the middle of the night to the police-station, and while he was dressing struck his wife, who was pregnant, such a violent blow in the back that she swooned, and next day suffered a miscarriage.

By these means Kapgar collected the amount in two days, and it was sent to the Governor. The troops were withdrawn; General Loschkarjev reported in St. Petersburg that the revolt had been quelled without firing a shot, *or the use of any violence*, thanks to the moderation and tact of *ispravnik* Kapgar, who talked the peasants into a proper frame of mind, and procured their submission to their lord's rightful claims. Loschkarjev was rewarded with special marks of the Tsar's favour, and Kapgar received a high military decoration.

As said above, so the matter would have rested, had it not suited Potapov's rival, who had a majority in the Cabinet, to take it up. But Potapov was so strong in the Senate that he escaped with a slight reproof. Then the Cabinet reported the matter to the Tsar, recommending a severe sentence. The Tsar endorsed this with his own hand in the words "Most decidedly." In spite of this Potapov's party succeeded in deferring the execution of the Tsar's orders for three years.*

Besides these illustrations, gathered from public records, we here give some notes specially written by a friend in Russia for our use, containing descriptions of cases that have come under his own personal notice.

A snowstorm is raging, with dismal howls. If we go out of doors we are at once covered from head to foot with driving, penetrating snow, or bitten in the face by a cold, sharp wind. If we sit in a warm room our thoughts turn with a sad unwillingness, with prickings of a half-wakened conscience, to the traveller who is overtaken by so terrible a storm. I do not know whether it is better for travellers on horse or foot. A pedestrian runs great risk of exhaustion and burial in some deep snowdrift; a rider may equally perish with his steed. But for us who are just now fighting a famine storm it is a day of rest. No applicants for aid throng our doors, and we can spend some hours in our own pursuits, giving ourselves up to thought, busying ourselves in household matters, reviewing the past, or planning the future work, bringing into coherence many of the impressions we have received. I will use the occasion to set down some of my experiences of the recent past.

     *       *       *       *       *

A glorious winter evening. It is more than 20° (Réaumur) of frost; the sun is overcast. Through the grey clouds is seen just one red streak of sunset. A frost mist fills the air, hiding,

* See *Poriadok* (the official Gazette), 1881, Nos. 330–340.

as with a rosy veil, the nearest as well as the more distant hills.

I go out by the shore of the Don. On the steep bank, opposite where I stand, is a village looking, in this evening light, as if of porcelain. I see an even row of cottages, with pink, round, overhanging roofs, and below these a ravine, leading to the Don, where piled-up snowdrifts seem to glide in finely-moulded shapes. And the outlines of all are softened by the translucent frosty mist.

Through this village I had to pass, and began to wander off in the direction of the bridge that crossed the Don. From the other side] a small figure came rapidly to meet me. Soon I recognised a little girl of about ten years. When she came near enough to see who I was she uttered in her small, childish voice the well-known, usual words, "I am coming to your grace."

"What do you want?"

"My mother is dying."

"Come, I will go with you."

We went up the steep bank, and as we approached the village the beautiful vision disappeared. To begin with, I saw that from several roofs the straw had been taken, so that only the framework stood there, like gnawed skeletons. Beneath the overhanging roofs the walls of the huts stood up, half buried in the snow. Openings were dug through the drifts to the small frosted windows which, however, were almost hidden behind heaps of dirt and refuse.

We entered the last cottage in the street; its owner had built it in more prosperous times, for it was of brick. Under present conditions it is more miserable to live in than those built of wood. Inside was darkness, damp, cold, and foul air. I recollected that the day before a little girl had come from this house to ask for money "for gas," *i.e.*, for lamp oil, and I had refused. They must then have applied to a rich peasant in the same village to lend them some.

The girl took a vessel and ran out, slamming the door after her. When my eyes became accustomed to the gloom I could distinguish the objects within. Doors, window, corners, and rents in the roof, with the lower part of the walls, were all covered with rime. The rest of the roof and the upper walls, that retained some warmth from the day just gone, were wet, and streams trickled from them in several places. On the oven lay a heap of rags and old clothes. From it came a noise, something between groaning and snoring. A hollow sound reached me from another quarter, but just where I could not tell. I could see no one on the bench.

The girl returned and lit the lamp.

" Where is your mother ? " I asked her.

" In the oven, and father is on top."

She opened the oven and put her head inside, calling, " Mother, come out, *barin* (the gentleman) is here."

I had known this family for some time. The girl was not their own, but the illegitimate child of a soldier's wife, and granddaughter of the old woman whom she called " Mother," because she had grown up under her care. The old woman " was dying," that is, was ill. Her husband had been so for a long time, and no one now troubled about him. When he heard our voices he rose up, groaned out something, and lay down again. The day before they had used manure as fuel, and had not yet recovered from the exposure to the fumes and smoke from it.

Soon after my entrance a young woman came in. She was a daughter of the old woman, and lived with her family at the other end of the village. Now she had come to visit her mother. At sight of me she burst out crying, and lamented her wretchedness. Her family, also, was suffering from lack of fuel.

" I came to move them to my place ; they cannot live here. But what a life is in store for us ! God help us ! I have seven children of my own. Our cottage is smaller than this, but it is built of wood ; with snow all round it is warmer, but here it is unbearable."

I approved her plan, and promised to help them with fuel. It was one of those families that were eating up their last resources, of which we have so many. This obliges us to adopt the method of crowding two or three families into one hut, and giving fuel for the one place, otherwise we should not have enough for all. But we have not ourselves the courage to tell them to crowd together in this way; this packing of people in polluted air is terrible. Still it is the only way of keeping them from freezing to death.

"We must move at once, because to-morrow my husband is going away," began the young peasant woman, putting some things into a sack, while she roused up the old people.

"Where is he going?"

"To the *volost*."

"What for?"

"The *stanavoi* (police commissary) is coming there to collect taxes."

"But why does your husband go there?"

"They are driving them all together, from the whole village district—all who have a plot of land."

I did not believe her, and could not understand her disconnected talk, but went to the *starosta*. He belonged to the "inhabitants"; that is, he possessed a cow and two horses, and was consequently regarded as "settled"; he had no need to go round looking for work, a condition that is becoming rarer every day. But his position was not enviable, for he had a large family. He had been a soldier. When I asked if it was true that they were driving them all together to the *volost*, he answered, "Yes, it is true, your high-born nobility."

But even he could not explain the whole matter. All he knew was that everyone had received orders to be at the office of the district by 8 a.m., and that the *stanavoi*, and perhaps the *ispravnik* himself, would be there.

When I left the *starosta*, the evening had cleared, and it was as light as day. The cold was more intense, and the moon flooded the hills and valleys with her pale beams. As I went homewards, the snow crackled under my feet with ringing sound. After crossing the Don, I turned again to look from my own shore at the beautiful village. It was more beautiful still in the gleaming light of the moon. Then I recalled the order of the village police concerning the next day's meeting, and determined to be there and see what would happen.

Next morning I meant to start in time to see the beginning of the meeting, but business hindered me, and I could not leave

till later on.   The meeting was called for 8 a.m.; I left in time
to get there about 11 o'clock, and was afraid I should be too
late.   The cold was still more intense.   When I came to the
village in which the district office was situated, my attention
was at once attracted to the great crowd.   At several *izbas* stood
teams of peasant's sleighs together, the horses taken out, but
not unharnessed.   They stood with heads hanging down, every
now and then shivering all over; some were munching a
handful of straw that had been thrown them; others had not
even this meagre fodder.   The sleighs were empty; only in a
few there was a layer of dried leaves at the bottom.   The
peasants were standing close together in groups in the street.
The villagers were not willing to receive guests in their houses.

I had visited this village a little while before, to inquire into
the condition of its families.   I knew well how cold and
damp were those huts inside—the usual winter condition in
that district.   They are very careful over their warmth, and
few will lend their huts to strangers.   It was only those with
relations there that could get shelter.   As I passed the groups I
recognised many faces.   I knew this district well, had visited
every village, almost every hut, and every face I recognised
brought to mind some special suffering, some particular
distress, that had brought about our acquaintance.   It was one
of the poorest districts in all that part of the country.

By some mistake it had been counted among those that had
had a good crop, and three *volosts* that had suffered more from
bad harvest than last year had been refused relief loans, and
now it was demanded that those received last year should be
repaid as well as the taxes.

As I approached the office the peasants were more closely
crowded, and there were still more sleighs with wretched-
looking horses and sad-faced men.   The vestibule and the
session-room were thronged.   I pushed through the press to
the table, where the local authorities, the *starshina* and the
*pisar* (scribe), were seated.

" Has the *stanavoi* arrived? " I asked.

" Not yet," answered the *starshina*, a short man, dressed in
a peasant's cloth coat, with thin dark hair, and a restless,

cowardly yet stubborn, look on his face. His small dark eyes sought mine, and his voice varied as he gazed, from fear to affected humility, and again to truculence and confidence in his authority.

The scribe was a young man, dressed in a kind of jacket, whose face wore an expression compounded of scepticism and routine.

"Where is the *stanavoi* then?"

"In the village close by. It is said that an old woman has been frozen to death there, and he is detained about the body," answered the *starshina*.

I left the office, having given directions that I should be sent for when the *stanavoi* came, and went to a hospital in the neighbourhood, where a physician of my acquaintance lived, in order to warm myself.

As I passed through the village I called at several cottages where I had business, and afterwards spent a couple of hours with the doctor, expecting the message, but none came.

I returned to the office. It was 4 p.m., but the *stanavoi* had not yet arrived. The hungry, shivering peasants were still standing in the streets as in the morning. Large numbers were grouped before the drink shops. What had they to spend in drink? Their last sheep? Their next harvest? I do not know. Cold and hunger had compelled them to have recourse to this poison. We may not judge them.

I approached one of the groups, and was immediately surrounded. "Has he not yet come?" I asked.

"No, and we do not know when he will come either."

It was painful to look at these people. Why had they gathered here in the morning? I went again to the office. The *starshina* was still sitting as before at the little table.

"When is the *stanavoi* coming?" I asked.

"I don't know. Something has detained him." He looked still more frightened and disquieted.

"Why do you not dismiss the meeting?"

"I cannot do it. He may come at any moment."

"But night is coming on already. What will the *stanavoi* do here then?"

"That I do not know; but I have no power to let the people go."

I advised him again to dissolve the meeting, and started for home. After I had walked some way I saw long rows of men and sleighs leaving the village; the *starshina* had evidently dismissed them.

Afterwards I learned that he had kept the *starostas*, and the chief of the police had arrived at 7 p.m.; he gave strict orders that the taxes were to be collected, threatening to sell up the peasants to the last stick. Then he left.

What is the cause and purpose of all these unnecessary sufferings?

It is night. The storm howls still more fiercely. I have had only one applicant for relief to-day. Through this terrible weather he had come a distance of six versts (about four miles). When he came in he fell on his knees before me.

"Let me not die of cold!" he said, in a quivering voice. "We have had no fire for two days. . . . My family . . . the children—barefooted."

I turned away. Hastily I wrote an order for five pud of wood, and gave it him, trying to avoid his look. He left.

So far, my friend's description. In another letter I was told that these peasants had been *publicly flogged in the cruellest way* by order of the authorities because they could not pay their taxes.

Count Tolstoi allowed me to use an extract from his book, then in preparation, which described the manner in which this flogging takes place, as seen by himself. This book has since been published ("The Kingdom of Heaven is Within You"), but we retain the description as fitly supplementing the narrative just given.

On 29th of September last (1892), as I was travelling to a famine-stricken place, I saw, at one of the railway stations, a General steam up in a special train, with a small company of soldiers; they were on their way to Tula, to punish several unruly peasants, who had dared to withstand a young lord, who had flagrantly trampled on their rights. . . .

18

I describe this occurrence, not because it was anything out of
the way, but because it was the only one I have myself witnessed, and for the truth of whose description I can personally
vouch. . . .

The troops were drawn up before the door of the courthouse.
A band of policemen with new red belts, in which were loaded
revolvers, were stationed round the little group of guilty
peasants, who were waiting the punishment of their misdeeds.
Some way off stood thousands of men, women, and children,
who were there as spectators. When the Governor-General
arrived, he stepped out of his carriage and made a short, sharp
speech, at the end of which he ordered a bench to be fetched.
This was not at first understood, but the police officer who
attended the Governor, and was responsible for seeing the
punishment carried out in an effectual and orderly way, explained with terse directness that his Excellency wanted a
bench on which a man could be thoroughly well flogged. This
was speedily forthcoming, a bundle of specially-prepared rods
brought forward, and the executioners called to the front.
These were two runaway convicts, since no soldier would
himself be used for this degrading work.

When all was ready, the Governor ordered the first of the
twelve peasants, reported by the landlord as originators of the
riot, to be brought out. The victim was a man in the forties,
the father of a family, whose uprightness had become a
proverb, and who enjoyed the respect and confidence of his
fellow-citizens. He was told to undress and lie on the bench.
The peasant made no attempt to beg for mercy; he knew the
uselessness of such a prayer. Silently he made the sign of the
cross and lay down. Two policemen ran to hold him in his
place. By his side stood a physician, to render medical aid if
necessary.

The convicts spat in their hands, struck a blow through the
air with their rods, and began the flogging. The bench was
seen to be too small, so that it was difficult to hold the writhing,
tortured man upon it. The General ordered a wider bench to
be brought, and a plank fastened to each side. One of the
soldiers saluted and answered, "Aye, aye, sir," and hastened

with all humility to fulfil the great man's command. Meanwhile, the poor, half-naked man stood there with doleful mien and sunken eyes, his under-jaw shaking, and his bare legs shivering. When the other bench was brought, he was fastened more tightly to it, and the floggers resumed their work. At every blow the gaping wounds became more frightful and ghastly. Back, sides, and limbs were streaming with blood, and after each fresh stroke the victim uttered a hollow moan of pain, which he strove in vain to repress. From the thronging circle round came the sobs of the martyr's wife, mother, and children, besides the frightened, quickly-checked cry from those whose turn was to come next.

The miserable Governor-General, who in the intoxication of his power persuaded himself that he was obeying the call of duty, counted the strokes on his fingers, as he calmly smoked a cigarette, which an obsequious adjutant lighted in the flame of a match, held up aloft.

After more than fifty strokes, the peasant ceased to cry or move. The skilled physician, who placed his services and knowledge at the disposition of the Provincial Government's hospital, stepped forward to the tortured being, felt his pulse, stooped to listen if his heart were beating, and informed the representative of the Imperial might that the victim was unconscious, and that further punishment would be at the risk of his life.

But the Governor-General, more than ever intoxicated with his brief authority, maddened like some wild beast at sight of blood, commanded the punishment to proceed, and the torture was renewed until the seventy strokes were complete. It seems as if, from some unknown cause, this seventy were a sacred number, to fall short of which would be an affront to justice.

Then the Governor took his cigarette from his mouth and said, " Enough! Bring out the next! "

That this is not exceptional, but carried on to a frightful extent, may be seen from these statistics. In two villages in the district of Slobodski, in the year 1878, no fewer than 618

heads of families were flogged for not having paid taxes.*
Between 1878 and 1881, out of 1,200 heads of families in a
single village district, 797 were flogged.† In 1884, 178 out of
415 peasants were flogged in three villages in the province of
Kiev, for arrears of taxes.‡  In a period of less than six
weeks, in ten villages of the district of Nova Ladoga, in the
province of St. Petersburg, 224 heads of families out of a total
of 517 were flogged, for their inability to pay the taxes
demanded by the " paternal Government."

* "Sketches of Self-Government." S. A. Priklonski, St. Petersburg
1882. p. 173.
† "Annals of the Fatherland," May, 1882, p. 159.
‡ "Sketches of Self-Government," p. 356.

# CHAPTER XVII.

## IS THERE A REMEDY?

A Conversation—A Russian's Views—The Fatal Breach—True Division of Labour—Healthful Development—Paramount Claims of Life—A Revolution Inevitable—" Go to the People."

CAN anything be done? is the question that must be uppermost in the minds of those who have read the preceding pages and in any degree formed a living conception of the state of things there depicted. It is not for us to give an answer, but we may fitly close with a presentation of the views of many Russians themselves as to the right way out of the evil conditions that sap the life of that unhappy country. The conversation here given is fictitious only in that the real names of the participants are withheld, and many things are brought together which were said at different times. Otherwise, the substance is a true record, and the occasion is historical and not imaginary.

"The essential cause of the general and constant misery among the masses," said our friend Kudrin, filling a glass with tea from the boiling *samovar*, " is the unnatural gulf that yawns between the so-called 'upper' and 'lower' classes." He spoke in his usual quiet manner, with a depth of conviction that was born of wide experience, extending over many years, both among the peasants and in "society." Of aristocratic birth and education, he had, as a young man, moved in the highest circles, but had afterwards abandoned both rank and property, and " gone to the people," among whom he had lived a long time, working hard to help them both in material and moral things. My other companion in the low and damp *izba*, where we had gathered round the *samovar* at the close of a day's relief work among the famine-stricken, was a jovial physician, who, in character, opinions, and appearance, presented a strong contrast to the serious Kudrin.

"The terrible distress among the peasants can be permanently remedied in no other way than by abolishing this unnatural cleavage between the masses and the so-called people of 'intelligence.'"

"Explain your views as to the cause and cure of this misery more fully," I said to K.

"No, rather let us have a consultation," he answered. "We are like quack doctors, working daily side by side with the recognised physicians of society. Let us then have a consultation."

"*Bien, allons!*" chimed in the doctor, breaking off his humming, and beginning to drink another glass of tea.

"We start then," said K., "from the proposition—that, at least, as far as I am concerned, has the force of an axiom—that it behoves every man to think and act according to his true nature, to satisfy the real wants of his body and soul, and promote his healthful development."

"Excuse my interrupting you with a demurrer to your axiom," I said. "You know that Professor Metcherkajeff denies this proposition in his criticism of Count Tolstoi and his views in the *Vestnik Europi*, pointing out that man possesses rudimentary organs which have lost their functions during the process of his evolution. Therefore, he argues that the presence of an organ does not necessarily imply the duty of using and developing it. What do you say to that?"

"This atrophy of any organ takes thousands of years," he answered, "and it is only when the use of one is superseded by that of another that it takes place. In all probability, should the present conditions of civilisation hold good for some thousands of years, man would lose both arms and legs——"

"Yes," broke in the doctor, jestingly. "The descendants of our well-fed friend, Tikvov, will then look like pumpkins on toothpicks, those of Professor Metcherkajeff like puffballs, and our ladies of the *beau monde*, after looking for centuries like wasps, will finally break in two at the middle."

"I believe, though, it will be long enough before we reach that stage," went on Kudrin. "Even the professor and his friends seem to agree that man must exercise his body as well as his brains, if he would be really healthy, since they praise gymnastics so highly, and that is merely a substitution of artificial exercise for natural work. To-day, among upper-class people, it is considered a great achievement to handle iron balls with ease and skill, to exhibit extraordinary powers of climbing, jumping, running, &c., without any other object than that of excelling others. About these matters telegrams fly round the world, long newspaper articles are written, books are published, and costly institutions are established, while our fellow men, who need our help in their struggle for mere existence, are left to themselves."

Here the doctor made some objections, which Kudrin answered, and then went on:

"I stick to my proposition, that it behoves man to live and work in accordance with his true nature; to procure for himself the sustenance for his body, to protect it against hurtful influences, keep it in a healthy condition, and give to both soul and body the power to use, create, and enjoy life, thus attaining to the highest good.

"But in this work, that should be harmonious, an unnatural division has arisen, so that one part of mankind uses only the brain or mind, and the other only the body. But, just as an engine cannot work well without an engineer, so it cannot be good for physical work to be done without the mind to guide it. As the mind can do great things within the sphere of imagination and theory, but cannot provide the body with its necessaries, so the brain-workers have become men of imagination and theory only, while the bodily toilers, deprived of necessary mental culture, have sunk to the level of beasts of burden, or soulless machines.

"If the engineer leaves his engine, it may certainly run for a time, but sooner or later it will stop work; the water in the boiler will be exhausted, the bearings wear out or perhaps take fire, or something will happen, and the machine either come to a standstill or be destroyed. Now we see that the great mass of labourers, deprived of the advantages of intelligent labour, go on working long and usefully, but sooner or later their *force inerte* is used up.

"The engineer, on the other hand, who leaves the machine he was set to manage, may go on for a long while dreaming and constructing clever theories, finding satisfaction in his works of genius, but at last he must die of want and hunger, unless he returns to the machine that produces the things needful for the sustenance of life. So we see the so-called intelligent classes engrossed in their brilliant theories, that float in the air like balloons without ballast. But the decisive crisis is approaching. 'The kingdom which is divided against itself, &c.' The kingdom is man, the engineer is his reason, the engine his physical body. Through the division of these elements in his nature, the individual man must perish, and so, also, must the society that consists of individuals so divided. This is the state of things at the present time. With one class of men reason is dead and inert; with the other, the bodily organs have become unable to be used for their purpose, and these men have become unproductive dreamers."

"But your analogy is not quite exact," I interrupted. "Your opponents themselves, the dreamers, assert that they are the engineers of humanity, and look on the physical workers as machines. According to them, this is one of the first principles of the division of labour, and is of axiomatic force in their eyes."

"Wait a little; I will soon explain further. I know that all comparisons are defective; every figure illustrates only a part of the truth. We know, well enough, that a small minority exert themselves as 'engineers' over all the rest, whom they manipulate as machines at their pleasure, but that this should have the force of an axiom is absurd. My comparison is defective, for in the case under discussion the machine and the engineer cannot be separated. I wanted to enforce the idea, by means of this figure, that the engineer must not be set over the machine except *in one and the same organism*. It is only when their mutual work is free and natural that they can fulfil their true ends; apart, they will never succeed. Mutual and harmonious work will never be effected through compulsion. When violence puts the engine in motion it soon destroys the whole machinery, bringing with it general ruin.

"But there are other means than compulsion for achieving this end; there is one that does not hurt, but gives life and strength. This is *the co-operation of love.* True moral love can unite the different elements, but it is very rarely given the opportunity of showing its strength.

"I do not object to division of labour in general, but most decidedly do reject that at present in force. There are two radical vices in the prevailing division. First, it is not based on free exchange, but on the slavery of the weaker, under the rich and powerful. Secondly, the specialisation is made without regard to considerations of health, or the conditions of life in general.

"There is no other cure for the evil than the union *in the same person* of these two kinds of work. In this way only can they become powerful for good. The division of labour, whose one justification is the greater production of the special brand of work, will always take place. More than that, it will be greatly extended for the benefit of labour, but always on condition that violence and compulsion be suppressed, and a law established, enforcing due regard to the sanitary, moral, and intellectual needs of every individual worker. The truth must be inculcated that there is no 'black' and 'white' labour" (a Russian distinction for lower and higher labour), "and that there is no labour that is in itself useful or hurtful, no occupation that is moral or immoral, without taking into account the work imparted to it by the labourer himself.

"You cannot allot work to classes of men as intellectual or physical, for by such division human life is destroyed. You can distinguish between the intellectual and physical parts of each branch of production, and every man must share in both. Of course he cannot manage the entire work of production himself, but he must accommodate himself to that portion of it, both intellectual and physical, for which he has the greatest capacity, and this distribution must in no way be dependent on questions of caste or any privilege whatsoever."

"There always have been and there must always be class divisions and other differences in external conditions. It is a law of nature,". interpolated the doctor.

"In the face of such an awful chronic dearth in a land of such immense resources as ours, inactivity is unpardonable, and it is frivolous to talk of such a state of things as necessary and natural. Nothing can be more *un*natural ! But the remedies we propose are considered so new-fangled that they bring suspicion on both themselves and us.

"The famine now raging is not of yesterday; for many years its causes have been at work, and the bad weather was only the occasion for revealing the chronic misery and the constantly decreasing working power of the labourer, deprived of all mental culture, oppressed by violence, with his whole life distorted.

"They object that this calamity is only incidental and local; that a couple of good years will set all right; that this year there has been a good harvest in Caucasia, and in other parts of Russia, in Europe and in America there is corn. I reply that there certainly may come good harvests, but they will not remove the evil. The sudden leaping of the flame is no good sign. Not much discernment and honesty is needed to see that, if the present conditions continue, the life of the people is like an expiring candle flame : it still burns and sometimes flares, but it is nearly gone out.

"Occasional revivals of prosperity cannot remove the distress. They say there is much corn in Caucasia, but they have not been many years there at the process of exhausting the land, so that they still get large supplies. The same is true of Central and Southern Russia and America, but in Western Europe does not a large part of the population already depend on foreign bread, and perish with those who feed them ? This present distress has had a bad effect on Western Europe, which to a great extent lives by the production of articles of luxury, all kinds of trash, which they force on the rest of the world.

"If the present division of labour, or rather sundering of mankind into two parts, is to continue, it must lead to a not

far-distaut ruin. Salvation lies only in the reunion of the
severed parts, and the healing of the whole."

"If such a union between the spiritual and the physical, the
so-called 'intelligent' and 'working classes' is possible," I
said, "why has it never existed, generally speaking, and why
does it exist nowhere at the present day? Differences of caste
and class have always been the rule among all peoples and in
all times.

"That is true, but what has become of all those peoples with
whom caste has flourished? They have perished with their entire
civilisation, or been vanquished by other races. The Indian,
the Egyptian, the Greek, the Roman, the Spanish and Moorish
civilisations have all perished in this manner; the French is in
the act of perishing, and the same fate will overtake the
English and German civilisations. What remains of the
thraldom under the yoke of tyrants during those long
centuries? The Egyptian pyramids, the Roman Coliseum, the
stones of which are cemented with the sweat and blood of slaves.
The lasting inheritance which these peoples have left behind
them in the shape of useful knowledge and fruitful thought is
not the result of caste; it rather came into being in spite of it.
There will remain of European civilisation mere ruins of huge
fortresses, temples and palaces, monuments of the intolerable
dominion of militarism, priestcraft, and Mammon-worship, of
the calamitous severance of "upper" and "lower" classes, of
schism between intellect and brute force. Shall we follow the
disastrous example of these peoples?"

"What do you suggest, then, as a means of remoulding
your social life, and radically changing its direction?" I
asked.

"Just what is done with soil that has become barren and
covered with weeds. You plough it again, plough deep, and
turn up the clods so thoroughly that the upper becomes the
lower, and all is reversed, so that what is at present sustaining
the burden and pressure may come to the top and inhale fresh
air, life, and strength. The whole social order must be
reorganised, human life must be reconstructed—we must begin
to live afresh. Only in such a regeneration of society is

salvation possible. However great the sacrifices demanded, whatever terrible events may precede and accompany this reconstruction, there is no other way of salvation, and all that will compel such renewal of life we ought to welcome gladly. No change of outward form can deliver us; the very principles of life must be radically altered.

"As to the nature of this change, since the *causes* of this fatal class separation are moral—greed, lust of power, vanity, love of pleasure—so the true remedies must be sought in the moral sphere. The life of the upper classes in general, not only of the openly reckless and licentious, but of those who are regarded as orderly and pious, must be pronounced *immoral* when tried by the standard of Christian ethics. How can it be anything else than immoral to live in luxury and affluence while my fellow-man is perishing of want and misery?"

The doctor, who was pacing up and down the room, here interjected that luxury was necessary to the State besides being pleasant to the individual; that it was a spur to social development, and gave work to a great many people.

"You must pardon me for not taking you seriously," said Kudrin, "for every educated man knows now, or ought to know, that those are fallacies long since exploded. Emile de Laveleye and M. Say, not to mention other prominent economists, have amply proved the immoral and inhuman character of luxury, *i.e.*, of everything made to excite and feed artificial wants and tastes at the cost of much labour. When about 40,000,000 of our countrymen are in want of the bare necessaries of life, how can it be moral and useful to spend vast amounts of capital and labour in producing articles of luxury, that are not simply useless, but frequently directly harmful and productive of great moral evils? Where is the good sense of talking of providing them with work to satisfy your lusts, when you have first of all robbed them of the right of producing necessaries for themselves?"

"But," said the doctor, "the poor are contented and happy in their misery. Besides, they live according to Tolstoi's ideal and yours; they have no luxuries, and live on as little as possible."

"I should not answer your jest," returned Kudrin, "if it did not seem to many people a real argument. It is not true that these people are 'happy' in their misery. It is true that many have become so degraded that they are incapable of desiring to get out of these wretched conditions, but that is a so much stronger indictment against the present social order that creates and fosters such boundless misery. Can we blame these men who receive such small return for their labour that they are driven to live in hovels where a decent farmer would not house his pigs? Even in wealthy France the great majority lack the dwellings, food, and clothing needful for the health of the body. As for Tolstoi, his work most certainly does not prove that he considers the condition of the peasants normal and 'happy.' Is it not his life's aim to lift them out of their material and spiritual misery, though to be sure it is with far other means than that of luxury that he is trying to rouse them from their stupor."

Here the conversation was interrupted by the entrance of a peasant, who came in the middle of the night, crying bitterly, and entreated the doctor to come to his wife, who was dying of typhus. When the doctor had gone I asked Kudrin if he thought there were any prospects of this social regeneration of which he had spoken. He answered:—

"In Russian society there is a remarkable phenomenon to be seen at present, which is not found to any great extent in other nations. I mean the 'going to the people' (khoshdjenije v'narode). This does not date from yesterday; it is now almost half a century old. People of intelligence, men and women, young and middle-aged, go into the country among the peasants, devoting all their time and powers to helping them, in the endeavour to raise them from their degradation. The means they have used are of various kinds, and some have been attended with but slight apparent success, but this cannot hinder the growth of the movement. When these men and women find new methods they go and put them into practice. The 'progressive intelligence' of the nation scoffs at them, the Government persecutes them, the ignorant and superstitious people are sometimes incited to hostility against them. This is nothing to them; they are animated by an all-powerful idea, and they will continue to go to the people. At present their numbers are larger than ever, and what they bring with them is very significant—no learned theories, but a simple and natural feeling, the emotion of sympathy. Of all the movements of this kind, that of the present time is probably founded least of all on social or philosophic theory, but simply on the emotion mentioned, on this living force, and if they go in humility, with a true practical sympathy with their brothers, suffer and labour with and for them, it will not be in vain. Through suffering the character is refined, strength is confirmed, love is tested and made strong. It is this love that is to unite all as brothers, and work for the healing of the dismembered organism, for the reunion of those forces of intellect and physical strength. From this force that works for uplifting and enlightenment shall other forces spring, that will bring with them the practical solution of the difficulties that now face us. To all who have gone to the people I would cry, '*Remain there.*' Ye who have not yet gone, but in whose breasts a heart is throbbing with pity for your suffering brothers and sisters, *go now to them!* This is my answer to your question as to the fundamental cause and cure of the distress."

The night had advanced far into the small hours. The doctor returned, and we retired to rest. The conversation had awakened in my mind many thoughts, both old and new, that kept me pondering until the morning light began to break through the little window of the hut. Will Kudrin's beautiful dream ever be realised? Will this abyss that now yawns between the "classes" and the "masses" be filled before the whole gigantic fabric of our present social order collapses like a house of cards and is buried in its depth? Will this dominion of organised tyranny, enforced by laws, authorities, and official religions, ever be supplanted by "an association of all in love"?

www.ingramcontent.com/pod-product-compliance
Lightning Source LLC
Chambersburg PA
CBHW020845020726
47497CB00005B/1257